Chasing Dreams

Chasing Dreams

Larry Stewart

Order this book online at www.trafford.com
or email orders@trafford.com

Most Trafford titles are also available at major online book retailers.

Printed in the United States of America.

ISBN: 978-1-4269-5802-1 (sc)
ISBN: 978-1-4269-5801-4 (e)

Trafford rev. 05/20/2011

North America & International
toll-free: 1 888 232 4444 (USA & Canada)
phone: 250 383 6864 • fax: 812 355 4082

Chapter 1

Recently married at 21, Dusty McBride hummed as she decorated the new apartment. Wearing a bikini top and short shorts, she stepped onto a stool to hang a framed photograph of herself and her husband surfing in Hawaii on their honeymoon. Three years her senior, her husband, Clint, strolled into the living room combing his hair and whistling along with Peter Paul and Mary's "If I had a Hammer" coming from the hi-fi.

"Look at you, handsome and debonair," she said in her usual sophisticated voice, sweeping her long blond hair from her blue eyes, "all dolled up in a three piece suit. What's the occasion?"

"Honeymoon's over, sweetheart," he said in his best Bogey voice. "It's time to hunker down and get that castle in the sky."

"I told you, no castle. They're haunted, and we'd have to feed the crocodiles in the moat all the time. I like our apartment. It's cozy. No spooky ghosts. No creepy crocodiles."

"How about a palace," he said, "with turrets and a drawbridge and two pools?"

"And the dust, I'd be dusting all day. It's bad enough my friends are calling me 'Dusty Bride' now that I'm married."

"What about your maiden name, *Melon*?"

"Can you imagine being called 'melon-head' your whole life. Where are you going?"

"Dan's father called. Said he has a proposal he wants me to peek at. This might be our big break. Launch us into the upper crust."

"I told you I don't care about that!"

"Why deprive me? I've never tasted it like you have."

Dusty hopped off the stool and skipped over to him. "I'm sorry. I just don't want you to become like my father. All he ever talks about is money and deals."

Clint looked into her eyes, ran his hands down her long tan legs, and winked at her. "You've got to be the sexiest McBride on the planet."

She stood on her toes and kissed him. "Good luck, Mister Dapper," she said, fiddling with his tie.

"Thanks, baby. Don't worry, you're my number one priority, everything else is secondary."

Standing at the doorway, Dusty waved at Clint when he fired up his Triumph Spitfire and sped off. Ten minutes later, Clint drove into the parking lot of Clay Thompson's office in San Mateo on a warm mid-summer day in 1966.

Clay Thompson's secretary Sylvia was seated at the reception desk typing when Clint walked into the offices of Thompson Construction and Development Company. She was dressed elegantly, and her red hair was in a bouffant.

"It's good to see you, Clint," Sylvia said, looking at Clint with a surprised expression. "You're certainly looking tan and fit. Except for the tux you wore at your wedding, I've never seen you in a suit. You're always in shorts and T-shirts. What brings about this rarity?"

"I'm moving up the ladder," he said, "getting out of the ghetto."

She smiled. "How was your honeymoon?"

"A dream come true," he said. "I spoke with Mister Thompson earlier, and he told me to drop by this morning."

"I know, he mentioned he's expecting you. Clay's in conference at the moment, but he shouldn't be long. Have a seat."

Clint sat on a chair and picked up a recent issue of *Time* magazine and began perusing an article on the escalation of the war in Vietnam.

"How's your charming bride?" Sylvia asked.

"She's busy with summer school at Cal, getting ready for a full load this fall. She has her hands full with commuting across the Bay Bridge almost everyday."

"How about yourself, you back in college, studying architecture?"

"I got my degree," said Clint. "But architects make peanuts. I'm plotting a course in construction. That's where the real money is."

"You've chosen a lucrative field," she said. "Construction is booming in the Bay Area."

"That's why I'm mapping out a strategy."

They chatted until Clay concluded his meeting and escorted his guests out to the parking lot. As usual, Clay was dressed conservatively and impeccably well-groomed. Except for his salt and pepper hair, he appeared much younger than 50.

"You look good in a suit and tie," said Clay, as he entered into the reception area. "Come inside my office. That was some special wedding. Your father sure can wail on the horn."

"Yeah, he's good."

"Have a seat and don't pay attention to the clutter."

"That's the way I want my desk to look someday."

Clay's desk was piled high with architectural drawings and spec binders. They spoke briefly about Clint's honeymoon until the conversation shifted to current events.

"A friend of Dan's told me you're getting ready to take the contractor's license exam?" Clay said.

"Yeah, next week," said Clint. "The week after that, I'm taking the real estate test. I don't want to confine myself to architecture. I want to branch out beyond design and put the whole package together like you do."

"Better to use your brain and not your brawn. I see you haven't lost that ambitious drive of yours."

"I'm just warming up, Mister Thompson. How's Dan, I haven't seen or heard from him since Dusty and I got back."

Clay Thompson's face distorted and he shook his head. "He's in rehab."

Clint jerked up in his chair. "Rehab! What happened to him?"

"He's being evaluated at Cordilleras Mental Health Center."

"Oh, my God," said Clint, "that's a psychiatric hospital. Is he alright?"

"He suffers from delusions and paranoia, constantly having hallucinations. The doctors say he took too many LSD trips."

get back to you. I'm going to pass that stupid test because I not only want to design, I want to build."

"Just be competitive."

* * *

Dusty was busy at her desk cramming for summer finals when Clint sneaked up behind her and jabbed his finger into her funny bone.

She jerked and spun around. "Clint," she screamed, "you scared the life out of me."

Grinning wildly, he said, "Clay Thompson told me about a house he has for sale."

She rubbed her elbow and said, "A house! Where?"

"Up in the hills of Burlingame," he said. "You're going to love it, it's on Tiptoe Lane."

"That's my favorite street, but how can we afford it?"

"It's dirt cheap," he said. "Come on, take a break, let's drive by and take a peek. He also wants me to design a Gothic mansion and build it. And money's not an object. The man's a Saudi oil sheik. Oh, I've got some bad news."

"Oh, no, what?"

"Dan dropped some acid and flipped out."

"Good grief, he took LSD?"

"I'm afraid so. I stopped by to see him at a psyche unit."

"You mean a psychiatric ward?"

"Yeah. He never said a word to me. Didn't even know who I was. All he did was babble nonsense, stare out the window, swing his leg, and chain smoke."

She grimaced, "Oh, my God! Can they help him?"

"The nurse told me there's a slight chance. She mentioned the words schizophrenia and psychosis, and suggested he's had a deterioration of the mind."

"How terrible! Isn't there anything they can do?"

"She said it doesn't look good but he might come around. Doctors all around the world are doing research on the stuff."

"I know, I just finished reading an article about it," she said. "How awful. He's so talented. I thought you told me he was heading to the big apple to try out for a Broadway musical?"

"His dad told me he didn't get the part. That's probably what triggered him to take that crap."

"I don't know what's coming over this world."

"It's got me baffled," he said, rubbing her shoulder. "Come on, let's check out the house."

"I hope something can be done for him," she said. "He's such a nice guy."

"All we can do is pray."

She smiled.

Chapter 2

Three months after scrounging the money for the down payment, Clint was beaming the day he carried Dusty over the threshold into their new home on Tiptoe Lane.

"I don't believe this," she said ecstatically. "It's like a fairy tale, our own home in a forest."

"You and I being married, escrow closing, passing the state contractors and real estate exams, this is phantasmagorical. And you about to get your master's, and me designing a medieval Gothic castle all in the same year, and the year's not over."

He swirled her around and set her down.

"I feel as if I'm dreaming," she said. "This property is so big. My parent's want to help, new drapes and..."

"Hold on, precious one," he interrupted. "No handouts. We're doing this on our own. We have a four-poster queen size bed with a canopy, a washer-dryer, and I'm making decent money. Enough to get us new drapes. We can shop garage sales and estate sales up in Hillsborough for stuff from the old west."

"The western theme will compliment my tastes for Victorian and antiques. We need patio furniture first so we can eat outside by the goldfish pond and watch the cascade."

"I'll build a barbeque pit," he said.

Looking around imaginatively, she said, "The Oriental rug will fit perfect in the living room. We'll put the sofa and the loveseat by the fireplace. And the piano will fit in that corner. Oh, Clint, this is going to be so much fun."

"I'm going to mount speakers in the beam ceiling," he said.

"We can put your painting of 'Dead Man's Hand' over the mantle."

"First thing I'm doing is building bookshelves in the spare bedrooms. They're going to be our offices."

"Let's name it 'Lover's Nest,' she said.

"You're so clever. I love it."

* * *

On a drizzly December day, Clint sat having lunch at Marvin Gardens beer joint with his long-time pal, Matt Gallagan.

"The design I submitted to the town of Hillsborough got approved," said Clint. "It's a Gothic mansion with flying buttresses, pointed arches, and gargoyles. I'm going to need a good man to run the crew. You've honed your skills and I need teammates."

Matt scratched his shaggy mop of long, brown hair. "Things are pretty stable where I'm working."

"What would you say if I gave you a piece of the action and offered you a fat bonus?"

"It's beginning to sound interesting."

"There'll be more incentives," said Clint. "This is just the beginning, Matt. Starburst Construction and Development is going to be a powerful force in the Bay Area. I've got some big-time investors coming on board with wheel barrels of venture capital. Clay Thompson has a couple of shopping malls in the works and over a hundred housing units in the planning stages. This guy doesn't mess around. He's even doing a feasibility study on building a business park. Santa Clara Valley is busting loose. This isn't hype, Matt."

Matt grinned. "How'd you meet this cat?"

"He's Dan's father. You heard what happened to Dan?"

"Yeah, I heard he fried his noodles."

"Almost," said Clint. "He's a miracle, thanks to therapy. Now the guy's skyrocketing to stardom."

"What do you mean?"

"He's in New York rehearsing for the lead in Jesus Christ Superstar."

"You're kidding me. That's terrific."

"Yeah. Anyway, Dan's dad mentored me in my senior year at San Jose State. He's sharp, and he likes the unit prices I quoted him. Well, what do you think about teaming up and joining the force?"

"You and I go way back," said Matt. "I trust you. Heck, we've known each other since the eighth grade."

"Then jump ship and come aboard. There are going to be a hell of a lot of groundbreaking ceremonies kicking off next year."

"I've never built a medieval castle, might be interesting. Got a dungeon?"

"Yeah, and an orgy room," said Clint. "Look, Matt. You know every carpenter who's any good around here. I only want top-notch master tradesmen aboard this force. I want the best crews in the Bay Area."

"Count me in."

* * *

With the Gothic mansion under construction and feeling optimistic about the future, Clint drove to the Chevrolet dealership on California Drive and bought a new 4x4 pick-up truck. Stoked in a fever, he raced home to surprise Dusty.

"Don't you think you might be going overboard with all this optimism?" Dusty said as they lay on a rug in front of the fireplace, listening to Poco, sipping wine, and munching popcorn.

"It's better to be optimistic than pessimistic," said Clint. "While the guy was doing the paperwork, I walked across the street and ordered you a new red Jaguar XKE ragtop. Be here tomorrow."

Her elbow knocked over the popcorn bowl and spilt the wine from her glass as she rolled on top of him. "Clint! See what you made me do."

"I didn't make you do that. You pounced on me."

"A convertible; are you sure we can afford all this," she said, going into the kitchen to get a wet towel. "We've only been married less than a year."

"I thought you might think I was selfish and only thinking about myself. I know how much you love the open air."

"I think I'm breaking out in an ecstatic rash," she said. "My whole body feels itchy."

"I have a magic remedy for cases of itchy skin."

She came back into the room and winked at him. "Then why don't you shut the drapes?"

Grinning wildly, Clint got up and slid the drapes closed as Dusty scrubbed the carpet.

"Have you heard from Tommy and Joey?" Dusty asked.

"Matrix is off touring Europe playing acid rock."

"How wonderful," she said. "And Mark?"

Clint laughed. "He's a full-fledged hippie writing music somewhere in Marin County. I hear he has a mop of hair down to his waist. Aside from Matt and Mel, only Roy remains straight laced, and he's hard at work running the family newspaper, striving to make his fortune with Chrissie."

"I like Mel," said Dusty. "He calls you all the time and sends you all those deep thinking books. What's he up to?"

"He's transferred to Notre Dame and living in South Bend, Indiana. Mel's gonna make a darn good English teacher."

"You're very lucky to have such good friends."

"I'm lucky to have you as my best friend and lover."

"As a friend," she said, "may I offer you some advice?"

"Sure."

"Don't stress yourself out. You've been putting in long hours these past few months."

"You're always so thoughtful," said Clint. "I appreciate your concern. Actually, I'm kind of enjoying the pressure. But I could use a little relief. If it's a nice night tomorrow, why don't we take a whimsical cruise to

Haight-Ashbury. Check out the city that's being heralded as the melting pot of the new drug culture."

"We can disguise ourselves as hippies," she said excitedly. "I've got a pair of ripped and faded old blue jeans and a tie-dyed shirt. We can wear peace symbols dangling from our necks to blend in. I'll wear a wreath of daisies around my head. I have a black wig you can tie into a ponytail and wear. That way no one will suspect you of being a narc, mister straight arrow."

He laughed. "I think I'll pass on that one."

"One more thing."

"Fire away."

"Please slow down; you're hardly ever around these days with your newly acquired gluttony for prosperity. It's been nice being with you tonight, talking."

"I'm not doing all this for me; I'm doing it for us," he said, "for our financial security."

"I don't want to own the whole planet," she said. "I want us to be happy."

"Slowing down's going to be tough. Clay gave me the go-ahead on a couple of big projects. But I'll try."

"This is cause for celebration," she said and rolled on top of him. "After we make whoopee, let's gussy up and go night clubbing. I'm in the mood to dance."

Chapter 3

With amusing grins, the next day, Dusty parked her new XKE along the panhandle near Golden Gate Park, and they meandered up to Haight Street. Hand in hand, they stopped to check out the evolution of the hippie generation. In a gesture of peace they held their fingers in a V and said, "peace" and "Namaste, brother" in passing the hordes of wandering flower children.

They smiled, whiffing the scent of patchouli oil and the thick, pungent odor of marijuana that permeated the air everywhere they walked. Counter-revolutionary young musicians were strumming their guitars on street corners, in doorways, hallways, alleyways, singing about peace, ban the bomb, and making love, not war.

"Check it out," said Dusty. "It looks like an invasion of Martian freaks on a pilgrimage to the Holy Land."

"I can't believe the change," said Clint. "It's so drastic, so radical. The streets are swelled with glossy-eyed moonies, sage mystics, shaman prophets, and transcendentalist gurus."

"Maybe we'll find Mark among these odd species of the spiritually enlightened," she said. "Look! Check out those shaven-headed Hari Krishna in the orange robes, whirling around in a euphoric trance."

"They're nothing but shameless panhandlers."

"I like the ones playing ring around the rosy," she said, "handing out leaflets, claiming to have reached a higher state of consciousness, while chanting dogmatic mantras."

"Check out that masked dude in the tinted shades, peddling psychedelics and plastic baggies of marijuana from that doorway."

"The way he's shaking," she said, "that dude is wired to the max. He looks like a frenetic zombie."

At nightfall, mellow acoustic rock-and-roll filtered out from the tiny coffee shop they ventured into. Strobe lights circled the ceiling in the smoky room. Zigzag rolling papers, hash pipes, incense sticks, plastic baggies full of weed, and other drug paraphernalia symbolic of the changing times, lay scattered on top of the round wooden cable spool where they sat on pillows.

Sipping tea, their eyes roved inquisitively around the room.

"Can you believe this," she said with an astonished expression. "It's incredible, not one woman is wearing a bra and everyone is stoned out of their gourds, pawing each other in public, like wild beasts."

"I agree. This is big," he said. "The way everyone is letting it all hang out. Maybe we really are in a sexual revolution. Check out the people wearing saris and loin cloths. It's a regression back into the times of the Roman orgies."

"Don't be ridiculous. It's only a passing phase. It's the emergence of modern youth, a less inhibited culture challenging the assumptions of the past."

"That's your point of view, but I beg to differ," he said. "This is no passing fad. The same thing is happening in New York. It's going on all over the country and in England."

A glassy-eyed, peasant girl with frizzy, sun-bleached hair sitting across from Dusty lit a joint and passed it to her.

Dusty straightened up and shook her head. "Ahhh, not now, I'm already as high as I want to be."

"Come on, take a hit. It's totally bodacious," the girl said, holding the joint in front of Dusty. She turned and looked at Clint and waved it in front of him.

Clint looked to Dusty for approval.

She shook her head in displeasure.

He frowned. "Ah, no thanks."

The girl shrugged, inhaled, and passed the joint to another girl, who eagerly took it and sucked the smoke into her lungs.

"Have you ever wondered what it would be like to smoke marijuana?" Dusty asked.

"On occasion," Clint said, "but I've a bounty of foibles. No need in adding another one and going further astray. It strikes me odd why you'd ask me such a question. You've never displayed the slightest notion of wanting to smoke pot. You've always been so embodied with prudence and your pragmatic ways. Why'd you ask?"

"Oh, ah," she stuttered. "Idle curiosity, I guess. I'm not interested in smoking marijuana. It seems everyone is smoking it. Even my girlfriends are smoking it."

*   *   *

Sunrays were coming through the bedroom window when Clint woke the next morning. Half awake, he slipped out of bed and quietly went into the kitchen to make breakfast. He came back into the bedroom and set the two trays on the bed. He slid a Beatles' tape into the tape deck, opened the drapes, and sang out, "Breakfast in bed at Lover's Nest." Dusty sat upright, stretching and yawning, wearing a see through teddy.

After breakfast and a round of passionate lovemaking, wearing short-shorts and a halter-top, Dusty went out into the backyard to work in her vegetable garden. Clint came out with a pot of herbal tea and sat on the swing set under the redwood trellis by the goldfish pond.

"Come on over and have some tea and crumpets," Clint shouted.

"How sweet of you," she said, skipping over and sitting on a cushion beside him. "It's so comfy out here. I like listening to the frogs croak. I do all my homework assignments out here. Those lily pads you put in the pond really add a special touch. And the grape vines are beginning to weave through the trellis."

"Your zucchinis are sure getting big," he said, "you're good at growing things."

"We'll be eating a lot of zucchini bread," she said. "Thanks for breakfast in bed. That was a special treat."

Clint pulled out a gift-wrapped box with ribbon and a bow. "The treat came afterward."

She smiled. "What's that?"

"A surprise," he said. "Saw it on sale at that mystic shop, The Magic Theater. I couldn't resist." He handed her the box.

"For me?" She said and began tearing the wrapping paper into shreds. She opened the box and stuck her hand inside. "A brass Buddha. I love it. Thank you. You've converted?"

"Not yet," he replied. "I'm still trying to figure out the difference between God, Jesus, Christ, and the Lord."

"They're all the same," she said. "Hey, I've been thinking it might be fun to try smoking marijuana. What do you think?"

Taken aback, he said, "You're throwing me for a loop. What's up?"

"I don't know," she said. "I guess I want to know why it's become such a big deal. I've never seen anyone act crazy or get violent. Everyone always seems so mellow and laid back."

His brow furled, astonished and confused. "Wow! You're really blowing my mind," he said. "You must be on a contact high. Something's loosened your morals."

She looked him in the eyes. "Debby's tried it. She said it's great for enhancing visual perceptions and that you see and hear things much more clearly. Especially the natural beauty of mountain scenery, the beach, watching the waves, and listening to the surf. And music."

His cerulean eyes widened. "What a trip! I can't believe you. You're forever changing. I love you." He leaned over and kissed her.

She smiled and added, "Deb also said it greatly heightens sexual orgasms."

Any hesitation Clint previously had about experimenting with grass completely evaporated. "That does it! You've whetted my juices. I'll pick us up a baggy this week." He cuddled closer to her. "How ignorant of me. I once thought the fifties would never die out, but I was dead wrong. This hippie stuff is for real. Now you, a socialite, want to get high. What a trip." He shook his head. "Let's get on with this enhancing stuff."

"I'm not suggesting we make it a habit," she cautioned. "I'm only saying that it might be interesting. Deb said to only buy the female buds."

He laughed. "Ah ha, so it's the female bloom that does the enticing."

She laughed and smothered him with kisses.

* * *

A warm zephyr breeze filtered through the French doors the next weekend when they returned home from having Saturday brunch with Dusty's parent's. Barefoot, Dusty lay sprawled on the sofa absorbed in reading a textbook and licking a popsicle. Clint stood quietly at the other end of the living room at his drafting table, sketching a rough design for another custom house. Staring through the front window over the bushy hedge awaiting a spark of inspiration, he watched Clay Thompson pull up in a shiny new Cadillac. He was well-groomed as always and dressed casual with a smile on his imposing face.

"We've got company," he said. "It's Clay Thompson."

"I'll get it. I want to tell him how much we appreciate the rug."

Carrying a tube and a brief case, Clay followed along the narrow, brick path towards the house as Dusty went to greet him at the door with a big hug and a kiss on the cheek.

A bright smile lit Clay's face and Clint wondered what the reason was for his unexpected visit.

"What a pleasant surprise," said Dusty. "Please come in, Mister Thompson, and have a seat." She gleefully gestured toward the sofa. "Would you care for an iced tea or lemonade?"

"Iced tea sounds terrific," Clay replied. He set the tube and briefcase on the dining table. "I can only stay a few minutes."

While Clint and Clay exchanged greetings and shook hands, Dusty scampered excitedly into the kitchen to fetch some glasses and a pitcher of iced tea. Clay sank into the sofa, unsnapped the gold clasps of his briefcase, pulled out some sheets of paper, and removed a role of blueprints from the tube. From the breast pocket of his sport coat, he brought out a gold pen.

"It seems your designs are creating a bidding war. I brought over the changes my associates would like on the Stonegate Project." Clay leaned back. "Nothing major, just some exterior alterations."

Clint looked at the drawings. "That's easy enough, no problem."

"I was thinking the other day that you kids might want to consider investing in income property," said Clay. "Get yourselves a tax shelter."

Dusty glided out of the kitchen and set a silver tray on the table. "Just the other day my father suggested the same thing."

"Your father has good perception, Dusty," Clay said.

"Oh! Your oriental rug really makes this room come alive," Dusty said enthusiastically. "It adds a whole new dimension to the room."

Clay looked down at the rug. “A family heirloom wasting away in the garage. Glad you like it.” Clay began to talk about the tax benefits of depreciation.

“Interesting,” Clint said after Clay had finished. “We’d definitely be interested in investing in income property, and I appreciate your advice. Thanks, Mister Thompson.”

“Oh, I just made an offer on three vacant parcels further up in Hillsborough by the Caroline Mansion,” said Clay. “In fact, I have some clients who want you to whip up some preliminary schematics. They’ve seen your work and are interested if your design meets their criteria. Post-modern American architecture.”

“Usonian, I believe is how Frank Lloyd Wright referred to it,” said Clint. “I’ll drive by first thing in the morning.”

“One other item comes to mind,” said Clay. “There’s a dilapidated shack some acquaintances of mine have been using as a summer retreat and neglected to maintain. It’s a secluded hideaway, nestled in the hills of Woodside. But the foundation is reinforced concrete and strong enough to support a three-story building. Loads of possibilities with your acute visionary ability. You can pick it up for a mere pittance.” Clay snapped the clasps of his briefcase shut. “All the pertinent information is jotted on this sheet.”

“I’ll go over everything tonight, said Clint. “Later today, Dusty and I will take a drive and look at the Woodside house.”

They chatted a bit before saying goodbyes and Clay left.

“Why does he take such an interest in you?” Dusty asked.

"I'm not really sure," said Clint. "I think it has something to do with my being Dan's best friend. Dan's a gifted actor and has no interest in construction. It's like Clay has this vast reservoir of information and no one to share it with."

"I've grown attached to this house," she said, "and all the work we've done."

"It's horse country, and you love horses."

She beamed. "Yeah, let's drive down and take a look."

Chapter 4

That afternoon, Clint and Dusty drove to see the property in Woodside. Turning onto a tree-lined, bumpy driveway and driving a half mile, Clint stopped his truck in front of a decaying wooden bridge. They got out and sat on the tailgate to take in the surroundings.

"I'm glad you didn't try driving over that rickety thing," Dusty said. "We'd never have made it across."

Clint looked down at the small stream and said, "Can you believe this, a babbling brook."

She threw her hands over her head. "Oh, look! A rainbow trout," she said excitedly.

"That sucker's huge," he said, "must be twelve inches. Darn, I wish I had brought my fishing pole. This place is paradise."

"I agree," she said, swinging her legs. "I adore the scenery and the view of Crystal Springs Lake is magnificent. But that shack looks ready to fall over and crumple."

"Don't pay attention to that dump. It's the property that has me mesmerized. This spread is heaven. This is it. This is the site of our dream home."

"And the meadow," she said, "it's beautiful and so peaceful."

"Well, what do you think?"

"I don't know," she said. "I love how woodsy it is and all those towering trees."

"I'm making an offer on this place when we get back."

"But I love our house. I'm confused."

"Come on," he said. "Let's take a drive up to that bluff and take in the full scope of this property. This parcel is five acres in the heart of horse country."

Clint drove to the top of the hill, and they sat on a boulder while he pointed out the boundaries to her.

"You see that knoll above that grove of redwood trees," he said.

"It's spectacular."

"That's where I'm building our cantilevered home. I'll get my sketch pad and show you what I have in mind."

He came back, rolled up his sleeves and began drawing in a flurry of strokes.

"Clint, that's incredible," she said. "You're so talented."

"I studied it for four years. Now it's your turn to get creative and name it."

She thought a few moments. "What do you think of Zenith?"

"You're a genius, sweetheart. That's the highest point reached by a celestial body. That's so cool. Oh, I almost forgot; I've a special treat for us." He pulled out a plastic baggy and held it in front of her.

Her eyes lit up. "You finally got some!"

"Yep, and all female buds," he said. "It's time for some mind exploration and visual enhancement. This stuff will get us into orbit."

She smiled. “I could use some entertainment.”

Clint drove back to the property and parked in front of the decaying bridge. They got out and walked gingerly over the bridge to a log and sat on it.

They both sniffed the contents in the bag and grinned mischievously at each other, like teenagers about to smoke their first cigarette. With childlike anticipation, Dusty watched Clint clumsily attempt to roll his first joint. On his third try, he licked the paper and twisted the ends.

“Ladies first,” he said, handing it to her. “I should warn you, the guy I got it from said this is dynamite stuff. He called it Panama Red.”

Dusty squirmed and looked reluctant as she held it between her finger and thumb and raised it to her lips. Grinning, Clint struck a wooden match and lit it. On her first puff, she fell into a fit of coughing spasms and passed the joint to Clint. He raised his brow, took a small puff and choked from the harshness. In a mirthful manner, she observed him intently for symptoms of instant derangement.

They smoked the joint halfway down, taking small hits and quickly exhaling. When there was nothing left, they waited silently.

Looking befuddled, she looked at him and said, “I don’t understand all the fuss, I don’t feel anything.”

“Neither do I,” he said. “If it’s no big deal, why is it illegal?”

“Beats me,” she said, laughing.

He beamed. “Now that I think about it, everybody I’ve seen smoking weed takes big drags and holds it in their lungs as long as they can before blowing it out.”

“I think you’re right.”

He rolled another joint and lit it. He sucked in a big puff and held the smoke in his lungs for as long as he could before he began choking and gagging. Dusty did the same thing. The joint finished, they sat silent, hands clasped, staring at the old house, listening to it creak. Sniffing the air, they watched the house bend and sway in the wind until it seemed on the verge of toppling. The twitter and chirping of small sparrows and the loud cackle of crows grew louder. The distant barking and the rustling of leaves magnified. The small creek gurgled louder as it twisted its way down through the grove alongside the house.

"Wow, this is like a revelation," he said.

Giggling, she looked into his eyes and squeezed his hand. "I think I'm stoned."

"Me too," he said, pointing at the creek. "Tell me if you can see what I see."

She closed her eyes and after several moments, she reopened them. "I see children splashing and playing."

"That's incredible. Tell me what you see over by those trees."

She closed her eyes again and opened them. "I see a tree-house and two hammocks, a hitch-rack with a barn, a tack room with horseshoes and saddles and reins, and stables with horses and dogs."

He stared at her. "I don't believe this. You're reading my mind."

She giggled and looked at him demurely. "Maybe it's because I've grown to know you and we are one."

He shook his head in thought. "Okay. What's over there in that clearing, my mystical sorceress?" Clint pointed at the meadow of tall, bending grass.

She stared for a moment, which seemed like an hour. Looking dreamy-eyed, she said, "I see a fenced corral with a white claw foot bathtub filled with water, and bales of hay and alfalfa, and clover, and a compost heap, and a big pasture, and a riding rink with several standards, and jumping apparatus."

He stared intensely into her shiny eyes. "What am I thinking?"

She kept a straight face. "They're obscene thoughts."

"Wrong! I was thinking of an afternoon delight, but then I changed my mind knowing you'd say that. So I began concentrating on Einstein's cosmological constant."

They both erupted in laughter.

He turned serious. "You look even more beautiful than on our wedding day." He had a sudden thought. "Stop taking the pill. Let's start raising a family. This property is huge, and it will be ours. We're going to buy this place."

She appeared enchanted. "That sounds soooo wonderful. But can you wait for the babies until after I get my master's and I've taught for a year or two?"

He shrugged. "Oh yeah, guess I got carried away. Anyway, it'll give me time to build Zenith." He nuzzled her neck. "I can't wait for tonight."

She cut him off and said in a titillating voice, "Why wait until tonight. Let's do it right here."

He laughed. "I can't believe you said that. But I didn't bring a blanket."

With an illicit smirk, she tittered, "Who needs a blanket? Let's get naked and do it in the grass. God, am I stoned."

Stunned and gagging in laughter, Clint fell backward off the log. "I love how you've become so indecent," he howled. "I'm stoned out of my mind," he playfully muddled her hair.

She whiffed the air. "Can you believe the smell?"

"My senses are running amok."

They were laughing hysterically as they bumbled through the tall grass and she dragged him down on top of her.

Their taste buds running amok and their hearts thumping wildly, they made love, oblivious to the rest of the world.

Dusty was still talking dirty when Clint screeched to a halt in their driveway. They charged up the brick path and slammed the front door shut. Dusty scrambled into the kitchen and grabbed two strawberry parfaits and a can of whipping cream while Clint played a Beatles' "Magical Mystery Tour" album on the phonograph. After Dusty drew the curtains in the bedroom, she stripped naked by the bedpost, giggling.

"That stuff certainly heightens your senses," she said. "My head is spinning and my body is all tingly."

"You look empyrean."

With blissful expressions, they dove onto the bed.

Chapter 5

The year shot by in a flash. Starburst Construction and Development Company was on a kinetic flight pattern with a shopping mall, two posh apartment buildings, and more than two dozen luxury homes under construction. In mid-summer of 1968, the plans for Zenith received approval and construction began. Fully remodeled, landscaped, and expanded, 'Lover's Nest' sold for a hefty profit.

Compelled to claim a piece of the American dream, Clint continued to follow the guidelines he had learned from Clay Thompson. He wheeled and dealed with bankers and high-rolling financiers, cutting through the bureaucratic red tape, and employing the principles and tactics Clay had taught him. Only he used less of an iron fist in running his construction business than Clay.

He put the bonus system into effect to reward his partner, Matt, the general superintendent. Matt paid the field superintendents, foremen, and carpenters well above the prevailing wage scale. To keep everyone motivated in a team-spirit mode, Clint set aside time each day to stop and chat with the crews and pass out tickets to 49ers and Giants games. Matt organized the first annual Starburst golf tournament with prizes, planned basketball and flag football games, and sponsored a little league softball team. The result was finely polished workmanship and a harmonious morale.

* * *

When Indian summer arrived, Starburst was ticking with the precision of a Swiss timepiece. Clint was so bogged down with the drudgery of paperwork and high-powered meetings, dressed in a three-piece suit that he looked forward to the weekends working with Matt at Zenith.

On a scorching Saturday morning, shirtless and wearing cut-off jeans and work boots, Clint buckled the leather pouches and joined Matt up on the roof.

"You're just in time to help me set this 4 X 12 hip rafter in place," hollered Matt, who was standing on the ridge.

"Hold your horses, Matt, I'm coming," said Clint, climbing up the wooden cleats that were nailed to the studs.

"Man, you're gonna be king of the mountain up here," said Matt, "with this panoramic view of Shangri La."

"Got my eye on something for you just down the road."

"No kidding."

"I wouldn't do that," said Clint. "Not after all you've done to help spearhead this company. You're more than deserving of a fat reward. You're the best construction manager around. You don't know how much I appreciate your coming here on your weekends off."

"It keeps me in shape," said Matt. "This sitting in a truck, driving around from one job site to the next is boring. I need the exercise."

"How are you doing with the ladies?"

Matt laughed. "Struck the mother lode the day I met Bonny. Wait till you meet her. This babe will knock your eyes out."

"Bring her over for dinner next Saturday."

"I will. She's a tad young, but she's a hottie."

"How old is she?"

"She just turned 17."

Clint cracked up. "Man, that's robbing the cradle. She's jail bait. 17's a mite young."

"What about you and Dusty?"

"She's only three years younger than me. That chick's a little girl."

"That's the way I like 'em. Young, hot and horny."

After they set the hip rafter in place, Clint's Skil saw buzzed, sawdust flew, and the zinging sound of nails sinking into the soft Douglas fir filled the air. Clint thrived on their competition, but as hard as he tried, he proved no match for Matt's walking the hip rafters. Matt's willowy body and the deftness of his movements, balancing on the rafters were a wonder for Clint to behold. For Clint, watching Matt was like watching a gymnast perform on a balance beam.

Clint felt good working up a sweat, breathing fresh air, laughing, and joking with Matt. The redwood trees provided shade over Zenith during the stifling afternoon while the blazing sun beamed down on them as they worked themselves into lathers.

Clint felt even better at the end of the day when, beaded in sticky sweat with a wet handkerchief tied around his head, he sat with Matt by a cooler of cold beer, admiring their accomplishments. Two separate skeletal infrastructures cantilevered over the creek, with hip rafters, jutting outward above the redwood grove.

*   *   *

Arriving home later that evening with a dozen red roses, Clint smiled seeing Dusty sitting on the sofa playing her acoustic guitar and singing Joni Mitchell's "Both Sides Now." She had obviously heard the door open and shut, and he thought it strange that she didn't budge to acknowledge his presence. In grimy clothes, his hair scattered with sawdust and smelling of sweat, he walked up behind her and placed his hand gently on her shoulder.

She abruptly stopped playing and jerked around, glaring at him. "We had a dinner engagement at the club with Debby and her fiancé," she yelled.

He grimaced apologetically and dropped the flowers. "Darn! I completely forgot. I'm sorry. I'll take a quick shower and change."

Fuming, she shouted, "Don't bother. We were supposed to be there two hours ago. I called her and canceled. Twelve hours a day, seven days a week you're at it. I never see you anymore. It's like you've become a stranger around here." She stood up. "This has gone beyond bothersome. I can't take any more frustration."

"Sweetheart," he said, "I'm building our dream house for us and our family. I want our children to know that I not only designed it, but I also helped build it. It's our legacy to pass down to them. And they can pass it down to their children."

She folded her arms tight across her chest, unwilling to surrender her anger. "What about tomorrow? My parents invited us yachting."

He lowered his head and thought a moment, realizing he had been guilty of neglect. "I promised Matt I'd help him finish stacking the roof. He's busting his butt to get the roof on before winter sets in and escrow closes on this place. He's even putting in a seven-day week." His face suddenly beamed with an idea. "Look! After we move in, we'll take a trip to Mexico or the Caribbean. Maybe even Europe."

"You're always saying that," she shouted. "Talk is cheap."

"Look, honey," he said in an even voice. "Right now my company is erupting, and everything is chaotic. This is a feast or famine business. Who knows what will happen next year. Recessions, inflation, depressions, another war; heck, anything can happen to shift the economy into reverse. I know how difficult it's been for you, but it's a small sacrifice to pay. Think of it as our security blanket for the future. I'm doing this for us."

"I understand," she said in a bittersweet tone. "I don't mind your working hard. I've always admired you for your drive to be successful. It's our weekends together that I miss. I rarely see you anymore. And your late-night meetings have become intolerable."

"That's all part of the diplomatic ritual. I'd stop but escrow is coming up, and we have to be outta here."

"You're right. I keep forgetting about that."

He picked up the flowers moved closer to her. "Now can we make up and be friends?"

She hesitated a moment, then the crease of her dimples appeared. "Actually, now that you're home, I feel in the mood for some romance. It's been almost two weeks since we've..."

He interrupted her. "That long?"

"Yes, and it's not fair that I have to suffer. Your riding the bullet train to wealth is weakening our marriage."

"You're right," he said emphatically, "how cruel and insensitive of me. I'm sorry if I've been ignoring you. I love you." He set the flowers on her lap and put his arms around her.

"You've been away from home so much," she said, "I've been suspecting that you have a mistress on the side."

"Don't be absurd. That would be like substituting a ripe blooming rose for a weed of crabgrass. Tonight is your night to be pampered with a massage. I'll call Matt and cancel. We'll go yachting with your parents tomorrow. I won't go to the office on Monday. We can play golf or tennis at the country club."

"I have classes Monday morning," she said.

"We'll play in the afternoon and get a tan."

"I'd prefer tennis."

"Then it's settled," he said. "Tonight I'll cook your favorite dinner, tostadas and enchiladas."

She picked up the flowers and sniffed them. "Thank you for the roses, they smell nice."

"I'm really sorry about working so much. I'll make a point to be around more."

"I would appreciate it. My sister called and told me that Richard's been drafted into the Army."

"Ah, gees, that means he could be shipped off to Vietnam."

"I know. It made me sick to my stomach when Betsy told me."

"Can't your father pull some strings? He's a lieutenant general."

"He's also a gung-ho American and supports that ugly war."

"You've got that right. That war is bad news. I like your brother a lot. He has a great sense of humor. He's also smart. He'll pull through."

"He leaves for boot camp next week."

"I'll drive him down."

"He'd like that. Richard likes you."

The next evening after yachting with Dusty's parents, Clint stood at the butcher block dicing onions and wiping his eyes. Dusty glided into the kitchen wearing fluffy slippers and a satin negligee. He sniffed the intoxicating fragrance of honeysuckle when he kissed her neck.

"You always smell so good after a shower," he said.

She smiled. "Your dad came by this morning and dropped off a copy of your family tree," she said, filling a glass with red wine. "I read some. You don't mind, do you?"

"Of course not. It's pretty gory stuff."

"I found it fascinating, but you're right, some of it's very tragic, like that part about your great-grandfather William McBride and Little-Fawn drowning. It was so heart-wrenching, I cried. Then the part about your grandfather being killed by a gunslinger had me in tears. Are you keeping a diary?"

He laughed. "No need, it's all stored in my memory bank. Besides, all those stories ended in woe. If I ever do write about us, it'll have a happy ending."

"Good. Oh! I almost forgot. Your sister called and told me she is leaving the convent, It seems she's fallen moonstruck in love with a monk."

He laughed. "A monk? That's an interesting combination, a nun and a monk!"

She nodded. "She said he'll be coming down to talk to you after they've settled into their apartment in San Francisco."

"They're not even married."

"That's why he wants to talk with you," she said.

"About what?"

"It seems he's a man of principles, and since your father's leaving tonight to tour with his orchestra, he wants to ask your permission to take her hand in marriage."

He snickered. "They're heathen sinners."

"Neither had taken their final vow."

"I'll make them repent for living in sin before marriage." He scratched his head in wonderment. "A monk, huh? I can't wait to hear this guy's story; it's gotta be a good one. I think I'll make him do penitence, a hundred 'Our Fathers' and a hundred 'Hail Marys.' A monk and a nun, wow! Living together in sin, pagan blasphemers is what they are." He laughed. Dusty stared at him, shaking her head.

*   *   *

The aroma of fresh flowers wafted throughout the house in the ensuing weeks and Dusty's bitterness slowly dissipated.

"It's nice to be eating dinner with you these past weeks," Dusty said, seated at the dining table, "instead of alone." You were in such an engrossed rut."

"It's a feast or famine world we live in."

"It doesn't have to be," she said. "I'd be happier back living in that cozy apartment having a romantic candlelit dinner with you every night. Your forging in high gear to build this financial empire was taking the fun out of our marriage. All you ever talked about was cutting the big deal."

"It won't last forever, sweetheart. Right now, the economy is bursting. Who knows what's in store for the future."

"What do you think of going dancing after dinner, I feel like kicking up my heels."

"I'd love to," he said, "but I've an important meeting tonight."

"We haven't gone dancing in ages. Can't you at least compromise and have a change of heart?"

"Dusty, you're an heiress to a fortune. Let me have a shot. In five years we'll be dancing every night. We're young."

She gave him a look of discontent. "Do you remember your promise to me before we were married?"

"Which one, I made a lot of promises."

"You promised me you would never be like my father."

"I'm not anything like him."

"Yes you are," she said angrily. "Money is manifested on your face. I don't want to be married to a mogul. All they think about is money and power."

"Look, sweetheart, I didn't marry you for your money. I'm doing this for our family and children."

"I know that, but what about happiness?"

"You're not happy?"

"I'm always happy when you're home. What's wrong with wanting to have fun before our marriage wanes into nothing?"

"Alright, you have my immediate attention. I'll call and cancel. After dinner, we'll go to the Tiger A-Go-Go and shake our tail feathers."

"Are you sure you're up to it? You look beat."

"Dusty, I love you and want you to be happy. I never want to lose you. I'll work on slowing down and being home for dinner. I promise. Now let's go dancing."

Chapter 6

Two weeks before Thanksgiving, Clint and Matt were hard at work putting the finishing touches on Zenith. They were setting oak spindles on the handrail at the head of the winding staircase when Matt said, “Thanks for those plans.”

“No sweat,” said Clint. “You deserve them.”

“I submitted them to the city last week. I should get approval by the end of the month. The planning commissioners loved your solar design. So did Bonny. She especially liked the futuristic look and all the glass.”

“I’d like to help you build it, but the home front is on shaky ground about me working too much. But I should be able to pitch in a little.”

A loud crash startled them, and they looked at each other.

“Damn,” hollered Clint. “Go see what the hell happened.”

Matt took off down the stairs and ran outside. A few minutes later, he frantically darted back inside the house and shouted, “Quick! “Get down here fast.”

Clint turned and looked down at Matt, noticing that his face was pallid.

"It's Dusty! Hurry up," Matt hollered in a squeaky voice. "Something's happened, something bad. She's acting strange and screaming her lungs out."

Clint dropped his tool bags on the steps and wildly leaped down the stairs.

"Dusty crashed into the wishing well," Matt stammered, running astride of Clint across the terrace. "She's hysterical, and cussing up a storm. It's like something tragic has happened."

An array of woeful images rushed through Clint's mind as he bolted out into the courtyard. His heart fluttered when he saw Dusty sitting and twitching violently on the cobblestones, her back leaning against the wishing well. Steam spewed from out of her crunched XKE. Her head was tilted forward in her hands, and she clutched a handkerchief in one hand and a crumpled sheet of paper in her other.

"Call an ambulance," Clint told Matt.

Matt sprinted to the job shack while Clint checked for signs of blood or an injury and placed his arm consolingly around her shoulders. Her body convulsed, and her speech was incoherent as he whispered comforting words to her. Tears gushed down her reddened cheeks when she looked at him with dazed eyes and shouted, "My brother is dead."

Dusty's swollen lips quivered as she tried to speak but only gasped. She began to choke and then collapsed, unconscious. Jolted into a panic, hoping she was mistaken about her brother being dead, Clint quickly took her wrist, felt her pulse, and placed his ear against her chest. Listening to her heart thump wildly, he pried her fingers apart and removed the scrunched sheet of paper. He was about to read it when Matt ran up, handed him a wet towel and said, “An ambulance is on the way.”

“Thanks,” Clint said, holding Dusty next to him and patting her forehead.

“Did she tell you what happened?” Matt asked.

“Her brother’s been killed, but I’m hoping she’s wrong.”

Her face enraged, she shuttered and screamed, “My brother is dead!”

“Aw, geez! Button the damn place up, Matt, we’re done.”

Holding Dusty in his arms, knowing the closeness she shared with her brother, Clint felt a deep sorrow for her and wept as he read the letter of condolence from the United States government. He was holding her curled on his lap, stroking her hair and rocking her when he heard the sirens. Within minutes, an ambulance screeched to a halt, and two medics came running toward Dusty and Clint with oxygen tanks and medical equipment.

Dusty filled her lungs with air and cleared her throat. “Richard’s dead,” she murmured after the medics helped to revive her, and Clint sat beside her in the rear of the ambulance.

“I know, I read the letter,” Clint said, feeling powerless. “I know how you must feel. I grieve with you. I wish I could say or do something.”

Dusty remained traumatized and was shaking uncontrollably as she was being examined in the emergency room at Stanford Hospital. After having her prescriptions filled at the pharmacy, she swallowed a tranquilizer and sleeping pill before Matt drove them home.

At midnight Dusty and Clint were sprawled on the carpet in front of the fireplace. She was still shaking and sobbing as Clint held her tightly in his arms and listened to her vent her anger at her father.

She wiped her eyes and in a crackling voice, she said, "I feel all twisted inside, confused, stifled. I love my father, but at the same time, I hate him. He's partly to blame for Richard's death with all his gung-ho, die-hard, patriotic blabber and rah-rah propaganda. America right or wrong, take it or leave it. Now Richard's dead and for what? Nothing! There hasn't even been an official declaration of war. My brother was shot in the head by a fucking sniper."

Clint gently massaged her back and searched for comforting words. "And a senseless war at that," he said stiffly. "A damn repugnant blight on America, sending young kids to fight in a jungle, bombing and killing innocent people and children with napalm and Agent Orange, claiming communism is responsible."

Her anger fueled, she said, "A ludicrous travesty to this so-called modern civilization of ours, falsely claiming to be the world peacemaker. War should be abolished."

In a low voice, Clint said, "I loved your brother. He had spirit. It's a damn tragic loss."

Staring blankly at the fire, she said in a quivering voice, "They said he risked his life. Single-handedly, charging up a hill to destroy an enemy machine gunner in a foxhole, he saved his platoon. They're awarding him the Medal of Honor." Her head dropped.

"That makes your brother a hero in my book."

She lifted her head and scowled, "Dead heroes can't talk."

Her words sent shivers rushing down Clint's spine, and tears fell from his swollen eyes as he searched his mind for something to say. He could only think to hold her tightly as they lay in silence, staring into the fire, at last united in agreement on the brutal ugliness of war.

* * *

Dusty remained emotionally devastated and under sedation the dark day her brother's body was shipped home from Vietnam. Her misery worsened on the gloomy day of her brother's funeral. Hardly a word was spoken between them on the solemn morning they dressed in black with armbands, both wearing silver peace symbols. At the doorway, he patted her eyes dry. After a consoling squeeze of encouragement, they walked out into the bright sunlight to bury her brother.

"Richard had to have been a popular kid in high school," Clint said outside of the mortuary, in hopes of lifting Dusty's spirits, "because there are hundreds of his former classmates in attendance."

Trembling and sobbing, she said, "They've come here to look at my bother's body lying dead in an open casket; to pay homage to a dead hero." Her head flipped sideways, and she fainted in Clint's arms. Dusty's sister, Betsy, charged over and flanked Dusty. Wet faced and grim, Betsy linked her arm in Dusty's and helped to walk her unsteadily inside the mortuary to where their parents stood with their eyes shut beside the silver casket.

Feeling queasy, Clint looked down at Richard's face. He appeared to be in a tranquil sleep. Dusty's body twitched and shook violently, and Clint gripped her tighter. Then Betsy's legs became rubbery, and she buckled, collapsing like a rag doll. Two young men quickly grabbed her and lifted her from the floor. Dusty's anguish-stricken father held his wife tightly as her legs wobbled, teetering on collapse. Then Dusty opened her puffy eyes and flew into a flaming rage, ranting hysterically about the war.

Dusty, Betsy, and their mother never regained their composure well enough to walk without assistance. As deeply as they wanted to be pallbearers, the sisters were too weak from mournful despair to do so. Richard's closest high school friends gripped the silver handles of the casket. Teary-eyed, the young men slowly marched outside and slid the casket onto the rails of a black hearse.

The funeral procession stretched more than two miles to a military cemetery in San Bruno where the American flag fluttered at half-mast. Holding Dusty tightly, Clint stared out the window at the rows of identical white, wooden grave-markers that lined up and down the rolling green sod. A blustery wind swept through the cemetery when the procession entered and proceeded to the floral wreaths that encircled Richard's grave.

Clint held Dusty and Betsy in his arms. Two of Richard's best friends flanked Dusty's mother, holding her upright, while a military priest recited a eulogy. It was followed by Mister Melon reading a shorter eulogy before Richard's casket was lowered into the grave. Dusty quivered when six uniformed soldiers fired three volleys as a bugler played taps. Amid a showering of tears, screams, and a flurry of flowers, Richard's casket was laid to rest. Three soldiers stood in front of Dusty's parents. The two on the ends saluted as the one in the center presented Dusty's mother with a folded American flag. The sad-faced pallbearers took turns scooping spades of soil and tossing them onto the casket. Each visitor saluted before leaving.

* * *

Dusty remained stricken with grief on the day they moved into Zenith a few days before Christmas. It wasn't until Valentine's Day neared that her melancholia slowly began to diminish, and her spirits lifted. Immersed in decorating the upstairs master bedroom, her lovely face returned to its usual brightness when spring arrived.

Clint was downstairs in the sunken den when he heard the phone ring.

"Who was that, honey?" Dusty asked when Clint came into the bedroom.

"You'd never guess in a million years," he said.

She shrugged. "Don't leave me in suspense."

"Remember Misty and Doug we met in Hawaii on our honeymoon?"

She looked surprised and said excitedly, "Yes, of course. What did they want?"

"They're moving to California. Doug wanted to know if it would be okay if Misty and their son, Chip, could stay with us while he sews up some loose ends in Seattle. Said he would follow in a week or two and find a place for them to live."

"Let's see," Dusty said, "that would make Chip almost two. He'd be potty trained. It might be nice listening to the pitter-patter of little feet, and it would give us some family training and help prepare us. What did you tell him?"

"I told him I'd talk to you and call him back. What do you think?"

"Sounds fine. I like Misty. And this house is big enough for a symphony orchestra."

Chapter 7

Summer was setting in on the afternoon Dusty and Clint stood waving excitedly as they watched Misty step out of a tunnel chute at San Francisco Airport. She was smiling and carrying her son, Chip, and a diaper bag.

"Well, look at you," said Clint, "all cheery and bright-eyed. Welcome to the city by the bay."

"It's so good to see you two," said Misty in a thick Scottish brogue. "It's been such a long time. This is like a dream come true. I've always wanted to come to San Francisco."

"I can't believe, Chip," said Dusty after they exchanged hearty embraces. "He's so big, and so adorable. Can I hold him?"

"Oh, sure," said Misty, handing Chip to Dusty.

Dusty cradled him in her arms. "He's light as a feather and looks just like you," she said. "He even has your freckles and green eyes."

"I should warn you," said Misty, running her fingers through her long, wavy red hair. "He's just starting the terrible twos. He's not quite potty trained, so be careful."

"Can I change him when he's wet?" Dusty asked. "I've never changed a baby's diaper."

"Oh, sure," said Misty, "you can change him all you want."

Clint grinned, "What if the little bugger goes poo-poo?"

"Don't worry, Dusty," said Misty, "I'm still breast feeding. Chip's poop doesn't stink, but it gets a little messy at times."

"Oh, I wouldn't mind," said Dusty. "Does he ever use a baby bottle?"

"All the time, I feed him juice and stuff. You can feed him later if you want."

"I'd really like that. I've always wanted to feed a baby."

Misty beamed. "You can even breast feed him if you like."

Dusty appeared confused. "But I don't have any milk."

"Chip won't mind," said Misty, "he just likes to suckle."

Clint chuckled and asked, "Can he walk?"

Misty's eyes widened. "It's more of a lunge. I always think he's going to trip and fall flat on his face, but Chipper holds his balance real well."

The three were gabbing excitedly as they walked through the bustling corridor and stepped onto the escalator. Downstairs in the baggage claim area, Clint grabbed a cart and pulled off half a dozen suitcases from the revolving turnstile. The cart was stacked six-feet high when Clint rolled it out into the windy parking lot. Finished loading Misty's bags in the bed of his truck, Clint headed south to Woodside.

Misty's head was revolving back and forth when Clint turned off the highway and headed south on Canada Road, passing the Pulgas Water Temple and the Fioli estate.

"It's so beautiful here," said Misty, ecstatically, "so peaceful, and all the horses and corrals and barns."

"This is horse country," said Clint, turning onto a private dirt road and heading up the hill toward Zenith.

"Is today April Fools?" Misty asked.

Dusty laughed. "Why did you say that?"

"Whose house are we going to anyway?"

"To our house," replied Dusty.

"Holy smoke," said Misty as the iron gates between two stone columns started to automatically roll open. "You guys never mentioned that you were rich."

"We aren't rich," said Dusty.

"Is this all your property?"

"All five acres," said Dusty.

"And those horses grazing in that pasture, are they yours?"

"Sure are," said Clint. "And they're thoroughbreds."

"They're beautiful. And that house, it's so futuristic."

"It's not completely finished yet," said Dusty. "There's still a lot of work we need to do."

"That house must be worth a fortune," said Misty. "It's enormous and ultramodern, and it's the only house around. Gosh, this is darn near a kingdom. How big is your house?"

"A little over ten thousand square feet," said Clint.

"There's so much glass," said Misty, "aren't you afraid of earthquakes?"

"You get used to them after a while," said Dusty as Clint parked in the circular courtyard. "Not much you can do to stop an earthquake."

"I read somewhere that seismologists at Berkeley are predicting a *big one*," said Misty, "even bigger than the one in 06."

Clint laughed. "After the *big one*, as some have coined it, California will be an island, floating in the Pacific."

As Clint unloaded Misty's baggage and was bringing it into the house, Dusty, carrying Chip in her arms, took Misty on a tour of the property. They were leaning over the wishing well when Clint came back outside and watched Misty close her eyes and toss some coins into the water.

"After you've finished making wishes," said Clint, "let's go inside and let Chip meet Snippy and Venus."

Misty opened her eyes. "Who are Snippy and Venus?"

"Snippy's a parrot," said Dusty, "and Venus is a Golden Retriever."

Chip proved to be a speedy tike the very moment Dusty carried him into Zenith and set him on the marble floor in the foyer. As Clint went to open the back door to let in Venus, in a flash, Chip slanted forward and lunged head-first into Dusty's favorite antique lamp, toppling it over.

"Oh, my God," Misty shouted, bending over to pick up the broken glass as Chip began cramming all the knickknacks into his tiny mouth.

"Don't worry, Misty," said Dusty, stooping to pick up the lamp, "it's nothing."

Misty grabbed the trinkets and ornaments from Chip and slapped his hand.

Clint opened the back door and Venus charged across the house and skidded smack in front of Chip. It was love at first sight. After Venus had thoroughly licked Chip's stunned face, the two scrambled into the dining room, and Chip yanked down the tablecloth, spilling spaghetti marinara sauce onto the rug.

Misty threw her hands on top of her head and yelled, "Oh, no, the rug," as Venus fell into a state of bliss, licking the strings of noodles and sauce, dripping from Chip's head.

"It's my fault, I shouldn't have let Venus in the house," said Clint as Dusty and Misty ran into the dining room. Misty picked up Chip and whacked his behind.

Grabbing Venus by his flea collar, Clint said, "I wasn't thinking properly. The little rascal is fast."

"Lightning fast," said Dusty. "I've never seen anything like it."

Holding Chip in her frail arms while he was crying and sucking his thumb, Misty said, "You wouldn't by chance happen to have a playpen?"

"No," said Dusty, "but we'll run down later and get one."

"I know what they look like," said Clint. "I'll make one. I've got a ton of stuff in the barn and a volleyball net. Take me a few minutes to slap something together."

"What about the rug?" Misty asked.

"Not to worry, Misty, we have a shampooer," said Dusty. "This little speedster needs more than a playpen, he needs a leash."

*   *   *

Misty proved to be a spry, wispy woman with a bubbly personality and an absolute delight to have around the house. Dusty nicknamed her son Hotfooter, who proved to be a constant amusement in the household, even with all the destruction the little squirt brought about by bumping, slamming, and knocking over everything in his path. From the first day Misty and her son moved in, Dusty made a happy fuss over Chip, helping to bathe and spoon-feed him, and baby-proofing the house.

With so much energy, it was several weeks before Chip stopped having tantrums and adjusted to being confined in the playpen that Clint had built. In the little spare he had, Clint finished building a playhouse and a schoolhouse in the rumpus room, where Dusty and Misty read bedtime fairy tales to chip.

Overloaded with work and feeling contrite one night, Clint broke away from his nightly meetings to be home in time for Hotfooter's feeding frenzy and bedtime story-telling. Misty and Dusty usually read pleasant fairy tales to Chip, but this night Clint decided to read Hotfooter Tolkien's "Lord of the Rings. " He spiced the story up by deepening his voice and contorting his face in such an ugly manner that Hotfooter began to grimace. Feeling guilty, he closed the book and opened "Cinderella" and read until Chip's eyes closed. He kissed Hotfooter on the nose, tucked him in bed, and went downstairs.

"Where's Misty?" Clint asked, stepping into the sunken living room.

Dusty continued to play her acoustic guitar. "In the stables, feeding the horses. It's been almost two months, and Misty still hasn't heard a word from Doug."

"Something's not right," he said. "I was feeling leery about that guy after the first month of no contact."

Dusty nodded her head in agreement. "Me too, especially after his mother said she hadn't the foggiest notion where he was, or what to think. No communication whatsoever."

"You'd think he'd have the decency to at least call or send a postcard."

"I feel sorry for her," she said. "Misty's been so distraught lately and her spirits have taken a plunging nose-dive. Now she mopes around, acting nervous and flighty. And she's become evasive whenever I bring up Doug's name. What should we do?"

"I don't know," said Clint. "All I know is that I've got a strong suspicion something's awry. The jerk could at least call collect. It's free."

Chapter 8

Another month passed without a word from Misty's husband. Arriving home late on a Friday night, Clint noticed Dusty's car wasn't parked in its usual spot the moment the garage door rolled up. Misty was sitting on a rocking chair by the fireplace, knitting a sweater, when Clint stepped down into the den and greeted her.

"Your company sure is thriving," Misty said.

"Yeah, it's steamrolling along," he said, filling a tumbler with ice at the wet bar. "Run into some crags and potholes every so often, but things always have a way smoothing out. Been lucky, haven't run into a roadblock yet."

"What about the strain your work is putting on your marriage?"

"Its a little hardship," he said, wondering what she meant. "But you need to sacrifice if you want to reap that pot of gold at the end of the rainbow."

"You and Dusty hardly ever watch TV," Misty said quickly as if she wanted to change the subject.

"We watch the news and take in a movie every now and then. There aren't enough hours in the day to watch television. Anyway, I prefer reading, and so does Dusty. But she still watches her favorite soaps."

"I know," said Misty. "We watch them together sometimes when she's not studying in the library or down in the workout room. You two have so many books. Your rooms are floor to ceiling with books. Chip doesn't allow me much free time to read."

"Why did you comment about my work putting a strain on our marriage?"

"I'm glad we're alone and can talk. I know it's not my place to say anything, but you work too darn much. You leave here every morning at five-sharp, like clockwork, and get home so darn late, like tonight. And you're haggard when you come home. Seven days a week is too much."

"It's a builder's bonanza out there."

"I know, but you need to slow down. I feel it's your habitual tardiness that provokes the flare-ups between you and Dusty. You two get along so well when you come home at a decent hour. Like the other night, when you and Dusty read Chip 'Goldilocks and the Three Bears.' She was so happy that night. I could see it in her face. Why, heck, she was singing and dancing and playing music all the next day. And I could still hear her singing when she was in the steam room. And we both started singing when I took Chip into the Jacuzzi. Chip just loves all those bubbles."

Standing at the bar, Clint poured a couple ounces of Johnny Walker Scotch into a tumbler and swished it around with a swizzle stick. "She'll come around when the rewards kick in."

He walked over to the stereo and slipped a "Beatles Magical Mystery Tour" cassette into the tape player and lowered the volume.

Misty smiled and then turned serious. "I hate to bring this up, but did you forget something tonight?"

"I don't think so, why?"

"You and Dusty were supposed to go Betsy's house for dinner."

The tumbler slipped out of Clint's hand and crashed on the slate floor. "Damn it. How the hell could have I forgotten that."

The kitchen phone rang.

"Would you mind getting that? Clint said, "If it's for me, I'm asleep. Unless it's Dusty, I'll take that call."

Misty was crying, and her eyes were red and puffy when she came back into the den several minutes later.

"What's wrong, Misty?" Clint asked.

Misty frowned and spit into the fireplace. "It was Doug," she said disdainfully. "The lousy bastard told me he never had any intention of following me and Chip. Sending me and Chip to California was a ploy to get rid of us. Can you believe that?"

Looking appalled, Clint hollered, "What, you're kidding me. You can't be serious, nobody would do that."

"That wouldn't be a very funny joke," Misty said.

"Why that miserable son-of-a-bitch. What a no-good asshole." Clint looked at Misty, "Geez, I'm so sorry to hear that."

Misty slumped into the sofa, her eyes paralytic, staring at the ceiling. She looked numb with disbelief and shock when Clint sat beside her and draped his arm over her shoulders. The loud sound of the entry doors slamming shut startled them both. Over the sound of the music came the click-clack of Dusty's high heel shoes, racing across the foyer. She stopped and stood furious with her hands on her hips before she stepped into the den.

"What's happened?" Dusty snapped. "Why is Misty crying?"

"Her jerk husband just called," said Clint. "He ain't coming to California. Hey, I'm sorry about tonight, I got so wrapped up in piles of paperwork, I forgot all about our engagement at your sister's tonight."

"I'm not in the mood to talk about that now," she jeered. "We can discuss that matter later." She snarled at Clint and sat beside Misty. "Everything will be all right, Misty. You and Chip are more than welcome to stay with us for as long as you like, if it's okay with Clint."

Without hesitation, Clint responded, "Absolutely, I wouldn't have it any other way." He patted Misty's shoulder. "My heart goes out to you, Misty. What a vile louse," he said in a harsh tone.

Misty began to fidget. "I'm no freeloading mooch," she cried out angrily. "I can earn my own keep." Her jaw slackened, and a flood of tears gushed from her swollen eyes. She leaped up onto her feet and bantered out a tirade of vulgarity aimed at Doug. Dusty jumped up and held her until Misty stopped shaking and calmed down.

Clint looked compassionately at Misty and said, "Did the bastard leave a phone number?"

Misty handed him a crumpled sheet of notepaper.

Infuriated, Clint grabbed the paper and stormed out of the room. Cursing to himself, he went into his office and dialed the number, trying in vain to control his anger.

Without a trace of remorse, Doug admitted to dumping Misty.

"Okay, maybe I did have an ulterior motive," Doug said. "Look, Clint, Misty and I are sexually incompatible. Frankly, after she had the baby she turned frigid. I found myself a real hot number, a Cherokee Indian. This chick is hot-blooded."

Clint envisioned Doug grinning and unleashed a barrage of profanities. Outraged, he yelled, "If I ever see your pretty-boy face, I'll carve it into a bloody pulp. Not even your mother will recognize you, you slimy piece of dog shit. I just might get on a jet and fly up there. See how you look with your dick stuck in your mouth." He heard the word custody and slammed down the telephone.

Snarling, Clint stepped into the den and said, "What a louse. The bastard wants custody of Chip. Where's Misty?"

"In her room," said Dusty, sitting in a rocking chair playing her guitar. "Poor thing is a pathetic wreck. I feel sorry for her. She's so wafer-like and fragile, and now she's heartbroken, stranded here with a child and no money. Her only family is in Scotland, and they're poor." She paused and asked, "What do you think of hiring her as our housekeeper?"

"That works for me. You'd think the gutless bastard would have the common decency to come out here and tell her face to face like a man."

Dusty slapped the guitar strings. "It's hard to fathom a man who would send a small child and wife hundreds of miles away with a measly hundred bucks and discard them like trash. What a heartless, cruel bastard."

"How does Misty feel about working for us?" Clint asked.

"She doesn't find it demeaning, if that's what you're getting at. That's how she came to America in the first place. She was hired as an au pair for a family in Seattle. She did say that she doesn't want her and Chip to be an intrusion in our lives."

Clint shook his head. "What would she expect us to do, send her packing out into the streets with a small child, penniless, without shelter or food?"

"I told her we'd give her room and board and a small weekly stipend. And she could use our cars or one of your company trucks whenever she needs to."

He nodded in agreement. "I'll call Wyatt in the morning and have him add her to our insurance policy."

She sneered in displeasure and quipped, "Must you work seven days a week, day and night?"

"Hey, I'm sorry about tonight. Come on, sweet cakes, let's call a treaty and not quarrel. You wouldn't believe the pressure that I was put through today. I've been stressed out all week."

"You're going to burn yourself out if you don't stop this madness," she said. She set her guitar down and stood up. "I love this house and the property and all you're accomplishing. But I would be much happier living in a shack and being with you."

"One more year, sweetheart," he said, taking her in his arms. "Right now we're about ready to break ground on two of my designs. And they're big projects, close to a million smackers each."

She appeared to relent, giving off a vague hint of a smile as she turned off the lights. "One more year of your vacuous greed might be too late. Please, Clint, I don't care about money. I care about you, our relationship, our commitment. I'm not sure if I can endure much more loneliness and heartache. It's becoming too painful."

"You're right, I promise to slow down. This isn't fair to you and I intend to find a solution." he said, taking her hand and walking into the foyer and up the staircase.

Their bedroom door closed, Dusty went into the bathroom to take a shower while Clint turned on the stereo and stretched out on the bed. Johnny Mathis was singing "Chances Are" as Clint lay in a daze of fascination when Dusty swung open the door and stepped out of the bathroom, dripping wet and wrapped in a towel. He stared appreciatively at her, admiring her sex appeal, and how beautiful she looked wet. She looked at him with ravenous eyes before she dimmed the lamplight and slithered between the satin sheets. She snuggled her wet body against his and whispered, "I love everything you're accomplishing, but for the sake of our marriage, will you please stop this madness. You've become worse than my father."

"I've been formulating a plan while you were showering. It'll be over soon, you have my word."

An hour after making passionate love, they fell into a delectable slumber.

Chapter 9

On a cool New Year's Day mid-morning, Dusty and Clint lounged on the marbled terrace at the Peninsula Country Club after playing a grueling doubles tennis match with Roy and Chrissie Svenson. A network of cobwebs weaved through the dark green ivy, hanging from an arbor where they sat. The pearly dew clinging to the spider webs dripped down on the four as they sipped ice tea and laughed about the old times they shared.

"Look at you," Dusty told Chrissie, "a toddler at home and now you're three months pregnant and playing tennis. You're in such great shape, how do you keep so fit?"

"Why, you're in much better shape than I am," Chrissie replied.

"I haven't had a baby," said Dusty, tugging on a damp towel around her neck, "not yet anyway."

"I wish Roy and I had had a church wedding instead of eloping to Reno. People are still talking about your wedding."

Roy laughed. "You're the one who wanted to elope."

"I'd rather have faced a firing squad than have been scrutinized by your family as I walked down the aisle to the altar," said Chrissie. "The way my stomach was bulging, I would have been flushed with guilt."

Chrissie's blond tresses were braided in pigtails and fell halfway down her back. She stood up and leaned her tush against the stone rail next to Dusty. They were both wearing short white skirts and white blouses, their silky loins gleaming with perspiration in the sunlight.

"You guys heard about Dan?" Roy said.

"Yeah, isn't that great," said Clint enthusiastically. "I saw his kisser on the front page of the *New York Times*."

"The kid has it made," said Dusty. "He's hit stardom and fame."

"He's such a great dancer, and the critics are raving about his performance," said Chrissie.

"It couldn't have happened to a nicer guy," said Roy. "I miss him."

"What about Tommy and Joey, and their band Matrix?" Dusty said excitedly. "They have a platinum album."

"Chrissie and I were listening to it last night," said Roy. "It's amazing. I thought for sure those two had fried their brains."

"So did I," said Clint. "I'm glad they straightened out their lives."

"It's a miracle they survived," said Dusty. "My heart goes out to the ones who didn't. There are so many people strung out on drugs these days, living in squalor. It's a shame."

"I agree," said Chrissie. "It's a tragedy. For the life of me, I don't understand why everyone is in such a hurry to blow their minds with all these psychedelics." She took a sip from the straw.

"Pot's okay," said Dusty. "Clint and I have had some fun times."

Clint grinned. "We sure have."

"Stuff makes me goofy," said Roy, "I can barely talk. All I say is far out, trippy and spacy."

"Makes me horny as a rabbit," said Chrissie.

Roy grinned. "She isn't kidding."

"It's the mind-altering drugs you need to steer away from," said Dusty. "The brain is so intricately woven, so delicate. It's incredible how many people are walking around brain-dead these days."

"You got that right, Dusty," said Roy. "Half my college buddies are living in suspended animation on communes."

Appearing melancholic, Chrissie said, "Reminds me of the time I ran into my best friend in high school last summer. She was sleep walking on Burlingame Avenue, wearing a fur coat. It was during a sweltering heat-wave. She didn't even recognize me. It was so sad, I cried."

"Funny, huh, you two were so wild and now look at you, staunch pillars of the community," said Dusty, glancing wistfully at Clint. "There are times I wish Clint had a bit of his wild streak left in him. I miss it."

Clint retorted, "It's still in me, it's just dormant, in limbo, hibernating. Right now the world is for our taking, fill our coffers."

Dusty appeared annoyed and blurted, "Would you please stop talking about money. It's all you talk about."

"I'm sorry," said Clint. "I'm only this rut so we can buy a schooner or a clipper and sail the seas and retire at thirty to live the good life."

Appearing more irritated, Dusty gruffed, "I don't want to retire at thirty. I want to teach and save the mentally disturbed children on this planet, and raise a family after I earn my doctorate."

"We'll bring the toddlers with us and let them see the wonders of the planet," said Clint. "Freedom ain't cheap."

Fuming, Dusty said, "Your skull is impenetrable."

Grinning wildly, Roy interrupted, "Here, here, a toast to the good life. Now let's play golf, our foursome is on deck."

"My brother Carl and his wife, Bridget, are coming later for dinner," said Roy over the sound of the clacking of cleats as they walked to their carts. "He has a proposal for you."

"I can't wait to meet your brother," said Clint. "You've spoken so much about him. It's as if I know him."

The golf match was a seesaw battle through 16 holes and dead even. Three balls lay on the green at the 17th hole. Dusty's ball was buried in a bunker. Clint snickered watching her wiggle her hips and dig her golf shoes into the sand. Her face turned intense, and with a fluid back swing, she lofted her ball onto the back fringe of the green. With perfect backspin, he watched her ball spin backward and roll to within 10 feet of the cup. To a round of applause, she raised the sand wedge and tipped her cap. Coming out of the trap after raking the sand, Clint gripped her waist and gave her a big kiss.

The match came down to the wire on the 18th hole. Dusty's and Chrissie's balls lay 50 yards behind Clint and Roy's in the center of the fairway.

"Can you believe that?" Roy said. "They're both on in two from 150 yards."

"Nothing short of astonishing," said Clint. "We're a couple of lucky guys."

Roy's second shot landed pin-high, eight feet to the left of the flag.

Clint stood lining up his shot when Dusty patted his rump with her putter and said, "Drop this in for an eagle, and I'll have a special treat for you tonight, honey-buns. Remember, head down, eye on the ball, follow through, and finish high."

"Just like tennis," Clint said and blew her a kiss.

Clint never took his eyes off the ball until it hit the flagstick, and he blinked. In amazement, he thrust his trusty seven-iron over his head and dropped to his knees, staring at Dusty. "Well, that has to be deserving of something, huh?"

"I should say so," Dusty said.

"That almost went in," said Chrissie, still clapping.

Roy had a sneer on his face with his arms folded at his chest when Clint looked over at him.

Dusty's ball was the furthest away and she dropped on her haunches, carefully studying the lie. She rose up and walked slowly to the flag and studied the right to left break. Then she slowly walked to the opposite end of the green and gripped her chin.

Roy pulled out a small book from his back pocket and waved it above his head. "This is flagrant unnecessary delay of game," he chided in a futile attempt to rattle Dusty's nerves. "A breach of rule 36; it's a two-stroke penalty. Says so right here in this USGA Golf Etiquette handbook."

"Blow it out your ear, Roy," said Clint. "Take your time, sweetheart. Big bucks are riding on this putt."

"I'm not playing for money," Dusty said angrily. "You're playing for money. I'm playing for the enjoyment."

With an intense expression, Dusty walked to her ball, bowed her head, and delicately tapped the ball with her putter. Seemingly locked on radar, the ball rolled and rimmed the cup 360 degrees before plunking in for a birdie. Dusty thrust her putter high and curtsied.

"You're right, sweetheart," said Clint. "Roy and I called off the bet. Now can I give you a congratulatory hug?"

Looking exulted, Dusty tossed her putter at the cart. "Can you believe I made that?"

Dusty threw her arms around Clint, and the two danced exuberantly around the flagstick.

Roy and Chrissie each two-putted for par. From a foot away, Clint tapped in for birdie.

"You two were on today," said Roy.

"Yeah, great round," said Chrissie.

"Karma never stops moving," said Dusty. "Next time we play, karma may be with you, and you'll be the lucky ones."

Later in the evening, dressed in formal attire, the four met back at the country club for dinner and a night of ballroom dancing. They were seated at a table sipping cocktails when Roy waved to his older brother Carl.

Unlike Roy, who was lanky, Carl was a brawny hulk, with the youthful face of a lettered first-string college quarterback. He came lumbering towards the table, dressed sharply in pressed and pleated khaki slacks, tasseled penny loafers and a tight-fitting shirt. The sleeves of his sweater looped over on his chest. Carl's wife, Bridget, a petite pageant queen, at best five feet tall followed closely behind him. She had a short blond, pixie hairdo that flipped outwardly at the sides. The rest of her hair was bunched together on top of her head, like tufts of golden straw. Bridget looked like a blond Barbie doll in a ruffled blouse, seemingly tiptoeing on a cloud in red go-go boots. Everyone stood and gregariously greeted one another.

Carl, roughly 6 feet 6 inches tall, stood an imposing mass of steel-like muscle with enormous thighs. His voice was much deeper than his brother's and resonated, and was in sharp contrast to his petite wife, who spoke in a high-pitched twitter with a German accent. Bridget let it all hang out with the upper half of her almost see-through blouse barely concealing her nipples.

The women got along amiably, and as Bridget had just found out she was pregnant, the three women talked mostly about babies during supper.

After dinner, the men excused themselves to discuss the business proposal Roy had mentioned earlier in the day, and they ambled over to the bar. Carl ordered a round of straight shots of Jack Daniels and put them on his tab. Their shot glasses emptied, Carl jabbered about the hiatus he spent romping around Europe for a year where he met Bridget in Germany. Then he rambled about his experiences during a stint in the Navy, touring the South Seas on a destroyer.

Carl slammed his glass on the bar, ordered another round, and hunched toward Clint, looking at him point-blank.

With his beady, steel blue eyes piercing into Clint's, Carl rumbled, "Let's get down to business and straight to the point. My brother's spoken highly of you. Roy tells me you've got a knack for making things happen."

Clint shrugged and nodded his head sideways, "I've been lucky."

"Luck has nothing to do with amassing the properties your company is developing," said Carl.

"Starburst is doing okay."

"I've done my homework. Your company is flourishing."

Clint squeezed his jaw. "We're rolling along steadfastly."

"More like an express locomotive," said Roy.

"That might be an exaggeration," said Clint. "It could happen if Dusty wasn't so altruistic and didn't despise money. But I'm happy. We have a storybook union."

"Clint's a mover and a shaker," Roy said with adulation. "He's got good business savvy. He knows how to chew the fat with those banker guys. Clint's been raking in big bucks the past couple years."

Clint laughed. "I should hire you as my PR man." He sized up Carl and added, "Let's cut the praise crap. Maybe I have been prone to some good fortune. Who knows how long it will last?"

Carl's face tightened. "I'm talking about getting into the big leagues," he said with authority.

"I'm already in the big leagues," said Clint.

"I'm talking the majors, not the minor leagues," said Carl. "Do you want to hear me out?"

Clint laughed. "I'm all ears; lay it on me."

"Lately our dad's been pissing the family newspaper business away with his damn boozing, womanizing, and gambling addictions. The damn debts are draining what's left of the company." Carl took a swig.

"I confronted him last week. Our dad's agreed to let my brother and I develop some of the family's land holdings. One parcel is huge."

Clint listened intently as Carl continued to describe the property.

"It's mostly grazing and pasture land," said Carl, "but the area is like a molting volcano on the verge of erupting. My brother says you have heavy connections in regional planning down in Silicon Valley?"

"I keep abreast with what cities and counties want."

"You're an architect?"

"I dabble in it," said Clint. "There's no money in the design profession. I have a staff of engineers and architects with rubber stamps and presto, they churn the work out dirt cheap. They're mostly my old colleagues from school. Architects are a dime a dozen and don't make shit."

"I know that," said Carl. "That's why I'm here talking to you. I'm looking for a builder who can make it happen. My brother tells me you make things happen. Construction and development is where the real money is made."

"I agree," said Clint. "What do you have in mind?"

Carl's eyes riveted on Clint's as he ordered another round. "I went down and checked out a couple of our parcels in Santa Clara. The area's a breeding hot spot."

"You mentioned huge," said Clint. "Just how much land are you talking about?"

"All totaled, over a hundred thousand acres in the heart of Santa Clara Valley. It's prime land, and the surrounding area has gone sonic!"

Clint's mind was made up. "Hell, man, that's the size of San Francisco. That area is a spawning ground for high-tech companies. I'll be truthful with you. I'm inundated with work these days. Seems I'm on the run day and night, and Dusty's been on my case for not being around the home front in the evenings, but this has me intrigued. Roy filled me in a little about your plan while we played today. I've always dreamed of building an entire city. How can I or my company be of service to you?"

"I need someone with contacts in high finance," said Carl, "somebody who'd be willing to jump in and whip up some viable conceptual drawings. Someone who's not afraid to take a risk."

Clint kept his growing excitement in check. "Look, I can't promise you two anything; I can only tell you that if I can squeeze in the time, I'll drive down and take a peek this coming week. If I like what I see and hear after nosing around and I think I can be of help to you, we'll meet again and I'll tell you what I think. I've a couple people in mind who I believe might have some powerful sway on the county board of supervisors down there, as well as packing clout with the zoning and planning commissioners. It'll help if we have some leverage on our side during the bartering over land usage."

Carl seemed pleased. "I like the way you talk, Clint. My brother tells me you're a pretty good golfer."

"Fair to middling," said Clint.

"Lady Luck was on his side today," Roy complained, his usual exuberance overshadowed by his older brother's significantly stronger presence. "He and Dusty creamed our butts in tennis and golf today."

"That was sheer luck," Clint said. "I've never in my life hit a flagstick and I've been playing golf since I was twelve. "How about yourself?"

"I've had a couple of eagles and a hole in one," Carl responded lackluster. "I'd like to brainstorm a few other ideas with you. You got time in the morning to squeeze in a round?"

"Let's make it next weekend," said Clint. "Dusty and I will be dancing the night away. She's been pestering me to try this ballroom dancing stuff. She'll have me dancing all night. Are you sticking around?"

Carl grimaced. "That ballroom crap bores me stiff. I'm saving that stuff for the golden years. Bridget and I are going to the Tiger-a-Go-Go." With a devious grin, he added, "About that golf game, why don't we make it interesting. Say, five a hole, ten a bird, pop twenty on an eagle, and fifty on the match?"

Clint snickered, quaffed his glass empty and said with a straight face, "Let's make it a real challenge. Up the ante to twenty a hole, fifty a bird, a c-note on an eagle, and a grand on the match. To make it even more interesting, how 'bout five grand for a hole in one?"

"You're on." Carl grinned and shook Clint's hand. "I like your ballsy style." Carl turned to Roy, "You in?"

Roy scrunched his lips and said, "Ain't nothing like a high-stakes game to get my adrenalin fired up."

Dusty and Chrissie were listening to Bridget tell them how she always wanted to dance the mambo, the fox trot, and the tango when the men rejoined them at the table. Carl thundered out his disdain for ballroom dancing. But Bridget held her ground, casting her finger at Carl like a magic wand until he fell under her spell. Carl sniveled and grumbled in protest to no avail.

Chapter 10

At the crack of dawn the following Monday, Clint and Matt sped south to Santa Clara County. Clint stopped the truck in front of the abandoned, red brick building that Carl had told him marked the northern boundary.

"I've ridden my dirt bike here a whole bunch of times," said Matt. "The land's mostly flat with gentle rolling hills. I'm impressed."

"So am I," said Clint. "With all the commercial and residential developments sprouting up all over, this is a gold mine."

"The immensity of such a project boggles my mind," said Matt. "This property's ripe."

"I've seen enough," Clint said. "I'll get you back to the office. I've some investigating to do."

After dropping Matt off at Starburst, Clint spent the rest of the day snooping around the county planning and zoning departments in Santa Clara. He checked the maps and made inquiries. He made copies of the plot plan, noted the boundaries, the major streets, arteries, highways, utilities, and existing and surrounding land usage.

Determining the property to be a diamond mine, he drove back to the site the next morning. A brainstorm came to him when he noticed the road was named Sunshine Road. With a sketchpad and a mechanical pencil, he sat on the tailgate and began sketching the theme for Sunshine City. He combined traditional nostalgia with futuristic design for Sunshine Mall, Sunshine Business Park, Sunshine Gardens, Sunshine Square, Sunshine Amusement Park and Sunshine Estates.

In a few weeks time, his sketchpad resembled giant canvases linked together. He designed a front façade of polished brass columns set atop marble pedestals, supporting an arcing, amaranth canvas that jutted dramatically over the parking lot of Sunshine Shopping Mall.

His passion for design returned, and with the skillful hand of an artist and a flurry of strokes, he drew amber-tinted reflective glass panes set in brass mullions above the rotunda. He sketched a stained glass dome with prisms of cascading sunbeams, falling onto a refracting geyser that shot upward from a five-tiered fountain in the center of Sunshine Amusement Park.

Pumped with enthusiasm and inspiration, he worked into the night at his office, standing in front of his drafting table. He drew in people toting shopping bags and women pushing baby strollers throughout the shopping mall. He added a well-lit three-level parking lot with old-fashioned lampposts and enough room for 10,000 cars.

He penciled in a network of high-profile, futuristic office buildings of steel and green and blue tinted glass that stretched across Sunshine Boulevard south to north through Sunshine City. In the center of the city, he drew a park-like setting with a lagoon and swans, cranes, geese, and Canadian honkers, encircled by low profile town-homes. He filled the winding streets on the rolling hills with Hawthorn, elm, and birch trees in front of thousands of homes with vernal lawns. His eyes weary, he sketched in a playground, tennis courts, a picnic area, basketball courts, soccer fields, and a baseball diamond.

Several days later, feeling satisfied, he rolled up the rough sketches and left the office to seek the guidance and advice of Clay Thompson.

Seated at his desk in his study at home, Clay slowly turned each page, carefully reviewing Clint's conceptual drawings. The only sounds were their breathing and the turning of pages.

When Clay finished examining Clint's drawings, he gazed at him and said, "I must say, this is a mighty bold endeavor for someone as young as you. You could be getting yourself into oceanic depths."

His voice confident, Clint said, "I studied the surrounding area thoroughly. From speaking with some higher-ups in regional planning, the project suits the needs of the county. It meets the required criteria of zoning in Santa Clara. I set aside land for a state college, high schools, junior highs, elementary schools, churches, and a city hall. There's much more, but I think this will suffice for starters. You always told me there's no success without risks."

Clay rubbed his brow, paused for a moment and in a fatherly manner, he patted Clint's shoulder. "It's a whale of a concept. I always knew you had good moxie."

Clint looked pleased.

"I'm quite familiar with the area," said Clay. "I agree, a project of this magnitude is quite viable." He rubbed his earlobe and thought a moment. "It's a mammoth undertaking, yet highly conceivable. We'll need to bring in people with powerful influence and clout to launch this project off the ground. I can't guarantee anything, but I've some business associates in the area who remain indebted to me. I'll see what I can do to help bring this to fruition. You might have found yourself a cache of nuggets."

Clay went on to rave about the concept and thumped Clint hard on the back. Clint knew he was on the right track, walking out the door into the brisk night air.

Chapter 11

Dusty was sitting on the sofa by the fireplace strumming the strings on her Martin D 23 guitar on the late Friday evening Clint arrived home from a meeting. She was facing away from him when he stepped down into the living room, holding a bouquet of fresh pink roses. Misty sat in her favorite rocking chair with her feet on top of an ottoman. Her hair was up in curlers and she was plucking on the strings of a zither that rested on her lap. Considering the lateness, Clint had anticipated a cold shoulder from Dusty. But Misty's sullen expression and lack of a friendly nod or wave caught him by surprise.

Misty had gotten over the woe of her ex-husband's betrayal and had been in bubbly spirits during the recent weeks. Most of the time, she bounced up for an exchange of friendly hugs when Clint came home. Venus, coiled up by the warm fire, gnawing on a bone, didn't race across the room and pounce on Clint, knocking him off balance as she was accustomed to doing. Even Snippy, inside her birdcage, appeared discontent and didn't squawk a friendly hello.

Clint knew he was in serious trouble and forced a smile as he walked over to the bar. He took a deep breath and said in a cheerful tone, "That's a nice piece you girls are playing. I like it. Did one of you write that composition?"

Dusty and Misty ignored him and continued to play as Clint unwrapped the green wax paper and filled a crystal vase with water from the spigot.

"Okay, I'm late as usual," he said. "I'm sorry. I had a rough night. You two aren't going to punish me with the shun treatment. I said I apologize. I'm not invisible."

Dusty stopped playing and shouted, "It's almost midnight. No phone call, nothing. You walk in unfazed by the late hour. What do you expect, a grand welcome home party."

Misty set the zither down and picked up a navy blue cap and began crocheting.

"No need to raise your voice," Clint said, filling a brandy snifter with cognac. "The meeting went longer than I expected. I didn't know it would take up the whole night. Clay brought a group of powerful, influential real estate tycoons from around the country."

"It's always one lame excuse after another," Dusty said in a harsh tone. "I'm tired of you justifying your lack of consideration."

Misty rose up. "It's late, I think I'll turn in, see you two in the morning." She gathered her stuff and went to her bedroom.

Dusty set her guitar on the rug and stood up, akimbo, "I've had it with you and your broken promises!" She yelled.

"Be reasonable, Dusty. I'm not a robot. I can't be programmed to know what's going to happen one minute to the next. Anyway, what was I to do in the middle of a major presentation, proposing the development of an entire city to a roomful of entrepreneurs? Say, 'I'm sorry, but will you please excuse me. I need to call my wife to tell her I'll be late."

"What's wrong with that," she shouted. "It's the proper thing to do. Where's your sense of decency, respect, courtesy?"

"Get real. I'm under siege with an extreme case of the jitters, sputtering, afraid I'm going to choke and blow the whole deal. Make a fool of myself in front of a table full of scions with attaché cases stuffed with checkbooks. And they're impressed and listening intently, poking the keys on their miniature calculators."

"I don't want to hear any more about your big deals," she said in a loud voice.

"This is an entire city," Clint said. "And not one of them flinched when Clay and I began talking about the staggering costs. The good news is they liked it. They liked the preliminary schematics. Sunshine City is going to happen, everything is moving forward in synchronicity. The county loves the concept. The council members have given us the green light."

"I don't care! You've become a stranger, an alien around here."

"You should because Clay is in the process of putting together a limited partnership. We're forming a joint venture. It's the beginning of the snowball effect. Starburst is gaining momentum. When this deal is sealed, Starburst will be rolling downhill like an avalanche."

"We didn't go skiing all winter," she hollered. "Marriage is not supposed to be all work and no play. Marriage is a joint partnership. We need our time together.

I hardly see you anymore. You're gone sixteen to eighteen hours everyday. You need to get your ears unplugged."

"Let's sit on the hearth and work this out," Clint said, reaching for her hand.

She jerked it away. "I'm not in the mood to be touched. I'm fed up with your fanatical drive to build an empire of riches."

"I know how you must feel, but what I'm doing is for us, for our children, for our freedom, for our retirement."

"I don't ever want to retire. Not at thirty, not at seventy. I want to teach until I die."

"I admire you for that, but starting up a school takes beaucoup bucks."

"Not really. There are plenty of government grants. I'm researching it right now. And my parents have offered to help."

Clint cut her off. "I will not tolerate handouts from them. We're doing this on our own."

"My parents want to help me achieve my dreams. You're not even interested in what I want."

"I am too. I admire you wanting to teach autistic children."

"Then why can't you break away for one weekend so we can go somewhere remote and be alone. We could go down to Big Sur, find a little hideaway, walk on the beach, play games, and have fun. Do the things we used to do before we got married. Or, if you feel up to it, we could go up to Tahoe and ski for a weekend or even just a half day. It will help relieve the strain you've put on our marriage. And we can relax together for a change, instead of all this tension and bickering every night. We don't even go out dancing or see a movie anymore. And we haven't even gone out for a romantic candlelight dinner in ages."

"Honest," he said, "I would love to do all those things, but Starburst is on the verge of exploding. Come on, let's sit down."

"And I'm on the brink of erupting," she said, sitting beside him on the hearth. "I didn't marry you to be left home alone every night. Making a marriage work in harmony takes two people."

Clint rubbed his temples. "It's the pressure, my mind has been stressing out lately. Everyone is talking astronomical figures. I feel out of my league sometimes, like a featherweight in a ring with super heavyweights, a David with a toy slingshot pitted against a one-eyed Goliath; a damn nobody trying to peddle a whole city."

"Didn't you just say they like it?"

"That's the high part. They do. The funny thing is these greedy bastards want the city completed by tomorrow. I should have taken a course in coping, but I never saw that class listed in any of the schedules."

"They're right next to the marriage counseling classes."

He smiled. "I got an A-plus in sex education."

She threw her hair back and laughed. "That's a joke. Then why is it we haven't had sex in over two weeks?"

"Come off it, it hasn't been that long?"

"I'm not counting. I just know that I came home tonight and busted my tail to make us a nice romantic dinner with candles, put on soft music, dressed sexy, and you don't show up. California's in the midst of a sexual revolution, people are having group sex in bathhouses with total strangers, wife swapping, orgies, free love.

Everybody is screwing everybody, even animals. Now people are going to sleazy movie theaters to watch pornographic films. How do I know what you're out doing every night?"

He lowered his head into his splayed fingers. "Why would you suggest such a thing; what happened to our trust?"

"Because I'm still in school and see what's happening everyday. Everybody's popping psychedelic pills like they're going out of style. Half the students come to class stoned out of their minds. It's a whole new generation of dope fiends."

"I'm not blind, but you never answered my question. What does that have to do with us?"

"I don't know what you're out doing every night. You could be screwing some whore because you're certainly not screwing me."

"For Christ sake, would you back off," he huffed.

"Morality has diminished to nothing, dissipated, evaporated into thin air. You can't have a free sex society without consequences. Catastrophic consequences, like the plague of sexually transmitted diseases that are sweeping across the nation right now. It's an epidemic worse than syphilis and gonorrhea. I don't want to be the victim of a contagious disease."

"Dusty," he said softly, "I'm not playing around. There's no need for me to play around. Your eyes are too scintillating, and your body drives me nuts."

"Then what are we going to do to resolve this situation? I can't take much more of your neglect. I don't like solitude."

He took a deep breath. "I can't just walk away from Sunshine City and the myriad of other projects. I suppose I can toss in the towel, but darn it, I don't want to. You were once upon a time a far-fetched dream, and now we're married. Now another dream is becoming reality. Why can't I have both? Darn, I wish I had the mind of a sage."

She calmed down slightly. "You make it seem like it's my fault."

"I didn't mean to," he said apologetically. "You're absolutely right. It's one hundred percent my fault. I haven't been around much. I've way too many things to do. It would be a lot easier if we lived three score and ten like that Methuselah dude. That way we could set aside a few years to accomplish our dreams and still have 900 plus years of bliss."

She laughed. "960 years of youth and 9 years of old age to be exact. Have you tried delegating responsibility? What about Matt?"

"Matt's my biggest asset, and he's way too overloaded. He's in charge of field operations, running all the superintendents and coordinating the subs, and we're always ahead of schedule. Everybody loves the guy. We've got the best tradesmen in the state working for us. But Matt ain't cut out for wheeling and dealing. And he doesn't want any part of it. I don't know what I'd do if I lost him."

"He would never quit," she said in a softer voice. "Not after all you've done for him. The house you designed for him was on the cover of *Architectural Digest*. Do you think I'm being too hard on you?"

"No, I guess I need to start bringing my work home, but the phone in my office would start ringing off the hook. The line would be busy, and they'd start calling the house phone. It'd be crazy."

"Then you need to re-establish your priorities," she said in a soft voice, "because this relationship is at extreme risk. I mean it."

"You're at the top of my list. I guess I just forget. Give me a couple of days. I'll put my head to the grindstone and come up with something."

"That sounds scratchy," she said. "Why don't you hire a key man? Someone like Carl, he's the one who started this mess."

"Hey, that's a good idea, Carl. I never thought about him. But he doesn't have my eyes."

"Nobody has your vision," she said. "Your eyes are one of a kind."

"I'll talk to him first thing in the morning," he said as they stood up. "Right now, let's deal with the issue at hand. Let's get into the Jacuzzi and see if we can change the tide."

She rubbed her chin, tugged her ear, flicked off the light switch, and they walked slowly to the spiral staircase.

"Whatever happens tonight will only bring a temporary solution," she said. "What our marriage needs is a permanent resolve. Please, Clint, establish new priorities before this union disintegrates."

"You have my word."

"Let's take a vacation before our marriage dissolves."

"You're right," he said, opening the door to the work out room. "Let me get things into motion. If Carl comes aboard, we'll take a second honeymoon."

Chapter 12

Two weeks later, Clint signed the partnership papers at Clay Thompson's office. With the powerful force of the financial backers, Starburst breezed through the red tape process, giving birth to Sunshine City. In less than a month's time, stage one of the project received formal approval by Santa Clara County, and the first sets of plans for Sunshine Technology Center were approved.

Late one night after a lengthy meeting at Starburst's new headquarters in Silicon Valley, Clint sat slouched back with his legs stretched on top of his desk, chewing the fat with Carl, who had eagerly joined the force.

"Everything is happening so fast; my head is in a whirlwind," said Clint. "And now ground-breaking ceremonies, I'm starting to feel like a slave to Sunshine City."

"You've been looking under the weather lately," Carl said. "You need to take some time off and relax with Dusty. Take her on a cruise to a tropical isle somewhere."

"You're a mind reader," said Clint, "that's exactly what I'm planning on doing when I can squeeze in the time. Now with you aboard, maybe I can. Think you can run the whole shebang for a few weeks or a month?"

Carl leaned back in his chair and clasped his hands behind his head. "No man in his right mind would want that position. Think of all the aggravation and strain. A guy could get burnt out and be gray-headed by the time the scope of this project winds down."

"It's your property. You'll be well-rewarded."

"In that case, take off tomorrow."

"I wish I could," said Clint, "but I gotta get this thing airborne first. I'm moving Matt up the ladder and making him a full partner. Bobby Sherdel is a well-seasoned pro and more than capable of running The Gables and Green Hills. I figure to give Dennis a fat bonus and give him a shot at running the Evergreen and West Ridge projects."

"That'll help ease the pressure," said Carl.

"Well, I'd better get going. Dusty's been on the warpath about my putting in all these long hours."

Pulling into the driveway, Clint pressed the garage door button and glanced at his wristwatch. He cringed when he saw it was nearing midnight. He knew in all likelihood Dusty would be on a rampage. Battles between them had escalated to a nightly affair.

Not wanting to awaken her, he left the light off and walked quietly into the bedroom. The room was eerily silent as he undressed and slid onto his side of the bed. He reached his hand across the bed and found Dusty's side empty.

Having seen her car in the garage, his mind began to race. He flipped on the bedside lamp and jumped out of bed. He turned on the light switch and searched for a note. Cursing aloud, he scrambled downstairs into the kitchen in hopes of finding a note on the counter.

Finding nothing in the kitchen or in any of the rooms, he hurried to Misty's bedroom and knocked on the door. She opened it wearing a terry cloth robe and yawning, and her face smeared in white cream. She rubbed her eyes and asked, "What's the matter?"

"Sorry to disturb you, Misty, but did Dusty tell you where she was going tonight?"

"You and Dusty were supposed to go out to dinner with her parents and later go to a recital."

His body twitched and he clutched his head. "Ah, crap, not again. How could I forget? My memory has gone out of kilter. I must be high on nepenthe."

"She waited, and then she left with them."

"Damn it. How mad was she?"

Misty seemed reluctant to speak. "I hate telling you, but she was fuming. Never seen her so angry. She got madder the longer they waited. Come in and sit."

Feeling regretful, he slumped down on a chair by her desk. He rested his aching head on his knuckles and silently cussed at himself.

"I know it's none of my business," she said, "you've both been so kind and supportive. I like you two so much that I feel caught in a triangle. But I have to tell you," she paused briefly, "Dusty's been acting funny lately. Tonight, she started talking about divorce and attorneys."

"Divorce!"

"Her parent's and I stuck up for you. We told her you've overextended yourself. Dusty wouldn't listen. She was really infuriated tonight and stormed out of the house with her parent's."

The sudden banging of the front doors jolted them onto their feet. The echo was still ringing when they heard the loud shattering of glass crash. Clint bolted for the door and froze.

She's pissed, he thought and cringed. Standing at the doorway, he listened to the sound of fleeting feet bound up the staircase.

Hearing the upstairs bedroom door slam shut, Clint whispered good night to Misty and tiptoed out of her room. Passing by the entry, he looked down at the mangled picture frame and shards of glass. The soles of his shoes crunched the splinters as he walked to the den. He grabbed a pack of smokes he kept for guests and went outside on the deck and sat. With a worried expression, he nervously smoked a cigarette.

Clearing his mind of a million fragments, he took a deep breath and walked slowly into the living room and poured a stiff drink of brandy. He gulped it down and went upstairs and stood by their bedroom door. He stared at the brass knob, sucked a deep breath, dreading having to face the consequences.

His hands moist, he opened the door and walked in. "You have every right to be angry," he quickly blurted. "I can't believe I'm so darn absent-minded that I forgot about tonight. I must be suffering from early symptoms of amnesia."

Dusty stood facing the vanity mirror, clad in lingerie. One leg was bent on the cushioned bench as she brushed her hair. "I see you've decided to start screwing Misty too." Her reflection in the mirror looked like she had eaten something sour.

"That's outrageous!" Clint fired back, incited by her accusation. He could sense she was well past the boiling point. "Don't be ridiculous. What the hell's come over you. It's preposterous. How dare you accuse me of screwing Misty."

Her face scathing with hostility, she turned and shouted harshly, "It's not so absurd if you think about it. I saw your shadow on the wall in her room." She slipped on an embroidered silk kimono. "Look at you. Almost naked in Jockey shorts and it's after midnight. What do you expect me to think? I want a divorce."

He felt a sting of pain pierce his heart as waves of shock surged up his spine. "Divorce! I don't believe this. This is turning into a haunting incubus nightmare. But you're way off base now," he glared at her. "I came home and undressed in the dark so I wouldn't disturb you. I got worried when I found out you weren't in bed and went down to ask Misty where you were."

She glared at him. "It doesn't matter. I've had it with you. This is the last straw. This nexus is over, done, finished. There is no other option except divorce."

"What do you mean over, divorce. I'm busting my butt and have to come home and listen to you accuse me of screwing Misty. This is utter nonsense!"

"Nonsense," she spouted, her face in a rage. "I haven't seen you in two weeks. You've become a foreigner."

He bowed his head. "Hey, this is insanity. I shouldn't have to make excuses." He regained his senses and attempted to control his emotions. "Look, I was only asking Misty where you went."

She stepped in front of him and held her hand open as if to slap him.

"Can't we sit down and be rational about this. I'm truly sorry I forgot about tonight," he said. "My mind has been clogged lately. This project is draining me."

"Just exactly how many women are you screwing these days?" She said bluntly.

"This is moronic," he shouted, not believing his ears. "You've gone bonkers. You've slipped off the fringe. Your mind is warped. I'm only trying to make life comfortable for us. So we can enjoy life when this project gets completed."

"It's all about money," she scornfully persisted. "I've told you a thousand times, I don't care about money or material things. You're so wrapped up in greed your brain has become polluted, infested with building an empire. Your mind is so preoccupied with money you've forgotten we're married. You've changed. You're not the same man I married. The insane emphasis you put on the almighty dollar has grown so far out of proportion, it revolts me!" She raised her hand and pointed her finger in his face. "Your alter-ego is perpetually in pursuit of cutting the big deal."

"Don't you point your finger at me like some rich bitch," he blurted out.

She raised her hands. "Rich bitch!"

"You've been fed with a golden spoon all your life." He grabbed both of her wrists. She broke a hand free and slapped him hard across the face.

Her face loathing, her lips quivering, she screamed, "Rich bitch - why you miserable - egocentric bastard."

Exhausted and regretful for his words, he lowered his voice, "You were handed your legacy, I'm only trying to make ours."

Her face enraged, she slapped him again hard on the face and then began pounding his chest with clenched fists until she wore herself out and shrank onto the bed, weeping hysterically.

He sat beside her and in a low tone, he said, "This kind of fighting hedges on lunacy. I swear, Dusty, there's no one in my life except you."

Her body trembling, she began pummeling him.

He didn't resist as a river of tears rolled down his face. His eyes pleading, he stared at her until she finally stopped, dropping her face into her hands.

"For God's sake," he said in a low voice, "calm down and hear me out. Look, sweetheart, you have every reason to be angry. I admit to forgetting about tonight. But I'm only guilty of absentmindedness, nothing else. I've been so absorbed with getting this damn city off the ground. Let's call a time-out."

"This is not a game," she blurted. "Divorce is inevitable because I can not take any more of your broken promises. Your neglect is too agonizing. I can't take living in isolation."

"Come on, I swear to you, it will never happen again. I don't want a divorce or even a separation. I love you."

She could not be placated. "It's not only tonight," she shouted in his face, "what about all the other nights you come tiptoeing into bed at all hours of the night?"

For the first time, Clint realized the harsh reality of the truth. "For that I plead guilty, but it's all work, no extramarital affairs, honest. I don't even look anymore, no woman compares to you."

She stood up and walked to the dresser and leaned against it. Her arms folded over her chest, she frowned and listened to him.

"I owe you a big apology, Dusty. I've been half-nuts the way everything's been moving so fast. I'm not saying things were perfect, but our lives were running smoothly, until Carl shows up one day and boom - a gigantic atomic bomb blasts off. The magnitude of this project is far beyond anything I ever conceived."

Appearing aloof, she said, "You're delusional. Our marriage is on the brink of collapse. We'll be divorced long before that city is completed. I'm thinking maybe we should consider a trial separation."

His nervous system went erratic with prickly bites, as if an outbreak of hives was attacking his entire body. His hands were now sticky with sweat while he listened to her repeatedly mention the words separation and divorce.

"Separation, divorce," he said, "our nexus is over. What are you talking about?"

Her expression of anger changed to confusion and the whites of her moist eyes were streaked with red veins. "I don't want to end our marriage," she stuttered. It's just that you refuse to change. You're not even willing to compromise."

He patted the bed and said, "Can we call a truce. Come and sit. We can work this out. You're right, my ears have been clogged, but hearing you mention divorce or even separation has finally opened them to the seriousness of my behavior. I'll call a travel agent. We'll take a romantic vacation. It'll also give me time to re-establish my priorities, rethink our lives. You're right. I need to change, steer a new course. I married you to share my life with you, not to torment you. Maybe I have been overly zealous about money."

She laughed in mockery as she sat beside him. "Obsessive, compulsive gluttony would be more appropriate."

"That bad, huh," he whimpered contritely, looking into her eyes. "I'm only doing what I was taught since I was a little kid, that women want financial security. It's the American dream. That's what all men are led to believe women want."

"I appreciate that," Dusty said evenly, sweeping her hair back. "I married you so we could grow together in harmony. You've been like an interloper this past year. Don't take me wrong. I admire what you've accomplished, and I truly want you to be happy in whatever endeavor you pursue. However, your greedy ambitions have swollen so much that they've put a mounting strain on us."

Clint shrugged and sat speechless.

"Tonight, I felt a rupture inside me waiting for you," she said, her voice turned soft. "I'm not sure I can take any more punishment. It's too brutal. My mind can't take anymore contamination. Then I come home and find you in Misty's bedroom."

"I'm guilty of everything, but not guilty of playing around. It's only been business that's kept me away from you. But I also suffer from spurts of jealousy when I see you all dolled up, dressed like a sex-goddess in your miniskirts going off to school, knowing guys must be coming onto you all day long. It's a two-way road. How do you think I feel?"

She looked surprised. "I've never thought you capable of jealousy."

As glum as the situation appeared, he laughed. “Take off your clothes, and go stand in front of the mirror.”

The slight hint of a smile appeared on her face, and her voice softened. “That’s the first compliment you’ve given me in weeks, or has it been months. You’ve been so remote. I’ve lost track since the last time you displayed any affection or compassion. I must admit that my doubts about your fidelity could partly be attributed to petty jealousy. And then tonight, I completely freaked out. I’m sorry for slapping you. I don’t want a divorce, but you need to change course. I can’t take any more neglect. I don’t like feeling abandoned.”

He felt a glimmer of hope. “I had it coming. Your actions tonight have awakened me to the pain I’ve caused you. I never want to lose you. I’ll steer a new course. Now can we make up?”

“As long as you’re willing to make an effort to slow down,” she said.”

“You’ve unplugged my ears. Will you please forgive me?”

She shifted her body closer to him and whispered that she forgave him. Both weepy-eyed and their voices turned to buttery atonement, they conversed calmly and Clint pulled the brass chain on the bedside lamp.

“No,” she said, “leave it on.”

Moonbeams filtered through the window onto the bed as they caught their breath and forgave each other. Their vows of love and fidelity renewed, she nuzzled her head against his neck and whispered, “Do you really feel jealous, or did you just say that to appease me?”

"It's the truth," Clint murmured in her ear. "You're a seraphic twelve on a scale of one to ten. What do you think of going to Tahiti?"

She beamed. "My parents always go to Venice to reinvigorate their love life. My mother says there's nothing more romantic in the world than a midnight gondola ride along the canals under a full moon to rekindle the fire in a marriage."

"Venice it is," he grinned.

She drew closer to him. "I'm sorry for behaving the way I did tonight." Her voice was soft and low. "I really do appreciate all you're doing, this house, the gym, the swimming pool, the wishing well, your business, everything. You've surpassed anything I could ever have imagined. All I ask of you is to share your nights and weekends with me. Without you, this house is a prison."

"You have my word. I'll call a travel agent in the morning and book our flights to Venus."

Chapter 13

Holding loyal to his promise to slow down, Clint arrived home on a Friday night at six. After taking a steamy shower and wearing a cashmere sweater over a turtleneck, Clint walked into the kitchen and said, "Smells yummy."

"Don't you look spiffy," said Dusty as she chopped a mound veggies. "It's a real treat having you home so early these past weeks."

He brought out a bunch of daisies from behind his back. "Ta-da, and I've the weekend off. Everything is running smooth, and no one blinks an eye when I leave at five. And we fly off to Venice in three weeks. What can I do to help out?"

"Now that you've lifted my spirits," she said, "would you mind slicing that roast into thin strips. Oh, you'll never guess what's happened?"

"Lay it on me, honeybunch."

"Do you remember that artist, Joshua, Misty met down in Big Sur?"

"Yeah," Clint said, "the Zen Buddhist guy with the shaved head, who kept babbling all that contemplative gibberish that Misty went bonkers over."

"Well, he just got back from India where he was staying at an ashram and called her. He wants her and Chip to move down with him. Misty's gone wild. She's in her room packing right now."

"This is sudden. She hardly knows the guy. There was a harem of worshippers following him and dropping flower pedals in front of him the day we met the guy."

"I remember," she said. "All those groupies pawing on him, like he was some kind of idol or something."

"Maybe this isn't such a good idea," he said. "It sounds like she's rushing things. The guy calls, and presto, she's packing to move in with him."

"They've been writing to each other for a couple of months. He wrote her love letters and poems every day while he was in India. Anyway, Misty was so distraught and depressed for such a long time and now she has so much pep and enthusiasm. It's not like they're getting married. People are starting to live together to find out if they have a common ground. Not that I agree. It goes completely against my principles. I guess in today's Age of Aquarius, I'm considered old-fashioned, and I'm only twenty-three. They'll live together in a commune to see if they have mutual interests. He's a very talented artist and has his own studio in Carmel. You were there."

"Yeah, I liked his work," he said. "He does good sculptures. I loved that brass dragon, and there was one marble piece I especially liked – 'Mother and Child.'"

"I liked that one too," she said. "Can we drive her and Chip down in the morning?"

"Sure, why stand in the way of love. Why don't we stay down there for a couple days, lull in the sun. Dilly-dally and watch the sunsets."

"Splendid, if it doesn't put a strain on your work," she said. "Oh, would you stir the gravy."

Clint walked over to the stove and grabbed a spatula. "Things are running smooth now that Carl's on board."

"Good. We can stop at Ano Nuevo and take Chip to see the sea elephants."

Stirring the gravy, he laughed. "They'll eat him alive."

A little after sunrise the next morning, with the bed of Clint's truck loaded with Misty's meager belongings and the gifts Dusty gave her, the four headed south down the coast highway to Carmel.

The sun was directly overhead when Clint parked a few shops away from Joshua's studio. "I'm going to miss you, you speedy pipsqueak," Clint said, squeezing Hotfooter's nose.

"Thank you for taking me to see the sea elephants, Daddy," said Chip. "They were funny."

"You're an irreplaceable bundle of joy, kiddo." Clint turned to Misty. "I'm going to miss you too, Misty. It's a pleasure to see you sparkling and bright-eyed again."

"I know what you're going to miss," said Misty as they got out of the truck. "You're going to miss Chip calling you, 'daddy.'"

Clint smiled. "You're right, Misty. I definitely will. Even though Hotfooter's a terrorizing scamp, I love the kid."

"I want that pirate ship in the window," Chip said excitedly, pointing at the galleon in the window of Joshua's shop.

"It's yours Hotfooter," said Clint.

"Thank you, Daddy."

"You see, Dusty," said Misty, "I wasn't exaggerating. Joshua works with stained glass too. He's so creatively gifted, so multi-faceted. His artistry is innate. He's a genius and so diverse. Joshua can do anything he sets his mind to."

"Wow, I'll say," said Clint. "Hope your new lover will take a check because I've gotta have that dragon and 'Mother and Child.' It will be perfect over the mantle."

"If he doesn't, I have our American Express card," said Dusty.

Misty shined. "I'll vouch for you."

Clad in a robe and long strings of beads, Joshua came out of his studio, bowed and said, "Namaste."

A polite exchange of "Namastes" and greetings followed.

"Please come inside and have some herbal tea," said Joshua as he picked up Chip. "My friends will help unload Misty's luggage and put it in my van."

Inside the large studio, a group of painted flower children, sitting in the full lotus position, busied themselves making making pottery, jewelry, trinkets, and leather headbands. Inside a smaller room at the rear of the studio was a fiery urn with artisans in leather aprons blowing glass bubble hash pipes, an assortment of glass bongs, hookahs, and other drug paraphernalia.

After tea, Dusty and Clint browsed around and bought the stained glass pirate ship, dragon, "Mother and Child," and two headbands. Following teary-eyed embraces and best wishes to Misty, Chip, and Joshua, Dusty and Clint waved goodbye.

"Did you notice those dark purplish scars on the back of Joshua's hands?" Dusty said on the drive to Big Sur.

"Good eyes, sweetheart. And the darn things went clean through. He had the same ugly scars on the palms of both hands. I saw them when I handed him the check."

"And those omniscient eyes of his," she said. "Man, they were spooky. It made me feel as if he could see through my blouse."

"Strange cat," he said. "I wonder if those wounds were self-inflicted. You know, like he's playing the role of a messiah."

"You mean like he made those to look like stigmata?"

"Yeah, stigmata," he said. "That's the word that was eluding me."

"I hope Misty and Chip will be okay living on that commune."

"Sounds like fun, living in teepees with totem poles, smoking peace pipes and that sort of stuff."

"Hotfooter will have fun making smoke signals, doing rain dances, and playing the tom-toms," she said.

With no more crashing and banging, Zenith fell strangely quiet without Chip when they returned home late the next night.

"It's so silent, it's creepy," said Dusty as they stepped into the living room.

"I know," said Clint. "There's only one thing to do, celebrate the return to privacy. It's time to loosen our inhibitions. Crank up the volume and go skinny-dipping."

Her eyes sex-crazed, Dusty started to undress. "You mean lower our morals and get nasty?"

"If it feels good, do it."

Shortly after midnight, they romped naked throughout the house as Clint chased after Dusty, feverishly wielding a feather duster. He was laughing like a madman, knowing the slightest touch of a feather against her taffeta flesh would send her into ballistic ecstasy. Two chocolate éclairs lay on a dish on the nightstand beside the bed where Clint finally tackled her.

Sounds of venery pleasure and gay laughter filled Zenith the next few weeks.

On a day when Dusty was cramming for tests, she flipped out with excitement when Clint walked in, waving the airline tickets and their itinerary in front of her.

"A week away, and we're off to Europe," he said, grinning wildly.

"Oh Clint," she said, jumping up and charging toward him, "our first vacation since our honeymoon, and Venice, it's going to be so romantic. I can hardly wait."

"On this glorious occasion," he said as they embraced, "you may call me the dream master."

Chapter 14

Dusty's excitement abruptly ended the day Clint postponed their trip to Venice during dinner a second time. Hostile bitterness swept across her face as their conversation turned into heated friction.

"Dusty, be reasonable," Clint pleaded. "In less than a couple of months, we'll be spending the holidays in Venice and skiing in the Swiss Alps. I swear to you on a stack of Bibles. I promise."

She stared at him morosely. "I don't want to talk about it. I'm fed up with your excuses. I've been patient long enough."

"This time I mean it," said Clint. "Carl's having to help his brother run the newspaper has put a damper on things. I've got two headhunter outfits searching for someone I can put in charge of operations. Nobody's found anyone suitable yet. Whoever he is, wherever he is, this fellow has got to be beyond reproach in honesty and integrity. Whatever it takes, I'll do it." He held up his glass and said, "A toast to Christmas in Venice and a European romp."

"Please, Clint, I'm not sure if I can take another broken promise," she said and clinked his glass.

* * *

Two weeks before Christmas during dinner, Clint postponed their getaway until spring. Dusty shoved her plate away and her head slumped forward when he told her. She sat silent.

"It's not my fault that people are buying all the buildings before they're completed," he said. "We've got deadlines to meet. It's totally crazy."

She raised her head and looked disdainfully at him and then hurled her glass, smashing it into the China buffet. Looking lurid, she got up, stormed into the foyer and turned, "I've had it with your megalomania," she shouted. "Don't bother coming up. I've no interest in sleeping with you tonight."

"We'll go this coming spring," he shouted. "I promise."

Not saying a word, Dusty charged up the stairs and slammed the door.

* * *

With Carl on board only part time, running Starburst Construction and Development as Sunshine City rolled along at full-throttle, the demand for Clint's nocturnal time increased. Pressure and stress continued to mount. Nightly meetings began running longer, and time ticked well past the hour of supper when he returned home. Deadlines, coordination, and scheduling became critical issues and caused his mind to suffer from a swirl of conflicting emotions as he skittered to the phone each night until Dusty stopped answering.

Amidst a city of concrete, steel, and glass being constructed, Buckingham Estates, a 160-unit garden apartment complex, broke ground in Sunnyvale, along with 180 townhouse units in Morgan Hill. Clint's greed multiplied like a drug addict. A part of him felt compelled to attain wealth; his other half wisely advised him to chuck the whole works for the sake of love and marriage. Unknowingly, greed won out, and the household battles worsened.

Bing Crosby was singing "Silent Night" from the stereo a week before Christmas when Clint arrived home early, carrying an armful of presents. Ignoring him, Dusty lay stretched-out silently on the rug in front of the fireplace reading a novel. She had a blasé expression on her face as he placed the gifts around the Christmas tree. He ignored her and went out to his truck. He returned with bundles of daisies and carnations and filled a couple of vases.

"Matt stopped by earlier and dropped off some presents," she said. "He told me by the way everything's moving that you'll be far too overloaded this spring to break away for our trip."

He rubbed his chin. "Matt's wrong. I hired a project manager a couple hours ago to lighten his load." He sat on the hearth in front of her. "I've been meaning to talk with you about this trip. Maybe we could trim it down from a month to a week or maybe two. It seems like every day turns into an emergency or a damn crisis with the investors. The high tech companies want to move into their new offices tomorrow and the buildings are only half finished. It's impossible."

Her face turned livid and she slammed the book shut, hopped up, and shouted, "You made a commitment, Clint!"

He looked at her sheepishly. "I know, but I never imagined all this would ever materialize. Now it's mushrooming like a hydrogen bomb. I've been tormented by this so much that it's driving me crazy. I spent a great deal of time thinking this out. I can't turn my back on everything and run away."

Her anger exploded in a tirade. "I'm fed up with your lies and the way you come waltzing in here making one excuse after the next. I'm tired of listening to your metaphysical insecurities and your phobias. Your ego eccentric maniac superiority is a superficial mask for your multitude of inferiority complexes."

"It's the season to be jolly," he said in hopes of calming her down. "Can't we put off this discussion until after the holidays?"

"I don't give a damn about the holidays," she blared. "I've had it, hearing about your vacuous greed. Your rapacious obsessions have destroyed our relationship. As it stands, this marriage is dangerously on the verge of a meltdown. For the umpteenth time, Clint, I have no desire to be listed in the Blue Book registry." Her eyes became penetrating and she scowled, "If it's a divorce you want, you've pushed it to the outer limits. The gist of it is I consulted with to an attorney this morning."

"You what?" He shouted and slumped down on the sofa as Dusty badgered him with threats. When she started talking about property settlements, he lost control and jumped up. "Give me some damn slack. You're way too demanding," he shouted. "Maybe divorce would be for the best. I'm not so sure I can stomach anymore of your badgering and your bitchy, cynical skepticism."

Fuming, Dusty jumped up and shouted, "That's it!" She stalked to the staircase. "Don't bother coming to bed. I'm not in the mood to sleep with you. I may never be. Sleep in Misty's old bed."

Teeming with frustration, Clint yelled, "Screw you and the magic carpet that blew you into my life."

"You and I are though," she yelled just before the door to their bedroom slammed.

Inside the kitchen, ridden with anger and sulking in confusion, Clint slapped a steak on an iron skillet, turned the knob to high, and went to the bar and poured a stiff drink. In a daze, he lowered his face onto his knuckles and began to weep.

He remained with his head between his legs until he sniffed the air and turned to look at the dark gray cloud of smoke drifting into the living room. Sprinting into the kitchen in a fit of panic, he burnt his hand grabbing the iron skillet and hurled it through the greenhouse window.

A short while later Clint threw the television through the bay window. His mind in a tenebrous haze, he sailed the onyx chessboard out another window. Unable to stave off his anger, he hurled the crystal vases through another window. He proceeded to go on a rampage until he lay curled up in the fetal position on the bed in Misty's old room. Regretful of his actions the instant his head touched the pillow, he wept like an infant.

Startled back to consciousness by Dusty's deafening shrieking and the slamming of the front doors, he bolted up as if from a nightmare. Racing out into the courtyard, he watched Dusty speed recklessly out of the driveway.

In the morning, Clint called a glass company and sat at the patio table in remorse. His head buzzing in agonizing guilt, he stared out at the redwood trees through the misty fog.

Regaining his senses, he went into the house and called the travel agency. He hung up the phone and drove downtown to pick up the tickets and do some shopping.

The glaziers were almost finished replacing the broken windows when he returned and began stuffing bunches of fresh lilies, holly and mistletoe into new vases. He went about placing them strategically throughout the house.

By the end of the day, the windows were all replaced and he was sweeping the broken glass. The house tidy, he lit a fire and turned up the volume on the stereo. His hands were trembling and tears flowed down his cheeks when he grabbed three silver candelabras on the dining table and lit the wicks. He placed the two airline tickets and their itinerary on top of Dusty's dinner plate before he went into the kitchen to prepare dinner.

Finished cooking a gourmet meal, he turned the oven on warm and put the plates inside. He filled two glasses with red wine, set them on the tablecloth, and sat waiting. Traumatized with guilt, he stared at the swinging pendulum inside the grandfather clock.

The night passed in repenting slow motion as he stared at the fire while writing Dusty a love letter. At the chime of the clock striking midnight, he rose up and nervously stoked the fire.

Watching the dawning sun creep up over the eastern hills and worried sick, he began pacing back and forth across the room like a wild-eyed zombie, regretful of his behavior.

"She might be staying over at Debby's," Dusty's mother told Clint on the telephone. "She's been in a terrible dither lately over your squabbling. Mind you, her father and I think you've far exceeded any expectations we ever fancied. We don't know what's come over her. She doesn't seem her normal self. You've been working so hard and have accomplished so much in such a short time. We're very proud of you. We hope the two of you can patch things up."

"I've been dwelling on our problems," he said, "Dusty's absolutely correct. All of our bickering stems from my lack of attentiveness and consideration. She's been working so hard to get her doctorate. And I've been in such a rut that I've been ignoring her. She deserves a break, and I intend to make amends. Will you please tell her there's a surprise for her in the dining room?"

"Why of course," her mother said cheerfully.

They chatted several more minutes about the power of love until Clint felt a catharsis and set the phone down. He sighed, knowing that her parents' supported him. In dire need to vent the pent-up tension inside of him, he called Carl and arranged a golf match at the club.

Later that morning, Clint sat next to Carl in a golf cart waiting at the first tee. "Same stakes?" Clint asked, trying to muster his lost enthusiasm.

"You've gotta be kidding me," Carl replied. "Bridget and I are practically on welfare because of you."

Clint forced a smile. "It's a risky game, but as the cliché goes, no balls, no glory."

"Hell, why not, you're bound to choke one day."

"On a serious note," Clint said, "I'm going to need to be reimbursed the 20 grand I lent you. The bulk of my money's tied up in building that city and all the other projects."

Carl winced. "What's the sudden hurry?"

"I need to save my marriage. Look, I don't like to haggle over something that's been agreed upon."

"Don't get yourself in an uproar. I'll rustle it up." Carl squinted.

"I need it today."

"No sweat. I've got a stash in my locker. You never know when a little payola is needed on the links."

After Clint played the worst round of golf in his life, they went inside the clubhouse and sat at the bar, and Clint explained his plight to Carl.

"I just hope Dusty and I can work something out," said Clint.

"You worry too damn much," said Carl. "Dusty worships the ground you walk on. She'll get over what happened last night. You just snapped because of the pressure. Same thing happened to my parents' when I was a kid. Striving to be a millionaire has its pitfalls. She'll cool down when she sees those tickets. That was a good move."

"I hope so. I went bonkers last night. I don't know what possessed me to do that. It's never happened before. I totally lost it big-time. I completely snapped."

Carl slapped him on the back. "Everyone has a breaking point, even me."

Before leaving, they went into the dressing room, and Carl opened his locker. From inside a cigar box, he pulled out a wad of greenbacks and peeled off the twenty thousand he owed Clint.

Clint wagged his head and handed Carl the grand he lost in their golf match. "This is like a clandestine operation."

"Call me anytime after you've had a lovers spat," said Carl with a snickering grin. "Now go patch things up and allow the lady to splurge. See you in a month. Don't worry, that lady loves you. Ain't no crisis can't be overcome when lovers are snuggled together in a gondola. And don't worry about Sunshine City. I'm jumping back in with both barrels. Enjoy yourself, you deserve it."

"First, I need to bring you up to speed on what's breaking loose this month."

Chapter 15

After briefing Carl on Sunshine City's upcoming schedule at the club, Clint drove to Starburst's headquarters and parked next to Matt's truck. It was twilight when he walked into his office and quickly peeked at the stack of spec binders and piles of banded plans that cluttered his desk. Matt was updating one of the critical path schedules on the walls when Clint came into the conference room and told him of his planned retreat to Italy. Matt's eyes expressed surprise when he told him he'd be gone a month.

"Think you can handle it?" Clint asked.

"You can bank on it," he eagerly assured him. "Carl's a good man, and this company's well oiled. It'll be smooth sailing. Have fun for Christ sake. You've earned it."

Clint forced a smile. "There'll be a generous bonus for you when I get back."

"But why a month?"

"As long as it takes until the old spark reignites. Keeping a marriage intact ain't an easy task, I've learned.

It's all about maintaining control when under pressure. And not spewing out a bunch of wrath. Last night was a real whopper. All hell broke loose. Dusty went ballistic and I totally lost control. I muffed it big time. I said and did stuff I can't believe. I've got to stoke the flame before it fizzles out, and our marriage dissolves inside a courtroom full of blood-thirsty leeches."

"I wouldn't worry too much. Dusty loves the pants off you," Matt said encouragingly. "Bonny and I have our fair share of spats, but they never last more than a day or two. Usually a little after we've slipped between the sheets, we've made up. Women have a knack of acting finicky every month. It's a cycle they go through."

Clint wagged his head. "You're right, because our marriage is a sticky mess. Enough of me burdening you with my troubles; hire a gopher to run errands. And get yourself a secretary to help with the paper work."

Matt grinned playfully. "Mind if I tell her that the mandatory dress code is hot pants, mini skirts, and bikini tops?"

"Go for it."

"No frocks or muumuu crap. And she has to have a hard body and a tight butt."

Clint chuckled. "Better yet, hire a frizzy-haired, Brazilian samba dancer in a dental floss bikini to teach you proper diction."

Matt's eyes lit up. "Hot damn. Hot and spicy. I've got the image. I can see her quivering, oiled and glimmering."

Clint played along, "How about a go-go dancer on roller skates to handle all the menial tasks and double your pleasure with a couple of succulent baits."

Matt beamed. "Now you're really talking. Let's get the show on the road. Leave tomorrow."

Clint shook his head and smiled. "I am. Now let's come down to reality and get serious."

They spent the next few hours reviewing critical path schedules, setting aside time to meet the next morning before Clint and Dusty would leave for Europe.

With things in order after a short visit with Clay, Clint sped home. Pulling into the courtyard, he noticed Dusty's car wasn't parked by the wishing well where she routinely parked. He pressed the remote control and when the garage door went up, he felt disappointed not seeing her car inside. Grimacing, he grabbed the flowers and walked inside the house. The tickets were untouched, and his love letter remained unopened. Feeling bereaved, he filled a green vase with water and arranged the flowers.

A glass of wine in his shaky hand, he sat on the sofa, his eyes transfixed on the telephone and waited. At midnight, he was pacing and mumbling incoherently. Without a wink of sleep in two nights, his mind was being sucked through a wind tunnel. Struck with an anxiety attack and distraught, he drove to Dusty's best friend's apartment building and pounded on the front door. Debby didn't respond. The only sound came from Debby's irate neighbors, who yelled for him to be quiet.

Returning to Zenith after ringing her sister's doorbell and finding no one home, Clint checked his message machine and called Dusty's mother.

"If she's not at Debby's, and Betsy and her husband are out of town," her mother said, "she may be spending the night aboard the cruiser. Why don't you call her?"

"Thanks, I will."

"The phone's a dead-end alley," Clint thought aloud. "Way too much time has lapsed and time is of the essence. Matters will surely worsen each minute we remain apart. " He grabbed the tickets and flowers. Outside, he jumped in his truck and raced to the Coyote Point Yacht Harbor where her parents' cruiser was tied up.

The tension he felt eased slightly when, through the thick fog, he saw Dusty's car and smiled. It was parked next to a ratty old Volkswagen bus that was hand-painted in floral graffiti. He figured the car belonged to Debby since she had recently converted from being a socialite to become a full-fledged hippie. He looked in the rear-view mirror and noticed that his face was puffy from lack of sleep. He rubbed his eyes, combed his hair, stuffed the tickets into his shirt pocket, grabbed the flowers, and made his way towards the wafting cruiser.

Whiffing the chilly sea air, he climbed aboard. The seagulls, standing asleep, scattered when he stepped on the wooden planks along the bridge.

The odor of marijuana lingered in the air when he walked into the galley. He looked curiously at the two wine glasses and ashtray full of half-smoked doobies and a roach clip that lay on the table. He smiled certain that Dusty was with Debby.

At the portal to the foreword stateroom, he straightened his posture and attempted in vain to relax as he softly knocked. The room was silent, and he knocked a little louder and heard only creaking and splashing. He knocked louder several times before he opened the portal and flicked on the light switch.

He smiled widely, expecting to see Dusty and Debby lying asleep. Stunned in disbelief, the flowers dropped from his hands when a bearded, long-haired hippie with a sallow expression raised his surprised face up from under the quilt. Clint blinked several times, then squinted and went into shock. His mind whirling in vertigo, his face twisted, his chin dropped, his mouth wide open, Clint stared at the shirtless man, who clutched the quilt in front of his neck. Dusty poked her panic-stricken face out from under the blankets and stared at Clint in a state of fear. So revolted at the ghastly sight of seeing the straps of her bra on her shoulders, Clint shut his eyes and vomited. Dusty's face was ghostly white when Clint reopened his eyes and saw her cringing.

"We haven't done anything!" Dusty shouted.

Clint stood paralyzed as surges of electrical shock burned deep inside his heart. His eyes blinked wildly, refusing to believe she was in bed with another man.

"It's not what you think," she ranted in a frightened voice. "We're just friends."

"She's telling the truth," the hippie shouted.

Feeling a sharp stinging pain as Dusty and the hippie continued to plead that they had done nothing wrong, he clutched the left side of his chest. Witnessing an unfathomable act of betrayal, the small room spun around in a blur. Dizzy from repulsion, his guts wrenching, Clint reeled backwards as his back slid down the wall. He slumped forward on the floor with his face burrowed between his legs.

Dusty lowered the blanket. "See, I have my underwear on." Clint raised his head and stared at her tangerine panties and matching bra. Staring at her horrified face, Clint struggled to stand up with the impulse to kill them. Taking a deep breath, he pushed himself up and leaned forward, spitting the phlegm and vomit that oozed from his throat into her face.

The long-haired hippie, sitting beside her, looked scared as he released the quilt and held his tremulous arms straight over his head and pleaded timidly, “She’s telling the truth,” he stammered. “Nothing’s happened. Look, I’m just a close friend. I only came here to comfort her. There’s no need to get violent.”

Unable to look at the man, Clint stared at Dusty, who was wiping her pitiful reddened face and screaming. Clint turned and staggered into the galley. He glanced at the meat cleaver that lay on top of a maple butcher block and grabbed it.

Instinctively, he whirled around and charged into the stateroom, wielding the meat cleaver over his head, compelled with the impulse to kill them. He stopped and stared at Dusty’s pitiful face as her shrilling shrieks of innocence echoed in his eardrums.

Voices rang in his head as Clint stared down at them as they clung to each other and screamed for mercy. His face loathing, Clint turned and hurled the cleaver across the galley into the main cabin, shattering the radar screen.

Grinning diabolically and laughing hysterically, Clint grumbled in a harsh voice, “What a vile, wicked, despicable thing to do. What a hideous joke. You pathetic bitch.”

“I haven’t done anything wrong,” screamed Dusty. “It’s the truth, I swear.”

Laughing, Clint stood above them. “I haven’t done anything wrong,” he mimicked Dusty’s shrilling voice. “Looksy, I have my underwear on.” His face tightened. “You miserable slut-bitch, you adulterous whore. With a ferocious expression, Clint slapped her face hard. He slapped her again while the cowering hippie shivered and covered his face. Shaking violently, Dusty's face swelled and turned a purple hue.

"I might have been snared in a web of greed," said Clint in a harsh tone. "But your act of betrayal is heinous. I hope the both of you fry in hell."

Laughing hysterically, Clint sailed the tickets at them and then turned and stumbled out of the stateroom. "Enjoy Venice with your scumbag lover. You deserve the bastard. You deserve the loser who would screw another man's wife. What a wicked act. You vile, wretched bitch. Merry Christmas and Happy New Year."

Dusty was still screaming they hadn't done anything wrong when Clint staggered out into the fog that engulfed the bay. Laughing hysterically, he walked to his truck.

Arriving back at Zenith, suicidal and emotionally distraught, Clint drove the truck up the steps and crashed through the entry doors, into the foyer and half way up the staircase. His hands trembled as he picked up the phone to call Matt. Then he called Roy and Carl. After he hung up, in desperation to prevent him from taking his life, he dialed his pal, Dan's number in New York.

"Good grief, dear friend," shouted Dan after Clint had spilled his guts. "Listen man, whatever you do, don't do anything rash or foolish. Killing yourself isn't the answer. Look, Clint, I have knowledge in dealing with trauma. It happened to me. Get on a plane and get your ass over here now. I can help pull you through this mess. You need long-term recovery if you want to survive. You need time to heal. Suicide is the easy route. Come to New York. Let me help you."

"I love ya, but I hate New York. You've already been a big help. Thanks for listening. See ya pal." Clint slammed down the phone.

Mid-morning, Clint dialed the travel agency and booked the only flight available to Europe that night. After packing two suitcases and a light travel bag, he went outside with a chain saw, a can of gasoline and a bottle of whiskey tucked under his arm. Lovelorn, he sat on the edge of the wishing well, staring in a trance at Zenith, wondering what he had done that was so wrong to deserve such betrayal. In a river of tears, he took out his lucky silver dollar and flipped it into the well. He watched it splash and laughed until he threw up. Gagging, he began to fill the chain saw with gasoline.

He listened to the engine of Carl's Porsche whine as he watched Roy and his brother race into the courtyard. Clint had just started recanting his horror story when he saw Matt riding up the driveway on his Harley. Later, his three friends sat at the wishing well, shaking their heads and appearing dumbfounded as Clint recanted his nightmare to them.

Matt stood up. "I don't know what to say, man, just that you can't leave all this. You've got an entire city in the works."

"Matt's right, Clint," Carl said. "You can't walk away. You've built this business into a damn empire. You'd be crazy to leave. Why give the bitch everything you worked your ass off for?"

Clint took a swig and stared at the orange sky. "Money doesn't interest me at the moment."

"What you need is a good attorney," Roy blurted. "No judge in the world would give that bitch a penny for what she did. Look at you, you're an emotional wreck."

Clint shrugged, detached. "There'd be a trial and I'd be forced to look at that traitor. I'd have to testify that I caught the bitch in the sack, screwing some asswipe.

And I'd have to relive the raging urge to rush over and mutilate the bitch's face. And the attorneys; God, how I loathe those bloodsucking bastards."

"Can't disagree with you on that," Carl nodded. "You got a passport?"

Clint took a chug and said, "It's in my back pocket."

"You can't just walk out on Sunshine City," Roy said.

"Your brother can handle it," said Clint. "Matt's a good man. And Clay Thompson's the best in the business. I no longer want any part of it. I need to breakaway, clear my head. I may not be back for some time." He stooped down and picked up the chain saw. "The American dream - what a farcical lie - what a crock of shit." He pulled the cord on the chainsaw.

"You're not going to do what I think you are?" Matt shouted. "This place's worth damn a fortune."

"Won't be when I'm finished," Clint said. His eyes crazed, he walked toward Zenith, pressing the trigger of the chainsaw.

His three friends continued bantering for him not to do it, but he didn't listen. Staring at the demolished entry, he slipped on a surgical mask and walked inside. The chainsaw only buzzed a few minutes before fumes and smoke flowed out the windows and entry.

An hour later, choking, Clint stumbled outside, covered in sawdust and sweat. Carl and Roy refused to take part demolishing Zenith and stood gaping as Matt reluctantly helped Clint wrap chains at several strategic locations around the house. Lost in thought, Clint locked the hubs of his four-wheel drive truck, and hooked the chains to the cable on the wench. His three friends grinned and pleaded for him not to do it as he pulled the chains taunt, backing up. Zenith began to creak, splinter, crunch, and snap. Following a series of thundering sonic booms, Zenith collapsed in a billowy cloud of smoke, reduced to a pile of crushed rubble and glass at the bottom of the hill.

Rain gushed and swirled sideways, and the sky rumbled on the drive to the airport after Clint had picked up his ticket at the travel agency. Lightning crackled and streaked, and the wind howled when Clint and his friends walked into the airport terminal.

Not listening to the voices of his companions, Clint perused the bookshelves and bought a couple of paperbacks and a dozen half-pints of scotch that he stuffed into his pockets. After checking in his suitcases, they walked to the boarding gate. Waiting in line, Clint became dimly aware of how grateful he was that his friends were with him. They were all shaking their heads in disbelief as he shook their hands and hugged each one of them.

"I love you guys, I really do," said Clint. "Thanks for all your support."

His friends stood with confused expressions, urging him to stay when he entered the boarding chute. He turned and waved, aware that it would be a long time before he would see the faces of his good friends again.

Chapter 16

Midway over the Atlantic on a stormy night, Clint was seated in the coach section with his head resting on his knees. A petite freckle-faced, redheaded stewardess, pushing a cart along the aisle, stopped and looked down at him. Appearing concerned, she whiffed the air and shook her head in disgust.

The stewardess politely asked the priest sitting next to Clint, "Is he okay, Father?"

The wizened priest looked up from a gilded Bible and replied in a refined Spanish accent, "He is fine, just weary."

"Are you sure?" She asked. "He's shaking so much. And he reeks terribly of alcohol."

"Yes, I know," said the priest, running his fingers through his grayish white hair. "The lad recently experienced some rather harsh, unexpected trauma. He is in the hands of providence. He will be fine."

The stewardess yawned and said, "The captain just informed me that the aircraft may encounter some minor turbulence ahead. I need him to fasten his seat belt."

"Wake him up," said the priest. "He is slightly inebriated, but harmless."

She leaned over and gently tugged on Clint's arm.

Jarred awake from a drunken stupor, suffering from a throbbing hangover, Clint opened his bloodshot eyes and grumbled, "What the hell's going on, what's happened? Where am I?"

"Everything's fine, Mister McBride," the stewardess said reassuringly. "There's nothing to worry about. I just need you to sit in the upright position and buckle your seat belt."

"Huh. Oh, yeah, sure," he mumbled. Disoriented, he sat up, his body twitching.

Discombobulated, dehydrated, and hyperventilating, he buckled his restraint and looked out the window. The stewardess smiled at the priest and braced herself as the plane rocked to and fro. She quickly caught her balance. Appearing relieved, she swiped her forehead and continued down the aisle, advising the passengers to fasten their seat belts. Clint rubbed his eyes until his vision cleared slightly and he stared at the fuzzy image of the sympathetic priest.

The priest's gray-green eyes were compassionate and penetrated deep into Clint's. Feeling strangely uncomfortable, Clint began to fidget. He stuck his hand inside his jacket pocket and fumbled, pulling out a half-pint of scotch.

"There is a better solution to healing than drinking spirits, my son," the priest said in a soft tone. "Your name is Clint, is that correct?"

Clint wiped the rivulets of sweat from his brow with his sleeve and stared at the priest's clerical collar. He shook his head and said, "How do you know my name?"

"We spoke briefly before you passed out. I am Father Bernardo."

Clint pressed his fingertips on his temples and said, "I don't remember talking to you."

"We spoke about your situation shortly after the plane departed San Francisco," said Father Bernardo, crossing his legs.

Clint leaned forward and studied the priest's pious face. "You do look familiar," he slurred, untwisting the bottle cap. "Oh yeah, now I remember. You're a monk, I mean a prior, an abbot, or something at a monastery."

"Yes, that is correct, I am all of those. As I was saying, there is another remedy to mend the heart and soul, an alternative to spirits. Unfortunately, there are two sides to spirits, much like the difference between good and evil. Taken in moderation is the good side of spirits. Drinking to excess casts a darker light on the harmful effects of spirits. The greatest healer for the agony you have suffered is time. Time, coupled with prayer and spiritual faith in the good Lord, will help hasten your recovery. Abusing spirits in a time of crisis only leads to a sorrowful road of desolation, misery and further wreckage."

Staring at Father Bernardo's collar, Clint nodded and screwed the cap back onto the bottle. He put it inside his jacket pocket and listened to the priest recant his plight.

Befuddled, Clint said: "Please forgive me, Father Bernardo, but this is all way too mysterious for me to cope with. I'm baffled. How do you know all this, are you some kind of clairvoyant?"

Father Bernardo gave off the hint of a smile and stroked his gray beard. "Oh, my goodness, I am most certainly not possessed with psychic capabilities. Most of what I know of your troubles, I learned while you talked in your sleep. The rest you told me in flight to New York."

Clint belched. "I did. You'll have to excuse me, Father, but I'm not feeling well. I think I'm going to be sick."

Dizzy and wavering, Clint fought the urge and restrained from throwing up. He managed to stand up, grab his toiletry bag from the overhead compartment, and stagger down the aisle to the bathroom. The moment he latched the door, he dropped to his knees and leaned his head over the toilet bowl. After vomiting for a couple minutes, he pulled himself up, rinsed the vile taste from his mouth, and stared at his swollen face in the mirror. Disgusted at the pitiful image he saw, he shoved his hand inside his trouser pocket and brought out a half-pint of scotch. He thought briefly about what the priest had told him before he gulped a small mouthful. Suffering from despair, he sat on the toilet and wept. He held the bottle in front of his face and shook his head before he emptied it down the toilet and discarded it in the trash. Standing up, he flushed the toilet and turned on the faucet. He splashed cold water on his face, scrubbed his cheeks, brushed his teeth and gargled. Shaking his head and crying, he combed his hair, exited the bathroom, and stumbled down the aisle to his window seat.

"If I told you what happened," Clint said, sitting beside Father Bernardo, "what provoked my wife to commit such an abominable act? Why did she do something so traitorous, so abhorrent?"

"I am merely a humble priest, doing God's work. I am not omniscient. Only God has the answer to your question. You will come to comprehend His reasoning in time. Do you remember my offer to you?"

"No, I don't remember anything, just vague remnants." Tears continued trickling down his puffy cheeks. "I only remember your face and your wisdom. Your face is unforgettable."

Father Bernardo gave off a faint smile. "Before you began to drink yourself into oblivion, you mentioned that you are an architect and builder. I explained to you that I am an abbot at an abbey near Madrid. There is a cloister area behind the chapel that is in shambles and in desperate need of rejuvenation. Some fellow monks and I thought to build a fountain in the courtyard as a central focal point to aid our retreat guests in their contemplative prayer. The abbey is ancient, and the chapel is also in need of restoration. I offered you a room at the abbey where you can attempt to rebuild your life, a place you can seek out a new meaning, a purpose."

"You did?"

"Yes. Of course, you are under no obligation if you wish to change your mind. But please consider it. Perhaps we can be of help to each other."

"I think I'd like that."

"I can only offer spiritual guidance in an atmosphere that is conducive to healing, finding solace and a new course of direction in exchange." Father Bernardo opened his black satchel and brought out a pad. "You made some sketches for me before you fell asleep. They are all very good. I especially like this one with the obelisk and the engravings, and the dove, with the wings of a butterfly."

His hands shaking, Clint took the pad and looked at the drawings. "I did these?"

"Yes, and very rapidly, considering your level of intoxication. You are a very gifted artist."

"I've never sculpted a fountain. I'd love to build one. It will be a challenge."

"Then I beckon you to come for a redeeming retreat."

"My head's so foggy, I don't even know where this plane is going, other than you mentioned Madrid. You mean Spain?"

"Yes."

"I have a question, Father. You said something a few moments ago about how God has a reason for what happens. I know I'm a little under the weather, but that statement boggled me. How can what happened to me be a good thing?"

"Unfortunately, my son, mankind is not infallible. I do not condone the contemptuous act by your partner. But we human beings are not created perfectly. In time you will view things through a different pair of eyes."

His sweaty hands quavering uncontrollably, Clint listened intently to Father Bernardo's soothing counseling until his eyelids became droopy.

When he reopened his eyes, Father Bernardo sat snoring lightly with his head tilted sideways. A Bible, clutched in his hands, rested on his lap. After swallowing four aspirins down his parched throat, he stared out through the rain-spattered window at the streaks of lightning slashing through the swirling clouds. He flashed back on the scornful image of Dusty sitting up in bed next to the creep and twitched.

A pleasant woman's sultry Spanish voice interrupted his slumbering thoughts as he stared out at the rising sun hovering over the horizon.

"We will be landing in Madrid in approximately twenty minutes," the voice said in English. "The temperature at ground level is 35 degrees Fahrenheit. Please refrain from smoking and secure all personal belongings."

Father Bernardo opened his eyes and stretched his thin arms above his narrow head. "You look much better this morning," he said. "Your face is less swollen, and the redness has faded to a mild pink. How are you feeling?"

"Hung-over, nauseous," he said. "I feel like a jerk, like an idiot, a complete imbecile. I failed. I'm a failure. I was so ignorant. My wife warned me a million times the dam would burst if I continued to place money above our relationship, and I didn't listen to her. I was like a glutton, engorged with greed. So wired, all I thought about was the almighty dollar. If she would only have been less subtle in the beginning before all hell broke loose."

"There is much truth in the timeworn expression that money is the root of all evil."

"I see it now. I saw it earlier when I demolished our house. I saw it again when I boarded this flight. Then I remembered meeting you. It all came back to me while I was sitting here watching you sleep. I thought back on your words and how they added clarity about how I allowed money to take complete control of my life. Funny thing is, Father, I'm really not a greedy person. It's like I was possessed by demons with dollar signs for ears."

Father Bernardo smiled. "If one believes in the feasibility of angels, then one must consider it inevitable that demons are not myth. Are you of a religious denomination?"

"I was raised Catholic. In keeping truthful, I'm not much of a religious man, but I believe there's a

God. Only a blind man without a brain wouldn't believe in the existence of God, someone born without the capacity to see the vast complexities of our universe, our brain."

"And the boundless intricacies of mortal life that mankind has yet to broach. The possibilities are limitless."

"I agree, Father. The creation of this universe was no accidental fluke. I've never fallen for the '*Big Bang'* theory. That's bull-dink. While you were asleep, I pondered over your invitation to stay at your monastery. I'd like that very much."

"I am glad."

"I want to build the fountain. I don't expect the magic of a miracle. I only know that I feel comfortable speaking to you. Perhaps if I listen closely, this suicidal tendency welling within me will be quashed."

As Father Bernardo spoke, he removed a small leather pouch from his black pants pocket and pulled out a string of wooden rosary beads. They prayed until the hydraulic sounds from the landing gear disrupted their concentration.

"Try not to dwell on the past negatives," said Father Bernardo. "Instead, focus on the positive episodes that have occurred in your life. Sometimes it is wiser to pass certain things by and let them lie dormant. For, in time, with proper nourishment, care and patience, even the worst wounds heal. Let the past be for the time being, and concentrate on the good things that have occurred in your life, and you will achieve salvation."

Peering through the window at the Spanish countryside as the plane began to make its descent; Clint made a steeple with his fingers in front of his face and listened to the abbot. Moments before the plane's wheels touched down on the tarmac, Father Bernardo and Clint exchanged smiles.

Chapter 17

Having passed through customs inspection, Father Bernardo and Clint walked outside under a light sprinkle of rain. A short jovial man greeted Father Bernardo with a warm embrace. The abbot introduced Clint to Brother Luke, who was wearing a sleeveless down vest over a tight-fitting, greasy white T-shirt. Brother Luke, a kindred spirit, who spoke broken English, nodded at Clint after they hugged and helped load their luggage into the trunk of a compact station wagon. Brother Luke's arms were slight, but his triceps and biceps were bulging.

A blinding rain began falling on the serpentine road that led to the abbey. It didn't seem to bother Brother Luke that the road was slick, he hydroplaned the small car toward the distant mountains as though tomorrow would fail to arrive. Brother Luke's reckless driving didn't appear to faze Father Bernardo. The abbot sat in the front seat, staring through the windshield as if he were in a trance.

Forlorn and submerged in an abyss of self-pity, and self-destruction, death appeared a relief for Clint. During a lull in the downpour, he stared solemnly out at the forest of verdant pine trees that flashed past in a blur. He tried to grasp Father Bernardo's profound advice on the meaning of forgiveness but wasn't able to touch it.

At the top of a rise, the rain turned to a light drizzle, and Brother Luke abruptly slowed the car. In the far distance, Clint stared in awe at the abbey.

"Valle de los Caidos translated in English is Valley of the Fallen," said Father Bernardo.

"It looks like a gigantic amphitheater on a pitted moon crater," said Clint as his eyes shifted to the right of the fortress where a mammoth cross rose some 500 feet from atop a mountain carved of jagged stone. It appeared like a giant parabolic antenna capable of beaming quasar signals up to the heavenly galaxies. Staring out at the countryside, Clint shook his head in wonderment and pondered the words '*Valley of the Fallen*.'

After Brother Luke parked the station wagon, a couple of happy-faced, robed monks greeted the abbot with embraces. Under an arched portico, Clint walked beside Father Bernardo to the underground basilica below the towering cross.

A strange sensation fell over Clint the moment they entered the basilica as if an aura of holiness hailed within the sanctity. As the abbot explained the annals of the abbey in a soft whisper, Clint looked over his shoulder at the altar. Listening intently to the abbot, his eyes rose to the grandiose cupola decorated with mosaic tiles.

"This place is colossal, Father," said Clint in a low voice. "My mind is staggered by the enormous proportions, and there's so much history here. It's beautiful and sacred."

"But, as you can see, the basilica is in dire need of restoration."

"Whatever I can do to help, I'll do," said Clint. "It would be an honor for me. I've never done anything like this. But I can do it."

"Amen. But the cloister area is my first priority. Come, I will introduce you to Brother Mark, the guest-master."

"Why were you in San Francisco, Father?" Clint asked as they began to walk.

The abbot reflected and said, "I was there to attend a conference on the human psyche and to give a lecture on subliminal spirituality."

"You've lost me, Father."

Father Bernardo rolled his eyes and half-smiled. "It is the subconscious transformation of kinetic energy into faith."

Clint nodded as if he understood. By the way the monks greeted the humble abbot along the way, it became obvious to him that Father Bernardo was well-loved and sought after for his spiritual savvy.

Brother Mark, a husky giant, wearing a hooded, reddish brown robe, reminded Clint of a jolly Santa Claus when Father Bernardo introduced them in Spanish. A chain of large wooden beads dangled down Brother Mark's side.

"Oh, I neglected to mention," said Father Bernardo in English to Brother Mark. "Clint does not speak but a little Spanish. So this will be a splendid opportunity for you and our fellow monks to brush up on English. Perhaps Clint will consider teaching a class in English."

"I'd like that," said Clint. "It'd be fun."

Brother Mark gave Clint a jovial grin and said with a heavy Spanish accent, "It is a pleasure to meet you, Clint."

Clint returned Brother Mark's robust smile. "Bienvenida, Brother Mark."

"Clint will be staying on with us for a time," said Father Bernardo. "Please see that he has a room and help him to get settled."

"Si, Padre."

"Perhaps show him around the cloister garden, so he becomes acquainted and feels comfortable." The abbot patted Clint on the shoulder. "My schedule is usually quite frantic on Sunday, and having been gone for a week, I am sure to be inundated the rest of the day. If you are not too worn out, I hope to see you at vespers tonight, at seven."

"Vespers?" Clint said.

"Evening prayer in the basilica."

"Ah, would tomorrow be okay," said Clint. "I think I need to clear my head."

"So be it. If you feel up to it, lauds is at six tomorrow morning."

"Lauds?"

"Morning prayer."

"Oh, I'd like that very much," said Clint. "I'll be there."

"Later, in the afternoon," said Father Bernard, "we will begin our therapeutic walks in the rose garden, and I will show you what I have in mind for the cloister area. Would three o'clock be a suitable hour?"

"Yes, Father. Three's a good time."

Father Bernardo and Clint hugged before the abbot departed.

"Please forgive my poor English," said Brother Mark as he and Clint set out on a tour.

Clint laughed. "There's no need for me to forgive you. I'm in Spain. I should be speaking Spanish."

"No, please speak in English. It is not often I hear someone speak with a native tongue. I understand you."

"To be quite honest with you, Brother Mark, English isn't exactly my forte. I'm not much good in grammar and punctuation. But when it comes to conversation, I'm pretty darn good."

"English is the universal language. It is a blessing that you are here."

Every monk Clint encountered gave him a curious look along with a friendly smile. After they toured the cloister area, Brother Mark escorted Clint to his new living quarters. Clint smiled when Brother Mark referred to the small room as a cell.

"You have stirred considerable excitement among my fellow monks," said Brother Mark as he set Clint's bags onto the cement floor. "They are very eager to learn English. When will you begin to teach?"

Glancing around the room, Clint said: "Soon as I clear out the incubus that's floating around inside my head. I need to get rid of it and get some clarity."

Brother Mark's face perked up. "Si. I know this word. It is similar in Latin. Incubare. Evil, wicked."

"That's right, Brother Mark."

A few moments later, Brother Mark squeaked the door shut, leaving Clint looking around the dank and dismal dungeon-like cell. *Things could be worse*, he thought to himself. *Small, but it's better than a prison cell, or solitary confinement, or death row had you killed Dusty and that pathetic bastard.* He stared up at the spangled silver and gold crucifix of Jesus nailed to a cross that hung on the stone wall above a small metal bed. His eyes continued to rove around the room until he looked at the thin mattress, neatly wrapped in a wool blanket and the small pillow that lay at the head of the bed.

Sitting on a rickety wooden chair, he rested his elbows on the walnut table in the center of the room. He scrunched his jaw with his fingers and with a blank expression, he stared at the gilded book with the title Santa Biblia that lay atop a desk next to a nativity scene and tin candleholder. He turned and gazed at a picture of the Blessed Mother Mary hanging on the wall and began crying.

He wept for almost an hour before he got up and peeked inside the meager bathroom and saw that it was clean and smelled of disinfectant.

Darkness was beginning to set in, and he lit a wax candle and turned off the bedside lamp. Crumpling old smelly newspapers, he crammed them into an old tin-lizzy potbelly stove in the corner of the room. Even though he was appreciative of the sanctuary, he was unable to erase the ugly memory of Dusty's deceit. He grabbed a handful of kindling and some pine logs from out of a crate, placed them on the pile of crushed papers, and struck a matchstick.

Later that cold wintry night, he lay on the hard bed, staring at the peeling paint on the plaster ceiling. Whiffing the burning pine, he heard the faint sound of a requiem filter through the open window. He wondered what laws he had broken when he destroyed their home.

The tolling of bells jarred him awake, and he lurched up from bed in a cold sweat, his mind in a torment from a nightmare.

Feeling stifled, he went to the window and stared out into the stillness of darkness. In the distance, he could hear the sound of organ music and the hum of a choir. He felt as if he had been cast under a spell and wondered to himself, *How could such a sweet woman commit such a contemptuous act*. Deep in thought, his hands trembling, he shook his head in bafflement. *You need an elixir to ease this damn depressive virus that's haunting you,* he thought. *Get on with your life. Listen to the abbot. Forget your hatred and resentment and forgive Dusty.* He unzipped his track bag and stared at the half-dozen small bottles of scotch. Setting them on the table, he caught sight of a small brown lizard crawling from behind a nightstand on the floor. In a flash, the lizard's long, slimy tongue snapped out of its mouth and snatched a spider in front of his eyes. Jolted, he fell backwards onto the bed. The lizard had fled by the time he pulled himself back up. He blew out the candle, laid his head on the pillow, folded his arms over his chest, and shut his eyes.

The sound of rain sprinkling onto metal woke Clint at the crack of daylight. Feeling empty and alone, he grabbed a bar of soap and a bottle of shampoo and took a hot shower. After toweling his face dry, he gazed out the window in sadness and wonderment at the magic of his new surroundings. He knelt by the side of the bed and prayed with the rosary beads that Father Bernardo had given him. Looking up at the crucifix, he made a solemn vow of solitude and fasting and looked forward to meeting Father Bernardo in the afternoon. *Only water, prayer, daily Mass, silence, contemplative meditation, sleep, and work, at least until you clear the jumbled mess that's spinning inside your head,* he thought to himself as he emptied all the bottles into the toilet and flushed it. Finished dressing, he went to the basilica for lauds.

* * *

"You have made excellent progress, and the foundation appears very sturdy," said Father Bernardo as he walked with Clint in the rose garden a month after Clint began working on the fountain.

"It needs to be, Father," said Clint. "This fountain is big, eight meters round and six meters high. I'm about to start sculpting the engraving forms for the outside perimeter of the first tier in the workshop. What did the archbishop think of the sketches of Angelwings?"

"He is quite pleased as I am. You are well-disciplined in adhering to your strict vows."

"Look, Father, my hands have finally stopped shaking, and they're dry. My thoughts are less convoluted. It's just sleeping that's bothersome. The moment I put my head on the pillow, the flashbacks return. They're incessant. And I wake up in a cold sweat, shaking, my stomach is twisted in knots, and my mouth is full of phlegm."

"Remember what I said, time is man's greatest healer. How is your meditation coming along?"

"Good, but the flashbacks keep returning when my mind is blank. Last night, I was making progress when my wife appeared in a bad dream. She was standing next to a monster with serpents and snakes wound through her hair. And the devil is standing beside her holding a trident and laughing."

A half-smile appeared on the abbot's face. "In time they will fade further away until they have vanished. Oh, I found my English Bible and a book on transcendental meditation. It is also in English. I set them by your door on the way here. There is a note inside with some psalms I would like you to read."

"Thank you, Father. I'll try. But these flashbacks are so contemptuous that I get sick and have to rush into the bathroom. I gag and heave until my throat's inflamed. I end up flat on my back on the floor in a deep quandary, wondering why I became so greedy."

"Remember our chats on forgiveness?"

"I'm working real hard on it. But it isn't easy, Father. I was so naïve, so stupid."

"Have patience, my son. The fountain is coming along splendid. Everyone is excited."

They sat down on a stone bench and continued to talk for almost an hour.

* * *

Another month passed, and Clint was on the staging planks setting forms for the third tier of the round fountain when Father Bernardo set a thermos of tea and two cups on a bench. Clint set down the hammer and chisel, and climbed down the scaffold.

"Good morning, Father."

"Good morning. The fountain is coming along wonderfully. You are a marvelous craftsman."

"I was a little rusty starting out, but it's come back. It's been years since I worked with my hands. I'm really enjoying building this."

Filling two cups with jasmine tea, the abbot asked, "How are you feeling within yourself, the inner soul?"

He thought a moment. "Better, Father, well, not exactly, but I feel I'm headed on the right path. I owe my life to you, Father. I might well have committed suicide and be buried if I hadn't met you."

"You have gained much headway in your short stay."

"I still cry every night," said Clint. "But my eyes are no longer swollen and puffy. Honestly, Father, I was on the verge of killing myself. But with your guidance, I'm now confident that I'll survive. I'm working really hard on forgiveness. Now that I realize it was me who was totally to blame, I'm working on forgiving myself."

The holy man beamed and gently squeezed Clint's hand as they rose and began to walk.

"Begin to eat," Father Bernardo said. "You are beginning to look deathly ill. Fasting is good, but going overboard could be life-threatening."

Clint nodded, "You're right, Father. My vow of fasting ends today on this glorious day."

"You have a presence about you that suggests you may wish to lead a monastic life, have you considered it?"

Surprised by Father Bernardo's question, Clint felt a light rumble inside his heart. He smiled and stuttered, "Ah, actually, it's funny you should say that. I thought about priesthood when I was an altar boy. It's so peaceful here, and everyone has been so helpful, so kind and supportive. I'm flattered, but I don't wish to mislead you, Father. There's not even a remote possibility."

"It was merely curiosity."

"Even if I were to consider it, I would beyond a doubt fail. I'm far too fond an admirer of a woman's anatomy. And sex, I couldn't live without sex. No, Father, the temptation would always be too great."

The abbot beamed as if he was dwelling in past memories, and his eyes began to drift and fade as they often did. “I understand, my son. At a very young age, I felt myself being pulled in two directions - my passion to lead a spiritual life and my compulsive desire to taste the nectar of a female.” The abbot’s eyes shifted back to Clint. “I was a mere lad of sixteen when I sustained a broken heart. It was on that day that I decided to forego lust and devote all of my attention to God, the Almighty, in preparation for life ever after in the Lord’s kingdom.” Father Bernardo paused in reflection. “I am proud of you and your effort to overcome your crises. It is good to see you smile. You have done much better than I originally anticipated. I remember watching you stagger down the aisle, coming back from the bathroom, smelling of whiskey when you collapsed in your seat.” Father Bernardo leaned over to inhale a Don Juan rose as they walked along the gravel paths in the garden.”

Clint whiffed the rose and smiled. “My wife was beautiful and talented, a gifted guitarist and smart too. Her big dream was to start up a school and teach autistic children how to overcome their problems and enjoy life. And I blew it. It was a riddle at first because deep down I thought I was doing the right thing, striving for success and riches. But now with what you’ve instilled in me, I’ve come to the conclusion that my greed destroyed our marriage. I was engulfed in chasing the American dream. But it was never for me, Father, it was always for us. I’m not a selfish man. I dedicated my life to us. I just wish I had looked in the mirror and seen what I’d turned into. Wealth, prosperity, what utter hogwash, anyway, it’s a lesson that I’ll never forget and never repeat.

"You have grown so much in such a short span of time. I am very pleased. I will see you at evening lauds."

"I look forward to it. Oh, Father. The obelisk to support the dove is nearly complete. When will the white marble that Gabriel found in Greece be here?"

"The quarry has shipped it by boat. It should be arriving any day. Brother Luke will pick it up as soon as it gets here."

"I'm excited. Brother Gabriel has keen eyes. I trust his judgment. I can't wait to begin. Sculpting the obelisk was easy. Now I can't wait to start on the dove."

"If you sculpt the way you sketch, the fountain will be a monumental masterpiece."

Clint smiled wide. "When I'm finished with the fountain, I want to continue to work for my keep. I want to help with the restoration of the basilica. And I feel that I'm now ready to begin teaching English classes to the monks."

A slight smile appeared on Father Bernardo's face. "Splendid. You are more than welcome to remain here for as long as you desire. It is important that the monks listen to the correct and precise pronunciation of spoken English. I shall post a notice in the refectory and set up a classroom."

Chapter 18

Along with the springtime sun, came the fragrance from the fresh budding daffodils and ginger lilies that Clint had planted throughout his cell. The smell from the blossoming roses in the garden filtered through the window and brought a smile to his face as he shaved and dressed before going down for morning lauds.

Later in the afternoon while Clint stood filing the wings of the dove, Father Bernardo walked into the workshop, "You told me an untruth," the abbot said. "You said you never sculpted."

"I'd never lie to you, Father," Clint said, continuing to file the marble, "this is my first attempt at sculpting."

"I spoke in jest."

"I didn't know abbots were allowed to joke."

Father Bernardo smiled faintly and shook his head. "Abbots are not prison wardens."

Clint bent in laughter. "That was a stupid remark. I know monks like to have fun. Your brothers clown around like little kids during English class. And they're always cutting up in Tai Chi and qigong. They crack me up the way they make funny faces, especially Brother Luke with his corncob pipe and mouthful of spinach, when he does his Popeye routine. Brother Mark drives me nuts with his Tarzan call of the wild yells while pounding on his buffed chest. And Brother Benedict's chimpanzee routine is a classic. Seems the better your fellow monks become at speaking English and watching American cartoons, the more they like to horse around."

"We are all children of God." Father Bernardo shifted his attention to the bird and softly stroked a wing. "It looks real. Will it fly?" The abbot half smiled.

Clint laughed. "Ah, I didn't take any Quantum physics or aeronautical jet propulsion classes, but I know that with enough force and energy you achieve acceleration and velocity. And with these wings, this butterfly dove will glide into the air and soar."

The abbot rubbed his chin. "Kinetic energy also produces motion. Butterfly dove. That is an intriguing thought for a name."

"I was toying with that and Butterdove or Butterwings, but I 'm kinda stuck on Angelwings. What do you think, Father, it's your fountain?"

"Then that is it," the abbot said excitedly. "Angelwings is befitting. We will set the timer to operate the pumps to coincide with the falling water and the Angelus bells for prayer. When will you set Angelwings atop the obelisk?"

Clint walked over to the calendar on the wall. "It should be functioning by mid-June if all goes well. With a little luck and if we find the proper mosaic tiles."

"Splendiferous," said the abbot. "But there is no need to rush. You have been working so hard, toiling around the clock, seven days a week. Take a deserving rest. You have earned a break. My conference on the phenomena of apparition is not until the middle of July."

"The fountain will be in full operation. You have my word. I can hardly wait. An apparition is sorta like a heavenly vision, isn't it?"

"Yes. It's a supernatural sighting created by a celestial higher power," said the abbot. "Similar to what the three peasant children saw at Fatima in Portugal. And not long after, almost a quarter million people witnessed a spectacular solar phenomenon."

"Oh, yeah. I have a vague recollection of reading something about that. Didn't the pope declare it to be a modern era miracle?"

"Why, yes, he did. He referred to it as a timely message from God. That humanity is in urgent need of peace. I will be making a pilgrimage to lecture at the caves of Tarbes-et-Lourdes. You are more than welcome to join me."

"I'd love to."

"If it proves to be a less exhausting ordeal than I expect, you and I will spend a few days in the Pyrenees Mountain range."

"I just the other day read about those mountains in the library. It's Basque country. A girl by the name of Bernadette witnessed an apparition there."

"Very good," said Father Bernardo. "There have been many sightings, but few have been authenticated by the church as miracles."

"Count me in, Father. I want to go."

Father Bernardo's eyes began to roll. "Shall we walk in the garden?"

Clint nodded and set the file next to the chisels and hammers on the workbench. The abbot picked up a pair of cutting shears and the two walked out into the cloister.

Engaged in conversation on apparitions, Father Bernardo stopped to prune the rose bushes of dead leaves and twigs. Since the abbot had abandoned the feminine gender for the hermit life, Clint suspected that the rose garden had become Father Bernardo's paramour.

"It's not that I don't believe in visions, or ghosts, or phantoms. I'm pretty open-minded," said Clint as they rested on a bench across from the fountain. "They come into my dreams, but they're only in my dreams."

"I will make sure you have a front row seat amongst the cardinals, bishops, and archbishops during my lecture. Oh, I am sending Brother Gabriel to the Vatican to personally request the pontiff's presence during the dedication of the fountain."

Clint's brow furled. "The pope. You mean the pope is coming to see the fountain?"

"If he finds time," said Father Bernardo. "He is a very busy man."

"Wow. This is too much. This is big. The pope is coming to see my fountain. I mean your fountain."

"God's fountain."

"This will get me into heaven for sure," said Clint. "No purgatory, no nothing. I'm going straight up nonstop, riding on Angelwings through the pearly gates."

Looking at the blue sky, the abbot's eyes began to roll again.

"I'm sorry, Father. I didn't mean to be disrespectful. It's just my facetious nature. It's starting to come back. Wow, the pope. You and your fellow brothers have all been an inspiration for me. You've taught me how to cope. I had no coping skills before I came here. The schools didn't offer classes in how to deal with hatred, anger, resentment, failure, depression, stress, and all that kind of stuff."

Father Bernardo sighed. "What splendid discussion topics. There is much for us to deliberate."

"I have to tell you something, Father. I was feeling imprisoned in self-imposed exile when I first arrived here, but now it feels good to be contributing something to this abbey."

"Your work is greatly appreciated."

* * *

Following Father Bernardo's conference on phenomenon at the caves of Tarbes-et-Lourdes, Clint and Father Bernardo set out to visit the grotto of Massabielle. A few days later, they waded out and dunked their heads into the water. The sound of thunder crackled the moment they raised back up and saw brilliant flashes of lightning streaking across the sky. Pallor-faced and stunned with disbelief, Clint lowered his eyes and stared at Father Bernardo, who stood with his arms raised high over his head.

His eyes hypnotic, Father Bernardo pointed skyward and shouted, "Look, the clouds. It's, it's..."

In a state of shock with his palms pressed tightly on his scalp, Clint watched two puffy clouds merge, being sculpted by swirling winds into the shape of a robed ghost. To its left, two more clouds united and formed another robed ghost. When the winds' swift carving ended, it was obvious it was a man and a pregnant woman, with two brilliant rainbow halos circling behind their heads. Amidst the twittering singing of birds and fluttering of wings, two clouds formed in the shapes of a small boy. Then two more joined and a little girl appeared and the four clasped hands.

"I don't believe this, Father," said Clint. "It's incredible. It's a miracle. There is a heaven. There's something more. There is life after death, a better place."

Father Bernardo, clutching his rosary beads, stood gaping, speechless. Clint made the sign of the cross and splashed cold water on his face as voices and images raced through his mind.

When Clint looked back up, the clouds had vanished.

"God's forgiven me, Father Bernardo," Clint cried out. "I'm purged. I've had a spiritual catharsis."

Just as Father Bernardo turned to Clint and placed his index finger over his lips, the sky darkened as if a solar eclipse was occurring. A beam of light shot down in front of them, and standing on the water before their widened eyes were the four robed images, enshrined in a ring of blazing fire.

"Listen carefully to the words and pictures I have instilled within you," said the echoing voice of the haloed young boy. "They come from our Father, your divine creator."

"Our Father has given you the opportunity to avoid the coming catastrophe," said the haloed little girl in a soft voice.

The children smiled, and the boy said, "Educate the children to end hatred and war."

"Show them," said the girl. "Go to Paris. There awaits the Miracle Meadow."

"More will come in your dreams," said the boy. "Paint them so the children can see the horror of war."

"Allow the children the choice between love and war," said the girl just before lightning crackled.

The images disappeared, and daylight returned.

"Can you believe that, Father Bernardo?" Clint shouted. "It was Jesus and his wife and their children. She was so beautiful. They were all beautiful. This is magic."

Father Bernardo remained frozen and mute while Clint sang, danced, and thrashed about like a raving maniac.

Father Bernardo's eyes started to flicker and he took a deep breath. Blowing it out, he said, "I need to find out something."

"Find out what, Father?"

"If anyone else saw this."

Back on the beach, Father Bernardo spoke in Spanish to a young couple walking a poodle.

"What did they say, Father?" Clint asked when the abbot had finished speaking to the couple.

His eyes appearing saddened, Father Bernardo replied, "They saw nothing."

"They must have seen the lightning or heard the voices."

"What did you hear?"

"Something about Paris and a Miracle Meadow, and I saw an image of a vast field with giant canvases. They told me more would come in my dreams. It's like I've been given a mission. What about you, Father?"

"I must go immediately to the Vatican and speak to the pope. We must hurry. Do not mention this to anyone."

"But why, Father. Why keep this incredible enlightenment a secret?"

"Disclosing this sighting may bring further condemnation upon the church."

"But the people of the world need to know what we just witnessed."

"I must talk to the pope."

After returning from the pilgrimage, nightly images began to appear in Clint's dreams. Each morning he awoke, he sketched what he had dreamt. The scope of his mission enlarged each day. He felt elated when Father Bernardo cabled him that the pope would attend the unveiling of the fountain along with a large contingent of bishops, archbishops, and cardinals.

* * *

On the day Father Bernardo unveiled Angelwings, Clint watched the admiring face of Pope Paul VI and the phalanx of Vatican members staring up at the sky, as if in hopes of another sign. Father Bernardo flicked the pump switch and cascades of water fell and splashed into the ponds. Amidst the ovation, Clint bowed before the pope and kissed his hands as Pope Paul VI congratulated and praised him for his work. Feeling on the verge of collapsing, Clint stared at the pope's face as he spoke.

"Go to Paris, my son," said Pope Paul, "and find your calling."

* * *

"I've got to go to Paris, Father," said Clint, sitting on the fountain ledge on an autumn afternoon. "I don't know what it is I am to do there, but I need to find out."

"You will be told in your dreams."

"The dreams I've been having are ugly, Father. They're vicious war scenes, full of blood and gore."

"Paint them, and show the children that love is better than war."

"They always end with the same beautiful woman appearing," said Clint. "She bears an uncanny resemblance to my wife. But there's something different about this woman's face. It's more innocent. And her eyes are so pure. Oh, skip it. Look, Father, I've spent considerable time thinking of joining the spiritual life since that apparition. But the truth is, Father, I am lonely for a woman. I'm also overcome with claustrophobia from living in that cell. I'm not cut out to be a hermit."

"Perhaps in return for your marvelous masterpiece, the monks could build you a small home. The property here is very sizable."

"That would be wonderful, but I miss the touch of a woman."

"After you have found her, bring her here to live."

"That could work. I can restore the basilica. Maybe I'll meet an artist and she can help."

Father Bernardo smiled widely.

A few days later, Clint packed his meager belongings inside his cell. He zipped the backpack and went down for Eucharist and his final chat with Father Bernardo in the rose garden.

"Memories of that horrid evening still fester in my mind," said Clint, sitting beside the abbot and staring at the spilling water falling from Angelwings Fountain, "but they're becoming less vivid."

"As long as you are emotionally rational, you will always love her. Love is everlasting. Mankind cannot erase love. Love is indelible."

"You're so right, Father," said Clint. "I practice what I've learned from you. I push out the negative and think only about the good times we shared. It works."

"One thing concerns me. Since you arrived here, you have been without communication. No mail, no telephone calls, nothing from the outside world."

Clint chuckled. "Yeah, you're right. I almost forgot there's another world, the real world. It's scary. It's so peaceful here. No one's in a rut about money. I get reminded when I see Brother Gabriel and Brother Bede busy in the business office."

"Yes, even theologians and monasteries must keep accounting records. Have you thought to make amends to your wife?"

"In time, right now, I have a mission to accomplish."

Father Bernardo gave Clint a disturbed look. "As in the aftermath of a vicious revolution," he said, "it is usually wise to sign a treaty, come to a mutual resolve. Write your wife an amend letter. It is of the utmost importance to convey to her that you forgive her. Express your gratitude and appreciation for the years you shared together. It will give her peace of mind."

Clint lowered his head and thought a moment. "You're right, Father. I'll do it. Faded dreams, faded glory. I'll write her a letter."

After Father Bernardo heard Clint's confession, they sat by the fountain and the abbot patted his knee. "The monks have enjoyed your classes and your facetious sense of humor. They will all miss you as I will." The abbot's eyes began to drift again. "You will always be welcome here." The abbot paused. "Take care with your hands. You are a master sculptor."

Clint laughed. "Master. I like how the monks are called master. Kitchen master, guest master, library master, automotive master."

The abbot smiled and continued talking about forgiveness as they rose and began walking to where Brother Luke stood grinning, waiting beside the station wagon. "In due time, your heart will be fully mended."

Clint concentrated, searching for the proper words. "This abbey has been a safe haven for me. You, Father, have given me salvation and rekindled my inspiration. I may not be a hundred percent recovered. I doubt I ever will be."

"Be patient, my son. You are on the right path."

"And I owe it to you. Without your intervention on the plane, I'd never have come to grasp my failure. I now realize the fallacy that money doesn't bring happiness. The only thing left is for me to fully regain my shrunken self-love."

"A little narcissism is healthy for the spirit. It's better than self-hate. I have watched you grow here at the abbey. Your recovery is God's miracle. You will find the woman you are looking for. This I am sure."

"Right after I awoke from another nightmarish war scene, the same woman appeared in another dream. I think she has something to do with the vision you and I had. I hope so because I need to love someone. I feel so lonely."

"Love will find you, because love seeks out love. You will face difficult challenges, intertwined with magnificent opportunities for a new life. Move along your new path wisely, with confidence. Remember what I told you when we first began our walks. I spoke of my bout with the soft-eyed gorilla who asked me to dance with him, and I foolishly obliged?"

"Yes, I do."

"When the gorilla winks at you and invites you into his cage, don't go inside. He is a sly devil, a real saboteur. He will flirt with you and tease you until he smothers you and drags you into his lair."

"Except for the wine I drink at communion," said Clint as he leaned against the fender, "I've had nothing else to drink."

"That is good. And thank you for your rigorous toil, 12 hours days, 7 days a week. Now go in peace and do God's work."

"I'll miss the serenity here. This place blooms with peace. That sure was something you and I saw. The mystery unfolded before our eyes. That was no hallucination. Now the intrigue that awaits me has captured my imagination. I feel all jittery."

"God will be with you on your journey. And remember, your mission is vital to this planet."

Father Bernardo beamed, and they embraced before Clint opened the car door and sat in the front seat with Brother Luke, wondering what God had in store for him.

Chapter 19

Brother Luke was barreling down the mountainside like a madman when he looked at Clint and said, "You are a good professor, Clint. How is my English, heh?"

Clint gripped the dashboard and said, "Excellent, but good grief, Brother Luke, keep your eyes on the darn road. You're giving me the willies, weaving all over the place. And slow down, will ya. Let's not topple this thing. I ain't on a death wish anymore. I've a mission to accomplish."

Brother Luke looked straight ahead and eased off the gas pedal. "Tell me one more time, how much money did you walk away from?"

Clint faked a smile. "You're one heck of a driver and a master mechanic. But come on, Brother Luke, pay attention."

"It is these leather gloves you gave me. When I put them on, I feel I am in a race car on the Formula One circuit."

"Then take 'em off. You can put 'em back on after you drop me off at the train station."

Brother Luke slowed the car down to the speed limit. "Now you sound like I did. You must practice sticking out your tongue when you say *these, them, this, that and those*. It is what you taught us, heh?"

"Oh, yeah, the digraph or consonant cluster, you're coming along well with those. You need to work on the diphthongs and contractions."

"How much money did you leave your wife?"

"Plenty."

"Tell me. I want to hear you say it, how much?"

"Never took the time to tabulate it, but I'd say close to 100 million bucks."

Brother Luke jerked his head around and grinned like a hyena. "Ai, yi yi, mi dios, ai carumba. Dollars, no pesetas, heh?"

"Yes, Brother Luke, dollars."

"A hundred million dollars. Ai yi yi. And you gave it all to her. I dios, so much dinero. I do not understand."

"I was obsessed with reaping sacks of money," said Clint. "But I've reached a new juncture in my life. Money doesn't matter to me anymore. Let's skip the past. What made you become a monk?"

Brother Luke turned serious. "It was like I received a telephone call, and the volume kept getting louder and louder until I answered it."

"Who was on the line?"

"No one, just bells."

"Maybe it was your girlfriend playing wedding bells, trying to give you a hint she was waiting for you to propose."

Brother Luke's face turned gloomy.

"Don't you miss sex?"

"Si, everyday."

Brother Luke's chest heaved several times, and he began to blab non-stop about his early sex life. Listening with an amused expression, Clint finally relaxed, thankful it was a clear and sunny day, and the road was dry.

Arriving in front of the train station in Madrid, Brother Luke parked the car. They got out and embraced.

"I'm going to miss you, Brother Luke," said Clint, slinging his backpack over his shoulder, "and the rest of your fellow monks."

Brother Luke squeezed his hand. "I will keep you in my prayers, teacher."

"Keep working on the contraction and diphthong. You've almost got it."

"You mean like *they're* instead of *they are*, heh."

Clint grinned. "You catch on quick."

"I wish you luck in your inward journey. Write often."

"I will," said Clint. "But I'll be back. Right now, I need to find out what my mission is."

"What is this mission you talk about?"

"Talk to Father Bernardo. I need to find a soul mate. I can't take any more of this loneliness."

"She'll find you."

"I sure hope so."

They hugged, and Clint drew in a long breath of warm air before walking inside the train station. After purchasing a ticket to Paris, he boarded the train. Seated by a window in an empty compartment, he stared out at the hurrying swarm of boisterous Spaniards, feeling instilled with new faith and inspiration. As the train started to roll and clank along the tracks, his thoughts shifted to the vision he and Father Bernardo witnessed in the grotto. He scrunched his jaw and began to dwell on the violent dream he had during the night. As he had been doing every morning since the apparition, he pulled out a drawing pad from his backpack and began sketching a bloody war scene.

He was in the middle of drawing a mass slaughtering of innocent women and children when the train crossed the boundary into France and a pack of scruffy gypsies barged into the compartment. Jolted in his seat, his eyes wide open, he watched the band of vagabonds spread a filthy blanket on the floor in front of him. With devious faces, shoeless and toothless, the scoundrels dumped burlap sacks of stale bread, soggy fruits, cheeses, and sausages onto the blanket.

For several minutes, he felt grateful for their intrusion and fought to control himself from falling into a fit of sidesplitting laughter. Speaking in guttural Spanish, one gypsy wiped the slobber from his face with his shirt and gestured for Clint to have a spongy, blackened banana. Knowing he was in need of a good perking up, he experienced an immediate uplift. He grinned wildly at the gypsy and politely wagged his head and said, "No, gracias."

Watching the gypsies devour the food like starving scavengers appeared like an animated cartoon. The scene began to sour when they brought out leather flasks and swilled red streams of wine. They were sprawled, spitting and gorging themselves like pigs when a half dozen grubby children garbed in soiled and torn rags charged into the compartment. Clint's stomach wrenched, noticing none of the children chewed. They only ripped, swallowed, spit and gulped wine. In a matter of minutes, food and wine was spilt, squashed, and splattered everywhere.

Picking up the scent of the rotten stench, a swarm of winged bugs, bees, and wasps infiltrated through the window, buzzing over the putrid spoils. The gypsies ignored the insects and continued to gorge themselves. The sight became repulsive when Clint watched one of the barbarian children swat a hairy-legged pest and cram it into his mouth.

Disgusted by the unsanitary sight, he rose from his seat and smiled politely at the gluttonous vultures just as a bumblebee plunged its stinger into his arm. Grimacing, he smacked the bee, gathered his belongings, and bid the gypsies farewell. He shook his head and slipped out of the stink-infested compartment.

Finding a more sedate compartment, he sat opposite an elderly woman whose withered face and gray hair made him think she was the grandmother of the young girl seated next to her. The woman was reading a magazine through thick eyeglasses. He figured the girl to be 6 or 7. She had splotches of freckles on her face, and curly red hair tied in pigtails and was reading a French comic book, and chewing bubble gum.

Wagging his head, Clint looked at the growing welt on his arm and chuckled about the band of gypsies he had encountered. He had just started to relax when the cute girl slowly raised her head, looked at him cross-eyed, and made a deranged face. He smiled when she stuck out her tongue at him. *So, the tiny tot wants to play, does she.* He retaliated and made a dopey face. When the girl made another funny face and blew out a big bubble, he began to dig back in his memory, trying to recall how to make the ghoulish goblin face he had made as a kid on Halloween.

When he remembered, he slipped his thumbs into his mouth and pulled his cheeks apart, inserted his ring fingers into his nostrils, and stretched them sideways. With his middle fingers, he pulled down the upper skin of his cheeks and crossed his eyes. The gamine little girl looked scared stiff and covered the comic book over her face. She scooted closer to her grandmother and snuggled, clinging to her skirt as if seeking protection. A few minutes later, the girl lowered the comic book and peeked at him. He winked at her, and she quickly covered her face.

He smiled when she set the comic book down and began trying to imitate the expression he had made. It wasn't long before the girl copycatted the ghoulish goblin perfectly. He pretended to be horrified and wished he knew how to speak French so he could thank her for raising his spirits. He felt good to be laughing.

Humming "Thank Heaven for Little Girls" and staring out at the French countryside, he brought out his sketchpad and drew her cute face.

* * *

The weather was overcast and the air chilly when the train rolled into the Gare d'Montparnasse in Paris in the late afternoon. Clint wanted to pick the little girl up, swing her around and squeeze her for bringing laughter back into his life. He blew her a kiss and said the only French words he knew, "Merci beaucoup." He made a goofy face and handed the portrait to the girl.

The girl stuck her tongue at him, turned and clutched the woman.

The train was slowly pulling into the Paris station when Clint grabbed his backpack and waited for the doors to open. His anxiety mounting, he disembarked and roamed through the busy station looking for signs in English. Thirty minutes later he was mumbling to himself. *Geez, you'd think they'd have signs in English. Not one darn sign. They could make it easy, instead of a darn chore.*

He began politely asking people if they spoke English. The surly replies and looks of scorn from the people when he asked them for directions to Montmartre began to gnaw at his temper. One woman snarled at him without uttering a word. Disenchanted with the language barrier and the people looking angrily at him as if he had disrupted their lives, he walked into a gift shop and bought a French/English phrase book. He sat at a bench and scanned the pages for several minutes. His hope rising, he stood up and asked a young man, Excusez-moi, parlez-vous English?"

The man flicked him a snide look and hurried off. Clint wondered to himself: *Why is everyone looking at me so darn weird, what the heck is happening?* His patience worn thin, he resolved to keep trying. Stunned, he froze when he saw the face of the beautiful young woman who had been appearing in his dreams every night since the apparition. She was carrying a couple books and an umbrella and appeared to be a college student when she and a young man walked briskly past him.

Clint quickly chased after her. "Ezcusez-moi, parlez-vous English?" His voice was anxious and desperate.

The young woman stopped and beamed, noticing the American flag Clint had sewn on his jacket sleeve. "Oui oui, monsieur. Yes, I speak English."

"Whew, thank God," Clint blurted. "I'm trying to get to Montmartre."

"Montmartre," the well-dressed woman giggled and corrected him. "The *t-r-e* at the end is silent in French."

"So that's why everyone was acting so strange," said Clint, "nobody understood me."

Her frail companion looked bitterly at him as if he was an intruder. Clint brushed it off.

"We are going in the direction where you may take the Metro," the woman said cheerfully and adjusted her red beret. "Follow along with us. My name is Christine, and this is Francois."

"I'm Clint. It's a pleasure to meet both of you."

Christine looked curiously at Clint as the three walked quickly and asked, "What city are you from in America?"

Clint slipped the phrase book into his back pocket. "San Francisco."

Her blue eyes turned excited, and her dimples creased. "Oh la la. San Francisco." A stream of frosty air flowed out of her mouth. "It is the city of my dreams. Is it as beautiful as people say?"

"Even more so," he said. Hearing her speak English with a French accent was a delight for him. He loved hearing her say, "Oh la la."

"I have wanted to ride on a cable car since I was a little girl. It looks like so much fun."

"It is. What's Paris like?"

"Why do you not stay and find out?"

"I intend to," he said. "I guess I need to learn to speak your language." He looked at the clock. "Please, one minute." He pulled out the phrase book and searched for the phrase to ask her and her friend to join him for a glass of wine. "Je suis tres heureux de faire votra connaissance," he said. "S'il vous plait. Vous voudrais un verrede vin?"

Looking to have not understood a word Clint said and giggling, Christine looked to where Clint was pointing and said, "Oui, Avec plaisir. I mean yes, I would like that very much."

Francois appeared disgruntled and never spoke. He just nodded his head as if he understood and seemed annoyed that Clint didn't speak French. Francois quickly embraced Christine, kissed her on the cheeks, and hurried off. Clint immediately felt relieved.

"That was very good except for your pronunciation," Christine said as they walked.

"I'm sorry for mispronouncing and not speaking your language," said Clint. "I really botched that, but it's my first visit to France."

"What is botched?"

"Make a mess, clumsy. Say something that makes no sense. Thanks for accepting. I feel indebted to you for helping me."

"Would you mind if I had tea instead?"

"No. Have whatever you desire."

"Thank you."

Christine took Clint to where his train would depart, got him a Metro schedule, and the correct change before they sat at a table inside a small cafe, speaking in English about Paris and San Francisco. Clint loved the way Christine rounded her lips when she repeatedly said, "Oh la la." Seated beside her, he studied her exquisite features and found Christine to be a near duplicate of Dusty. Even Christine's fastidious mannerisms were the same as Dusty's. The way she had methodically taken off her mittens one finger at a time, removed her wool coat, and placed it on the chair was so like Dusty. He smiled watching Christine unwind her fluffy scarf, sitting with her svelte legs crossed, and looking so ladylike. She was a carbon copy of Dusty.

He was still studying Christine's prim and proper mannerisms when the waiter returned and set cups and saucers on the table. He was getting a kick out of the way she sipped, stroked her wavy blond tresses, and patted her luscious lips. He found her to be the epitome of Dusty.

Trying to be nonchalant and dreading her response, he asked, "Was that your boyfriend?"

"No, no," she replied rapidly. "Francois is a classmate and longtime dear friend. How long will you be in Paris?"

He scratched his head. "I haven't the faintest."

"Faintest, I do not understand this word."

"I'm sorry, it's an abstract expression. It means no clue, indistinct, unclear, similar to, I haven't the foggiest."

She smiled. "Foggiest?"

He went on to explain that he didn't know how long he would be in Paris.

"Why are you going to Montmartre?" She asked.

Noticing the silver cupid anklet on her nylon stocking, he grinned and said, "If I told you the real reason, you'd laugh. Someone told me it's hilly, like San Francisco and loaded with bohemians and artists. And I'm kinda homesick."

She beamed. "Are you an artist?"

"I don't know," he said as his mind went into a swirling motion. "I'm here to find out. An abbot I met on a plane coming to Europe invited me to his abbey in Spain. I built a fountain and did some sculpting while I was there."

"You are a sculptor?"

"I didn't know until I finished it."

"I have a dear friend that I have known since childhood," she said. "who is married to an artist. He is also a sculptor. He is American but lives in Paris. He never speaks English to me. He only speaks French. I need to practice English with a native speaker, because I intend to teach English when I have finished the university."

"I taught the monks English at the monastery. They were practically fluent after only a few months."

She shivered and said, "Monks and hermits frighten me. They are so reclusive, it is spooky."

He smiled. "Naw, monks are like little kids, playful and fun-loving as well as spiritual and dedicated."

"How long were you at the abbey?"

"Almost a year.

"That is a long time."

"It was a learning experience. Hey, maybe while I'm here I could help polish your English, and you could teach me French."

Her blue eyes lit up like sunstones. "That would be so helpful. English is the international language of the future. Where will you stay in the Montmartre?"

"I don't know."

"Then how will I see you again?"

"You could give me your telephone number. That is, if you don't mind?"

"Of course not," she said. "I would like to see you again. I have already learned so much from you in such a short time. I have a hard time with contractions and diphthongs."

"Oh, I can help you. I'm good with those."

She brought out a pen and a small notebook from her purse and wrote her vitals in exquisite penmanship. She folded it and handed it to him. Clint took out his wallet and opened it to a string of pictures.

"Who is the lovely bride, is she your wife?"

"Oh, no, this is my sister," his voice squeaked, feeling guilty for lying to her. "I'm not married. I don't even have a girlfriend."

Appearing relieved, she studied the photograph. "Your sister is very beautiful. She resembles you. Oh la la, is that the fountain you made?"

"Yep, that's Anglewings."

She thrust her arms over her head. "Is that the pope?"

"Yeah, he was there to bless it."

"Oh la la, the pope blessed your fountain. It is magnificent. I adore the dove and the wings." Christine stared her sunshiny eyes into his. "You have extraordinary talent. You must meet my friend, Dominique, and her husband, Jacques. They are also gifted artists."

"I'd like that."

"Tomorrow is Saturday, and I do not have school. Perhaps I could take you on a tour of Paris."

"Wow, this has turned out to be one incredible day. I'd love that. If you're ever in San Francisco, you'll have a free tour guide and a ride on a cable car."

She smiled endearingly. "Call me after you have settled, and we can plan on meeting tomorrow. I had better hurry or I will miss my train."

His mind went haywire as they walked to her train. *The way she's been sending you signals with her eyes,* he thought. *This vivacious lady is telling you she wants to get intimate. It's written on her face.*

A horde of similar thoughts flashed across his mind when they arrived at her train. A peculiar sensation rushed through him as they embraced and she kissed him lightly on both cheeks. He stood frozen and tongue-tied, staring at her.

With her mitten held up in a dainty wave, she said, "Au revoir, my friend."

He stood on the platform as Christine stumbled and tripped up the steps. He waited until she took a seat and peered out the window at him. Her blue eyes were resplendent and tacit and seemed to say, "I'd like to know you better."

When the train began to pull away, he wanted to blow her a kiss, but didn't because he thought it a foolish notion. The train waning in the distance, he could see her arms waving out of the window. His eyes straining, he tittered aloud, "It's her. She's mine. I can feel it." Whistling happily, he threaded his way to his train.

Chapter 20

Early the next morning, Clint lay on the bed inside a small room at a quaint hotel in the Montmartre district of Paris, sketching another bloodbath he had dreamt. When he finished, he picked up the instructions Christine had given him the previous night when they spoke on the phone. Excited about meeting her and having had her in his second dream during the night, he jumped out of bed, showered, shaved, dressed, and slipped on a down jacket.

A light sprinkle of snowflakes slapped his face when he stepped out onto Boulevard de Clichy and hailed a taxi.

"Pigalle Metro Station," he told the taxi driver and grinned when the driver nodded that he understood him.

The snow had stopped, and visibility was clear when the taxi driver pulled in front of the train station, and he spotted Christine. She was standing beside a silver Citroen wearing a bright red woolen overcoat, black gloves, red beret, just as she told him. Her face lit up when she saw him and enthusiastically waved her umbrella. She greeted him as he was paying the driver.

"Look at you. You're dressed so fashionable," Clint said after they exchanged kisses on the cheeks. "I feel grubby."

Her dimples creased, and she swiped her curly blond bangs from her sparkling blue eyes. "You look fine."

He looked at his frayed blue jeans and dirty sneakers. "Everyone is so spiffed up. It's like a fashion parade here. I feel like a bum. I'd go back and change, but I don't have anything nicer. I'm sorry."

"There is no need to apologize," she said. "You dress casual like all the Americans I have met. My girlfriend's husband, Jacques, dresses the same way. It is the American way. What does spiffed-up mean?"

"Dressed up, spruced up, dolled up, gussied up, they all mean the same thing - well-dressed."

"That is why I like English so much," she said, looping her arm around his. "You are not restricted to one word. Come and meet my sister and her family."

Dressed impeccably with a beaming smile, Christine's sister, Juliet, wrapped her arms around Clint and they exchanged kisses on the cheeks.

With a look of amazement, Clint turned to Christine and said, "She looks just like you."

"We are identical twins."

Juliet's husband, Antoine, also impeccably dressed, grabbed Clint's shoulders tightly and nearly squeezed the life out of him. Following their embrace, a strange sensation fell over Clint when he felt the sharp bristles of Antoine's neatly trimmed moustache peck him on the cheek. It was the first time Clint was kissed by a man. Feeling even weirder, he reciprocated.

Clint looked down at the sharply dressed young boy, who appeared to be around 5 years old.

"This is Andre," said Christine, "he is their son."

With the look of a distrustful sleuth, Andre stuck out his hand and said, "Hello, nice to meet you."

Clint smiled at the handsome boy, shook his hand, and said, "Bonjour, Andre."

Juliet and Antoine started speaking rapidly in French to Clint.

Confused, Clint looked at Christine, "Did you tell them I don't speak French?"

"Yes, they are explaining to you that they are sorry they do not speak English. I told my father about you, and he is very anxious to meet you. He wants you to come for dinner after we sightsee."

"I'd like that."

They piled into the car and set out on a whirlwind tour. Antoine was hell-bent on showing Clint all the famous sights in Paris in a single day. After visiting the Palace of Versailles, they rode the elevator to the top of the Eiffel Tour.

"Why not get your bag from the hotel and bring it with you," said Christine, as they capped off the day with a slow promenade along the Champs Elysees toward the Arc de Triomphe. "You may stay at our house tonight."

"I couldn't do that."

"It is my father's wish," she said. "He asked me to invite you, and hotels are very expensive in Paris."

"I've enough money," he said. "Besides, it would be an imposition."

"My father just finished building a room. It has a fireplace, a small kitchen, and a private bathroom."

"It sounds wonderful, but it wouldn't be right. I'd feel like an intruder."

"On the contrary," she said. "It would please my father very much. He loves Americans and is grateful for your country's support during the war. He speaks a little English and has many American friends. Mostly the GIs he met during the war. They exchange letters all the time, and they come to visit. That is why he built the room. So his soldier friends could have a place to stay."

He scratched his chin. "I'd feel uncomfortable, and look at how I'm dressed."

"My father is a farmer."

"You live on a farm?" He said excitedly

"Yes, with a barn, chickens, pigs, cows, and horses."

"Horses!"

"I love horses," she beamed.

"So do I. You're sure it would be okay?"

"It would make my father very happy."

"Our serendipitous meeting has turned out to be a fantasy dream come true," he said. "So don't pinch me, I don't want to wake up."

"Pinch?"

He gently pinched her wrist.

"Oui, pincier. I have learned so much from you today. Please continue to correct me whenever I mispronounce a word."

"Sure. Maybe you could teach me a little basic French."

"I will on the way to my parents' home in Herbley."

Christine and Andre were giggling as Clint counted to 10 in French as they sat in the backseat of Antoine's car on the drive to the hotel to get Clint's belongings.

An hour after picking up his backpack, Antoine turned onto a narrow dirt road. Rocks pelted the underside of the car, and a pack of barking dogs followed alongside when Antoine pulled in front of a gingerbread two-story farmhouse and parked. The house had a thatch roof and smoke was billowing from a red brick chimney.

After getting out of the car, Clint's smile broadened when Christine pointed at a white-haired man with a weathered face and scraggly beard, and told him he was her father, Norman. Norman was wearing soiled coveralls, standing beside an old tractor, holding a pitchfork, and wiping the sweat from his face with a towel. Christine clasped Clint's hand and they walked over to her grinning father.

Noticing the American flag on Clint's sleeve, Norman's gregarious face flushed, and he hurled the pitchfork and charged toward Clint like an enraged mustang. Stopping short of plowing into him and babbling excitedly in French and English, Norman gripped his shoulders with his large calloused hands and kissed him hard on the cheeks. Holding back from breaking out in a fit of laughter, Clint pressed his lips against the prickly hair on her father's cheeks and kissed him.

"This is my mother, Eva Marie," said Christine.

With an astonished expression, Clint said, "It's amazing, she looks just like you and your sister."

Eva Marie was holding a broom with a blithesome smile, bundled warmly in moth-eaten clothing, a stain-blotched apron, and a faded bandanna. Clint leaned down and embraced her, exchanging kisses on the cheeks.

Clint turned to Christine. "This day is straight out of a storybook fable. It's unreal."

"Come," said Norman, grasping Clint's hand, "I show you quarters."

"I will be helping my mother and sister prepare dinner in the kitchen," said Christine before she turned and joined her mother and sister and walked to the house.

Clint shrugged as Norman led him to the rear of the farmhouse.

Barely understanding a word Norman jabbered, Clint followed him into a small room. The air was permeated with fresh paint, and the potbelly stove reminded Clint of the cell at the abbey.

With a jovial smile, Norman bent forward, patted the blanket and said, "Bed comfortable."

Clint smiled.

While Norman was busy stoking the fire and chattering in a combination of French and English about his American friends, Clint browsed the oil paintings hanging on the walls. When the fire blazed, Norman went over to a hutch and pulled open a drawer. He took out an old scrapbook and plopped it on top of a butcher block table. Clint sat beside Norman, who proudly proceeded to slowly flip the pages that were filled with black and white photographs of American troops. Norman's use of sign language and facial expressions proved helpful to Clint.

Amber flames were popping and fizzling when Antoine entered the room, puffing a briar pipe and carrying a crystal decanter of red wine and three fluted glasses. As Antoine filled the glasses, Norman continued to rave about the American soldiers that befriended him during World War II.

By the jocose expressions on the blackened faces of the soldiers ensconced in foxholes, snuggled close to

Norman, it was obvious to Clint that Norman had many cherished memories.

"How are you doing?" Christine asked, coming into the room with Juliet.

"I could use a quick lesson in French," replied Clint. "But by your father's facial expressions, I get the picture."

"My father liked the way the American soldiers all brought chocolate bonbons and silk stockings and wooed the young women with flattery. My mother still laughs about it."

"Hey," said Clint, "who's the artist who painted all these paintings, especially that one?" The model is beautiful."

"That is my best friend, Dominique. Her husband, Jacques, painted it. I love it."

"They're better than good," said Clint. "That's worthy of hanging in a museum."

"I agree. Oh, my sister and her husband would like to take you to the Louvre tomorrow."

"Only if they'll allow me to treat them to dinner afterward," he said.

Christine looked at Clint quizzically. "Paris is extremely expensive. That is not necessary."

"After all they have done, it is only proper that I take them to dinner. I have enough money and can afford to splurge." After Clint finished explaining the definition of splurge, he thumbed through his phrase book and did his best to pronounce, "Je profound reconnaissant. Merci beaucoup. Viva la France."

"Tres bon," said Antoine, clapping along with Juliet.

"Oui, very good," said Christine. "Dinner is almost prepared. Shall we go into the house?"

Tchaikovsky's "Swan Lake" was playing on an old phonograph when they walked into the humbly furnished farmhouse. Everyone immediately began sniffing the aroma of beef bourguignon cooking inside the kitchen. Clint liked that their home was simple, nothing ostentatious. The dining table was laden with a smorgasbord of tasty hors d'oeuvres. Clint was standing by the buffet, staring in awe at the artwork that adorned the walls when Christine gestured for him sit.

"Did Jacques paint these too?"

"Yes."

"I'm impressed," he said. "This Jacques is an exceptional artist. I'd like to meet him."

"He has a bistro in Paris. I go there after school almost every day. Maybe you can come with me one day next week."

"I'd like that very much. Wow, this has been one incredible couple of days. Meeting you and now being here, having dinner with your family. It's like a dreamscape."

While explaining what a dreamscape was to Christine, Clint sat beside her eating a gourmet feast with her family. When they finished, Eva Marie and Juliet brought out a silver platter of truffles and delectable éclairs. After dessert, Clint and Christine excused themselves and went outside to roam around the farm.

"My father is very happy you will be staying with us," said Christine as she and Clint fed the horses in the corral. "He wants you to stay as long as you like. He likes you."

"Tell him that I'm willing to work for my keep. I know how to operate a tractor."

Her eyes lit up. "Did you grow up on a farm?"

"No, I learned because I was a builder."

"You and my dad will get along fine."

Later in the evening, fireflies circled the outside light fixture next to the door when Christine walked Clint to the room at the back of the farmhouse. She looked so stunningly lovely standing under the prisms of golden light that his heart raced. The rays enshrining her silhouette created a halo behind her head. The sight was so arresting that he felt an overpowering impulse to hold her and kiss her.

"I'm at a loss for words," he said in a low voice. "All I can say is you have a wonderful family."

She swept her hair from her eyes. "Thank you. This has been a special day for me also. I would like to have you as a friend."

"Then let's mark this day as the beginning of a long friendship."

"I would like that," she said.

"Where do you go to school?"

"I am attending the University of Paris in the Sorbonne. We must leave early in the morning. The Louvre is very big."

"I enjoy watching the sun rise."

Blushing modestly, she wiggled her fingers and said, "Bon nuit."

"Pleasant dreams," he said as she turned and walked away.

He softly took her hand. "I know it's late, but could we sit and talk a few minutes longer. Maybe you could teach me a few important words in French. And I love listening to you speak French, your language is so melodic."

"Of course, I would like that."

They sat on a bench for almost an hour, and she had taught him several helpful phrases when he said, "You remind me of Goldilocks."

"Goldilocks?"

"She's the blond girl in "Goldilocks and the "Three Little Bears." The Mama Bear, the Papa Bear, and the Baby Bear."

"Oui, Boucles d'Or," she said excitedly. "I know this fairy tale. She goes into their straw house and finds three bowls of..."

"Oatmeal, grits, mush, or porridge."

"Oui, porridge or bouillie."

"I think it has something to do with your curly golden hair."

"My hair is not really blond. My natural hair color is auburn."

"That's what's so great about being a woman. Women are always changing their hair color."

"Oui, women are like chameleons. I should be getting in."

The impulse to hold her and kiss her he felt earlier returned with an overwhelming force. He smiled and watched her stride away until she rounded the corner, and he flicked on the light switch and shut the door. He stared at the paintings while thinking about Christine. *Wow. What verve. What dalliance. She's ethereal and those dimples and sparkling eyes. The pieces to the puzzle are fitting together. I can feel it. Something big is about to bust loose.*

The next day flew past like a hurricane.

* * *

A soft knock on the door brought Clint from out of wonderland early the coming Monday as he sat sketching another violent dream. The knock was followed by a sweet sounding, "Bon jour."

Smiling, he grabbed his jacket, opened the door, and said, "Bon jour, Christine."

"Good morning," she said. "Come, my mother is preparing breakfast."

A few minutes later, Clint joined Christine's beaming parents at the breakfast table, sipping coffee and munching on croissants.

"Did you attend university?" Christine asked.

"Yes, I did."

"What did you study?"

"Architecture, but I mostly partied."

"You are funny. Is college expensive in America?"

"No, it's cheap."

"What do you design?"

"Everything, but now I want to try my hand at doing something more creative - like art. I can't wait to meet your girlfriend Dominique and her husband, Jacques. I'm intrigued."

"You will like them. My sister and her husband wish they had studied English so they could have spoken to you. They like you. They said you appear to be down to earth. Not like all the snobbish Americans they see with fancy cameras around their necks."

"I don't even have a camera. My memory is my camera."

"I do not understand everything you say, but I understand enough. We should go," she said. "I will give you a French lesson on the train ride. And you can help improve my English when we come back. My problem is all the contractions."

"I'm good with that stuff."

When the train arrived at the Gar du Nord station in Paris, Christine slipped on furry red mittens and adjusted her wool scarf and beret before they disembarked. They walked briskly through the crowded station and out into the bustling street. Clint thought it funny that it was only half-past seven in the morning, and the sidewalk cafes were lined with Parisians sipping cognac from snifter glasses.

They arrived at the Sorbonne a few minutes early, and Christine's history professor readily allowed Clint to sit in the classroom. He took a seat in the back row and watched the students come in dressed as if they were attending a formal soiree. His smile began to fade when some of the students began to gawk at him with snide expressions. It vanished when almost everyone in the class sat glaring at him and whispering until the instructor slapped a ruler hard on top of his desk. Clint felt relieved when the students turned to face the teacher.

"What was going on in class, Christine?" Clint asked as they walked in the crowded hallway after class let out.

"What do you mean?"

"All the dirty looks, the way everyone was sneering and scrutinizing me. It made me feel as if I were some kind of heinous monster."

She appeared confused. "I do not understand."

"It's as if everyone in the class thought I had leprosy. There was a lot of anger and hatred on the faces of your classmates. Even right now. Look at them. They're staring at me as if I have a contagious disease like the plague."

Christine looked around and then nodded. "I see what you mean. I did not notice it until now. Let's go have a coffee. I think it has something to do with the American flag on your coat. I was going to mention it to you earlier.

But I did not foresee this. I think it has something to do with the war in Vietnam."

"Look, Christine, I've never supported that war. Most Americans don't. It's a travesty to mankind. I'm patriotic, but that war is all about warmongering ammunition dealers and profit."

Students continued to leer at Clint as they made their way to a small cafe and sat down at a booth.

"Go home, Yankee pig," an angry voice blared out.

"Do not pay attention to them," said Christine.

"Maybe I should leave. This looks like it can turn ugly."

Just as he finished his sentence, a mob of hostile black militants entered the café. They were dressed in African garb and stared at Clint as if they wanted to slit his throat. Two of the lethal militants strutted toward their booth, and Clint wished he had a weapon to defend himself.

Her eyes inflamed and her face flushed, Christine stood up, pointed her finger at the two men, and angrily lashed out a barrage of French. The militants backed away.

One vile brute twisted his convulsing face and pointed at Clint. "How dare you come here wearing the flag of genocide, while your countrymen are napalming women, children and innocent babies? Go home, you capitalist pig."

Sensing danger and trying to contain his temper from the harassment, Clint stood up and threw his arms above his head as if in surrender and huffed: "Okay, that's enough. Look, I may be an American, but I'm a peace-loving man. And I agree that the use of napalm and

Agent Orange is deplorable and inhumane. That war is a damn fiasco, an abomination, an atrocity, and a disgrace to modern civilization."

"Parlez Francais," an angry voice shouted.

"Speak French," another voice hollered.

"Please forgive my companion for not speaking French," shouted Christine in French, "but he has only been in Paris a few days. "She looked at Clint and said, "Please, let's go. I apologize for my classmates' horrible, rude behavior."

Christine took Clint's hand and dragged him through the sinister mob.

"I am very sorry," Christine said as they walked along the sidewalk on Rue de la Sorbonne.

"It's not your fault. It's mine for putting on this stupid flag. I must have been whacked out of my mind."

"I suspected the flag might cause some controversy, but nothing like that."

"That was pretty intense," he said. "I was thinking I'd have to fight my way out, and I'm not much of a fighter. I'm going incognito from now on. Look, you go back to school. On the way here, I noticed a shop with a bunch of flags in the window display. Think I'll buy the Canadian flag. From now on if anyone should ask, I'm from Vancouver."

She smiled and said, "That is very clever."

"I never thought the day would come when I'd be ashamed to be an American though I'm aware my country has a lot to be repentant for. Like how we scalped and slaughtered the Indians, stole their land, and forced them onto reservations. And how we went down and decapitated the peasant Mexicans and stole Texas and California."

"That was centuries ago. Let's talk about something else."

"I'm sorry," he said. "What time do you get out of school?"

"My last class finishes at three."

He pointed across the street. "I'll meet you by that row of chestnut trees along the river," he said.

"We can have a picnic. Do you like camembert cheese?"

"Love it. I'll pick some up and a loaf of sourdough and some wine."

"Water is better."

He grinned. "You're right."

Chapter 21

When Christine's final class concluded, they met by the chestnut trees and exchanged English and French lessons while picnicking on the grass. Nibbling on chocolate éclairs, they strolled alongside the river Seine, hand in hand until Clint hailed a taxi, and the two headed to Jacques' bistro in the Montparnasse district of Paris.

A thick cloud of bluish gray cigarette smoke hung in the high ceiling of the bistro when they walked inside. An attentive crowd of jazz aficionados sat at tables, snapping their fingers and tapping the soles of their shoes to the syncopated rhythm and percussion coming from the jazz trio. The trio was wailing out their rendition of Dave Brubeck's "Take Five" as Christine and Clint made their way to the bar.

Staring at the ceiling in amazement, Clint's jaw dropped. "Wow. Did Jacques paint that ceiling?"

"Yes," she said, "and Dominique and I and a lot of their artist friends helped. But we only painted and followed Jacques' direction. The ceiling is his conception."

"I'm astounded. The man's remarkable," said Clint. "I feel privileged just to be looking at it. It reminds me of the Sistine Chapel."

"Have you seen it?"

"No, only in books, but I'm gonna see it. I can't wait to meet Jacques. Is he here?"

"Yes. That is him behind the bar. Come, I will introduce you to him."

Clint was still staring at the ceiling as he stumbled behind Christine until they were seated on bar stools. Jacques, a ruggedly handsome man, appeared to be in his late 20s. He had a cleft chin and chiseled features and wore a faded dark green beret. A foot of stringy dark brown hair, banded in a ponytail, fell down the back of his tattered sunburst shirt. His sideburns were neatly trimmed, and a drooping mustache hid his upper lip. Jacques winked at Christine when he came over and set a case of wine down. He leaned over the bar, took her hands and kissed her on each cheek. Christine and Jacques spoke in French for several minutes when Jacques flicked Clint a surly look.

Wondering why Jacques looked at him that way, Clint stuck out his hand and said, "Hi, Jacques, it's a pleasure to meet you. I mean it's an honor to meet you. I love your paintings."

Jacques didn't say a word, nor did he extend his hand. He just scooted across the bar and kissed Clint on the cheeks with his scratchy whiskers. After Clint reciprocated, Jacques went back to talking to Christine in French. Other than a sullen glance when he set a glass of wine in front of Clint, Jacques continued to ignor him.

When Jacques walked over to serve a customer, Clint asked Christine, "What's his trip. He never said a word to me. Not even hello. Just gave me nasty looks."

"He kissed you."

"I know, but..."

"Jacques is a quiet man until he gets to know you," she said and politely excused herself to freshen up.

She had been gone less than a minute when Jacques returned and leaned on the bar in front of Clint. Jacques squinted, furled his brow, and in a gruff voice, he said in English, "Christine is like a delicate butterfly, very fragile. Don't hurt her."

Incensed, Clint looked Jacques square in the eyes and scowled, "Hey, bug off. Why do you insult me with such a rude suggestion? Why the hell would I want to harm that lovely lady. That's an outrageous remark. You don't even know me."

Jacques didn't say a word. He just glared at Clint, scratched his chin, and abruptly walked away. Puzzled and fuming, Clint got up and sat at a table, thinking, *what an asshole.*

Christine looked at Clint curiously when she came back from the restroom. "Why did you move to this table?"

"While you were gone, your jerk friend came over and said something strange to me."

Christine sat next to him. "What did he say?"

"Something about me intending to hurt you," he said. "It caught me totally by surprise and really irked me."

"I am so sorry. Jacques sometimes gets overly protective of me."

"He still had no right to say that. It wasn't justified."

"I agree, but once you two get to know each other, you will find he has a coeur d'or. A heart of gold."

"It still made me feel as though I had 'woman-killer' tattooed on my forehead."

She smiled. "He is an artist, and like most creative people, he can be extremely sensitive and moody."

"I understand, but it's no excuse. I'm one hundred percent nonviolent."

She studied his face and giggled. "It shows. I will talk to him when I get my purse. Oh, can I show him the picture of your fountain."

He wagged his head and took out his wallet. Confused, he removed the photo and handed it to her.

"Are you a jazz buff?" she asked.

"Yeah, I was raised on it. My father's a jazz musician."

Christine smiled enticingly. "You will enjoy Paris. There are many great American jazz musicians living here. I will be right back."

Christine had been gone about 20 minutes when Clint watched Jacques raise the wooden bar hatch and walk to where he was seated.

"Please accept my apology for saying that to you," Jacques said in English as he took a seat beside Clint. "It was totally uncalled for. It's just that I have known Christine for many years and have seen men put that sweet lady through hell so many times."

"Really, in that case there's no need for you to go any further. That explains everything. I might very well have said the same thing."

"She showed me your fountain. It's very impressive. It's even more so the way the pope is admiring it. Look Clint, I'm getting ready to start an art project. It's big. In fact, it's more than big. It's colossal. Maybe you and Christine could drop over for dinner this Friday. I can show you what I have in mind. I could use a man with your talent."

"I like the word colossal. We'll be there. What kind of art project?"

"It's a resurgence of the renaissance fresco."

"Really, this sounds interesting."

"You play chess?"

"Ah," Clint sighed, "yeah, I play a little."

"Then perhaps we can partake in a game after supper."

"Sounds good, I'd like that."

* * *

Feathery snowflakes fell from the sky Friday night as Clint and Christine stepped outside the metro station and walked gleefully along the narrow cobblestone sidewalks of Montparnasse to Jacques' bistro. Their hands clasped, and their arms swinging, they stopped to watch an artist painting a couple of seated lovebirds. Waiting for the light to change at the corner, they listened to a lingering poet recite prolific verse. After passing by a cathedral, they went inside a boulangerie. Christine gently squeezed a loaf of sourdough and sniffed the warm scent before she paid the clerk. At another small store, Clint purchased a bottle of red wine from the Bordeaux region.

The bistro was crowded and noisy as they passed by and walked up the flight of stairs to Jacques and Dominique's apartment.

Dominique, Christine's best friend since early childhood, opened the door. She was as beautiful as she appeared in Jacques' painting of her. Dominique beamed and said, "Sacre blu." Her long raven hair and azure eyes glistening, Dominique seized Clint's shoulders and kissed him on the cheeks. Clint followed suit. After exchanging embraces, Dominique spoke excitedly in French to Christine before she turned to Clint and switched to English.

"Please come in," Dominique said in good French-accented English and closed the door. "How are you enjoying Paris?"

"I have the greatest tour guide in the world. Christine took me to Notre Dame Cathedral today. She and her sister's family have been chauffeuring me everywhere. Saw da Vinci's "Mona Lisa." Man, the dude was a genius and eons ahead of his time. All of his designs of helicopters, submarines, and other futuristic stuff are incredible. That guy was from another universe."

"I agree," said Dominique. "Leonardo was a brilliant man, and exceptionally diverse."

"I'll say," said Clint. "He was into everything."

"Let me take your coats."

After Dominique hung their jackets in the closet, they went into the living room. Dominique and Christine began yakking up a storm as if they hadn't seen each other in a decade. A Thelonious Monk record was spinning on the phonograph as Clint's eyes scanned the artwork, which was everywhere. After setting down his leather folder, Clint's eyes drifted from the painted ceiling down to the painting of several women over the mantle. Hardly able to believe his eyes, he moseyed closer and looked at the inscription etched in a small gold plate. "Les Vierges Prenant un Bain Dans L'etang Sacre," said Dominique as she and Christine airily floated to his side.

"What do you think?" Christine asked.

Staring at the painting and realizing Christine and Dominique were on the canvas, naked and playfully dancing behind a cascade surrounded by genuflecting archangels, cherubs, and cupids with bows and quivers of arrows, Clint muttered, "Ah, well, I..."

"Does our nudity disturb you?" Dominique said.

"No," he said, still staring at the painting. "I'm just caught by surprise. It's superb, you're both very beautiful."

He turned toward Christine and Dominique. "Wow, it's like you two just stepped out of the canvas." Christine and Dominique appeared unfazed, not remotely embarrassed by their nudity. "Your husband, Jacques, is a master. He's really captured your playful innocence. This painting, heck, everything I've seen so far belongs in a museum. What's the title in English?"

"Virgins bathing in sacred pond," said Dominique.

"That's what I was thinking," he said. "By the way, where is Jacques?"

"Up in his atelier painting," said Dominique, pointing at the spiral staircase. Why don't you go up?"

"And tell Jacques what you just told us," said Christine. "He loves praise."

"But, not too much," said Dominique. "It swells his head."

Clint smiled and whiffed the aroma filtering into the room. "Whatever's cooking smells delicious," he said.

"Oh, I hope you like vichyssoise," Dominique said.

"I love French food, especially truffles."

The three spoke a bit longer before Clint grabbed his folder of sketches and made his way up the grated iron steps. Peeking into the large paint-splattered loft, Clint flashed back on his vision with Father Bernardo and what had been appearing in his recent dreams. Jacques stood in front of an easel with a brush in one hand and a palette in the other, absorbed in deep concentration when Clint quietly entered the loft. As if struck by a bolt of inspiration, Jacques suddenly began slapping paint onto the canvas in a flurry of brush strokes.

Without looking at Clint, Jacques hollered, "Pour yourself a glass of wine and make yourself comfy."

"Thanks. I hope I'm not disturbing you."

"You're not."

Paint was blotched and smudged everywhere in the atelier as if a swirling cyclone had blown through. Clint filled a glass with red wine from a crystal decanter and sniffed the sweet fragrance.

"Christine tells me you hail from Frisco," said Jacques as paint sprayed through the air.

"I was born in the city."

"Good thing you took off the stars and stripes and put that maple leaf on your coat. Christine told me about the incident at the Sorbonne."

"Yeah, that was spooky."

"It could've been worse. You might have been maimed or even killed. Best not to flaunt being an American while you're in France."

Clint chuckled. "Nobody bats an eye when they see the maple leaf. Most people react as if they've never heard of Vancouver when I tell them I'm from there."

As Clint's eyes roamed around the loft, he realized that Jacques was also a sculptor, a jeweler, and a metal worker. He picked up the brass queen from the chessboard and studied the exquisite detail.

"It's Dominique," said Clint.

"You've a good eye."

"Your wife is quite a lovely woman." Clint's eyes shifted to the two chess books by Boris Spasky and Bobby Fisher.

"Indeed she is." Jacques swatted the brush across his pants, set it in a bucket and walked over to Clint. "Let's forego the hugs and kisses routine, unless you care to look like a clown. Shall we play a game?"

"Love to," replied Clint as he sat at the table. "Christine mentioned you studied at Beaux Arts?"

Jacques nodded as he joined Clint at the small table.

"I've heard it's one of the finest art schools in the world."

"So they say. And you're an architect?"

"In another life," said Clint as Jacques grabbed two pawns and hid his hands behind his back. Jacques brought out his fists and Clint tapped his right knuckles. Unclenching his right hand and exposing a black pawn, Jacques won the privilege to move first. "Right now I want to paint. I think it's the reason why I'm here."

"It's also the reason I'm here," said Jacques as they set up the pieces.

"That painting above the mantle of your wife and Christine is a masterpiece. And I ain't exaggerating."

Jacques smiled appreciatively. "I enjoyed painting it. You planning to stick around Paris a while?"

"I'm thinking of getting an apartment around here or the Montmartre district. I don't want to impose a burden on Christine's parents. They're absolute gems.

I love 'em dearly. They haven't stopped smiling since I arrived."

The game commenced when Jacques moved his king pawn two spaces and banged his palm on the clock.

"This isn't a grandmasters' match," said Clint. "What's with the clock?"

"It's the European way."

"It makes me feel under the gun, and that ticking is annoying. It rattles my nerves and concentration."

Jacques gave Clint an astute expression. "Can't handle pressure, huh?"

"I like pressure. It's just that I've never played with a clock."

"You're finished learning. Is that it?"

"Okay," said Clint as he launched his pawn attack and quickly smacked the clock.

They were talking about French wines when their first hard-fought game ended in a stalemate. Jacques squiggled his cleft jaw and conceded the second game. The subject changed to the Renaissance period when their third game came down to the wire and Clint flicked over his king.

"You're a good player, Jacques. Mind if I borrow that Bobby Fisher book so I can brush up on honing my strategy."

"Take 'em both."

"Thanks. Now, what about this colossal art project you've got in the works?"

"Oh, the Renaissance resurgence," said Jacques. "Have you worked with plaster paint before?"

Looking dumbfounded, Clint said, "Plaster paint?"

"It's a plaster-based oil paint," said Jacques. "The type they used during the Renaissance era to paint frescos. Thick and gooey."

"Oh, yeah," said Clint. "You've got me going about this Renaissance resurgence and fresco stuff. Are you serious?"

Jacques' hairy eyebrows rose. "I've never been more serious in my life. The photograph Christine showed me of your fountain, Angelwings, suggests you have a creative gift. At least the pope thinks so."

"Art is deep-rooted in my family bloodline. I'm ready to find out if I have some of it. It's like I've got an inferno burning inside me to paint."

Jacques rose up from his chair and Clint followed him to a long paint-splattered table where he brought out a roll of paper and four bricks.

"Take a gander at this sketch," Jacques said unrolling the paper. "Bear in mind it's rough."

Clint's mouth widened and he blurted, "Wow, it reminds me of 'The Last Supper.'"

"This is 'Magnum Opus,'" he said setting the bricks on the four corners."

"It's your wife, Dominique, and she's pregnant. She looks about to burst." Clint went into shock when he recognized the two small children from his vision and choked.

"Are you okay?"

"Yeah, but who are the two children clutching your wife's gown?" Clint stuttered.

"This one is Simone, the first daughter of Mary Magdalene and Jesus. The boy is Joshua, their second child."

"Mary Magdalena!"

"They had a slew of children," said Jacques.

Completely blown away, Clint shivered and said, "How did you know what the boy and girl looked like?"

"Their faces came to me when I started to paint them."

Realizing he was on the path to accomplish his mission, Clint stared at Jacques and said, "Wow. This is humongous, Jacques. And the scale - forty by twenty meters. Where would you paint this?"

"Dominique's father is a wealthy land baron. He has a vast parcel of level land just south of Paris."

Jacques rolled out another sketch on the table.

"This one's even bigger. How would you move these?"

"That's for others to worry about. My task is to paint them."

"How many?"

Jacques grinned and rolled out sketches of "The Mystic Garden," "The Resurrection," "Noah's Ark," "God's Kingdom, " and "Heaven's Eternal Sanctuary."

"You don't mess with frivolity. This is a monumental undertaking. I want in on this. This will make history, Jacques."

"Welcome to the force."

"The force?"

"The response to the advertisements I've had posted around the globe has been overwhelming," said Jacques. "My colleagues at my alma mater have already begun screening work samples being submitted. Only those artisans with extraordinary talent, faith, discipline, dedication, tenacity, and willingness to accept a challenge of this magnitude will be selected. Artists from all walks of life will begin flocking to Paris this coming spring."

"Wow, a resurgence of the fresco," said Clint, "but I thought frescos were murals on walls and ceilings, not canvas."

"A fallacy, the canvas fresco has been around hundreds of years."

"This is going to require a lot of paint and canvas, and lumber for the staging. And money."

"It's all under control," said Jacques. "Dominique recently inherited a tidy fortune from her grandparents. Everything will be at prairie de miracle come spring."

"You mean miracle meadow?"

Jacques wiped his brow and took a sip of wine. "Yes, but everything is tentative. Dominique likes magic fields."

Hearing Jacques say the words *miracle meadow*, Clint twitched and stuttered, "I would stick with *miracle meadow*. How big is it?"

"A couple of kilometers square, and it's gentle."

"Man, Jacques, when this comes to fruition, it's going to shake the planet. Knock the gravitational force out of kilter."

"As to your apartment issue, Dominique's old apartment is nearly finished being renovated. It's very nice. It has a terrace with a marvelous view of Paris. And it's furnished."

"I'll take it. I have the money. What about me submitting a sample?"

"I've seen your submission. You qualify."

"But I want you to see them anyway," said Clint, walking over to get his folder. "I just happen to have some with me. They're completely the opposite of yours. Yours are peaceful, and mine are a tad more on the violent side, made me sick to draw them."

Jacques stood with his arms folded and a curious expression as Clint opened the folder and laid out his sketches.

"Nuclear mushrooms, rockets, missiles, bayonets, howitzers, decapitations," said Jacques, "this is a bloody slaughter. What do you mean a tad more violent. These are grotesque."

"That's what war is all about," said Clint, "a mass annihilation. That's what I want to depict. This one's titled 'Hell's Battlefield.'"

"This might work, Clint, a fusion of war and tranquility. This will allow the children of the future to make their own choice as to which is a better way of life."

Clint was further taken aback when Jacques mentioned the children of the future choosing a better life.

Jacques flipped another one of Clint's sketches and grimaced, looking at it. "This is gross, pure savagery, and barbaric. It's inhuman. What's it called?"

"Viking Warriors."

Jacques carefully studied the sketches of "Swashbuckling Buccaneers," "The Fall of Babylon," and "Lances and Swords." He turned to Clint. "You will be a great asset to the force."

"Why did you bring up children?" Clint asked.

"Because they fit and tie this project together. It's realism I want to show. And these are damn good."

"But I want to paint the peaceful stuff too. I intend to paint Christine. She's agreed to model as soon as I get settled in. I'd appreciate your dropping by for some feedback."

"It would be my pleasure," said Jacques, refilling their glasses with wine and swishing his glass like a convivial connoisseur. "Leggy and a fragrant bouquet."

"A little tart," said Clint.

Jacques gave Clint the look of a shrew. "It seems you think everything grown in California is superior. I suggest you rinse your taste buds and rid your mouth of impurities, such as fungi, decay, and other such rot."

Clint smiled. "Hey, Jacques, I'm not bad-mouthing French wines. But the soil in California is richer and more fertile. It's virgin. The roots of the grape vines in France have sucked out all the nutrients in the ground here. That's the only reason Napa wines have surpassed French wines."

"You make a valid point," said Jacques. "But remember, it was the notable French immigrant vintners who brought the saplings to America."

Clint raised his glass. "I'll toast to those guys. God bless the French and the grape."

Jacques smiled. They clanked glasses and chatted about Dominique's apartment. Coming to an agreement on a monthly rent, Clint handed Jacques some traveler's checks as a deposit and asked him, "Have you ever had a vision, Jacques?"

"Everyday."

"I mean recently?"

"I already told you," said Jacques. "What exactly are you getting at?"

"Never mind, let's skip it."

"Dinner is being served," Christine shouted from downstairs.

Jacques and Clint went down to eat.

Chapter 22

Chestnut leaves were swirling on the late wintry night Clint and Christine returned from the Moulin Rouge Cabaret. Bundled warmly, they parked their motor scooters in the garage of Clint's new apartment on Boulevard de Grenelle and rode the elevator to the seventh floor. Inside the penthouse apartment, while Christine was in the bathroom, Clint tossed some kindling and old newspapers into the fireplace and lit a match.

He was stoking the fire when she came out and stood silently, staring at him with a demure expression. "Everything has been moving so fast," he said cheerfully as he walked over to her and slipped his arm around her waist, "my meeting you and now this fantastic apartment with a spectacular view of Paris." He opened the door and they stepped out onto the terrace. "Yesterday we're on an outing," he said, wondering why she was so quiet, "riding our scooters with Jacques and Dominique and visiting boutique wineries in the Bordeaux countryside. And all of us play acting the roles of expert viticulturists. That was so much fun. And tonight a cancan show. It's been like a fairy tale." He looked at her, "Why are you so quiet? What's with the melancholic look? Hey, what's wrong, Christine? Why are you looking so sad?"

"I am wearing mistletoe, why have you not kissed me?" She said, standing beside him poised seductively in a black chiffon décolletage, black mesh nylon stockings, knee-high black patent leather boots, elbow-length black gloves, with a long white scarf wrapped around her wide-brimmed black straw hat.

"We kiss all the time," he stammered.

"I am not talking about friendly kisses on the cheeks," she said staring into his eyes, "I am talking of amorous kisses. Romantic kisses. Passionate French kisses on the lips, our tongues swirling."

Thrown for a loop by her quizzical expression and displeased voice, he said, "It's not that I haven't wanted to kiss you romantically. It's just that I... The truth is that I have a phobia about being rebuffed. Look, I felt the urge to kiss you the first day we met at the train station. I've wanted to hold you in my arms every day since then."

"Then why have you not at least you tried to kiss me," she said, stepping closer to him. "That way you will find out if I intend to reject you. Living would be a meaningless, sad, pathetic tragedy without love and sexual desires. Are you homosexual?" Her voice was blunt.

Caught completely by surprise at her remark, he stepped away from her and fired back, "Gay. Heck no. I'm not homosexual. What possessed you to ask me that, what's wrong with you?"

"I dress sexy. We see a cancan show. And you pay no attention to me when I flirt with you."

He took her hand. "Hey, Christine, I totally flipped out over you the first time I saw you. You told me you wanted to be friends. So I've been holding back because I want you and me to be friends forever."

Her eyes turned resplendent, and he placed his hands on her hips and pulled her tightly against him.

She nuzzled her knee softly between his legs and said in a sultry voice, "Friends can be lovers too."

"You're so right," he said. "How foolish of me. About tonight and my not saying how pristinely beautiful you look. I wanted to tell you how I felt the moment I saw you looking so sexy tonight. But I didn't want to lose you by moving too fast. Most men are aroused by concupiscent sex kittens. I get excited by a woman's sensual innocence and playfulness. You, my lovely ingénue, are the epitome of virtue and sexiness."

"Women can be both chaste and Carnal. Now will you kiss me," she said.

Clint pulled her tightly against him and slid his tongue into her mouth. Breathing heavily, their hearts throbbing erratically, their tongues undulating in a froth of tasty peppermint, Christine lowered her hands. Savoring her touch, he pulled away and stared at her. She appeared to have swallowed a powerful aphrodisiac as their hands raced in bodily exploration.

Whispering words of love and caressing each other tenderly, they turned and leaned against the rail, staring out at the glare of neon lights. They looked up at the sky and witnessed a waxing gibbous moon, lit by a corona, and a plethora of bright stars. They watched the moon turn gold, then fiery red, and listened to the night birds tweet as fireflies flashed around the fountain. Both were so entranced by such a magical sight, they danced, holding each other tightly.

Unlocking from a passionate embrace and sensual fondling, Christine stepped backward and melodiously whispered, “Je t’aime, mon amour.” Her eyes glimmered like diamonds.

Startled with surprise by her words, Clint took a deep breath. “God, how I love hearing you say that. “Je t’aime, mon amour. I love you, too.”

“I would like to freshen up. Would you mind?”

“Of course not,” said Clint.

“I will only be a moment or two.”

The ambers were red hot and crackling in the fireplace when they stepped inside the living room. Christine grabbed her tote bag and sashayed into the bathroom. Brimming with anticipation, Clint fluffed the pillows on the loveseat, lit the scented candles on the mantle, and put on a Cal Tjader album. Kicking off his shoes, he turned on the Christmas tree lights, and smiling, he filled two crystal glasses with Pinot Noir. Sinking into the loveseat, he watched the shadows of the flames dance on the walls.

He was staring at the fire when she airily floated out of the bathroom, running her fingers through her sparkling golden spirals. The dimly lit room exploded in a dazzling whiteout when she did a pirouette and danced toward him, fluttering and flinging colorful ribbons.

Completely enraptured by her unexpected transformation, he fixated his spellbound eyes on the tantalizing expression on her glowing face. She began to flail her arms seductively, twirling her fingers and shimmying her supple torso. She swayed and wiggled her willowy body in front of him to the melodious Latin beat of Cal Tjader and sailed her hat across the room.

He sat silent, hypnotized as she performed the most highly erotic peek-a-boo striptease he had ever seen until she wore only a sheer, lacy pink camisole, silk panties, and ballerina slippers. As her camisole floated onto the carpet, he saw the tattoo of a butterfly above her navel. His eyes shifted to a small glimmering gem lodged in her bellybutton when she slid topless onto his lap and began to unbutton his shirt.

Running his hands along her velvety thighs, he whispered, "That was highly evocative. You are a very sensuous lady. Where did you learn to dance like that?"

"Ballet school," she said, "I was studying to be a prima ballerina until my toes became inflicted with tendonitis. Did I pronounce that correctly?"

"Perfect. I'm so sorry to hear that."

"That is okay," she said as she removed his shirt. "It is too competitive. And I am voluptuous. You need to be very thin."

"But you're skinny as a rail," said Clint. "You have a beautiful body and you're light as a feather. Anyway, I love your curves. And I love the butterfly. I've never known a woman with a tattoo."

"It is my symbol of freedom," she said, removing his pants.

"I like the diamond in your bellybutton too."

"It is not real. I saw a model with one in a *Vogue* magazine. I liked it. It looked apropos. Now hush and let's dance. Oh, I should tell you that I am a virgin."

Completely blown away by her unabashed expression, he barely managed to utter, "Then I shall enshrine and treasure this night in my heart forever. You smell delicious. I want to paint you in the morning."

"You are so charming and charismatic. Everyone likes you." She smiled enticingly and held a finger to his lips before he could speak. "That is if we sleep. I do not plan to sleep. I intend to devour every inch of your masculine virility."

Stunned by her aggression and frankness and clad in his underwear and socks, he took her hand and raised her up. The two were dancing sexily as he watched their silhouettes move slowly along the wall toward the boudoir. He reached for the light switch.

"I would prefer candlelight," she said softly.

His heart racing, he said, "I'd like that too."

From the moment they lit a half-dozen bedside candles, their panting began to rise until it turned to passionate moans of pleasure.

Lathered in fruity oils, their bodies glistening from the morning sunbeams that filtered through the window, they gasped and screamed in orgasmic delight.

* * *

Two weeks flew by like a bolt of lightning. On a warm mid-morning, outside on the terrace at Clint's apartment, Christine untied her bouffant hairdo and mussed her tresses before she lay reposed on a hammock. She held the same demure expression and wore the same black décolletage she had worn on first day he began to paint her. A brush in his hand, Clint carefully studied the gold chain with an opal cameo and a heart-shaped agate that was wound around her neck before he started painting. He painted the looping jade earrings hanging from her ears and the gold heart-shaped anklet on her right foot and added nightingales swirling around her head. He dipped the brush in glossy rouge paint and dabbed the final strokes on her lips.

"We can talk now," said Clint. "I'm done with your lips. God, you have beautiful lips. And it's the same with your eyes. There's so much purity in them - the way they shine and sparkle."

"Did Jacques tell you that Dominique is with child?"

"Yes, he did, yesterday when he dropped off supplies. The timing is perfect. She'll make the consummate Mary Magdalene. And you, my sweetheart, will be the perfect Immaculate Virgin Mary. I can't wait for spring and this resurgence. I agree with Jacques. This is going to be gigantic."

"How do you feel about children?" she asked, remaining motionless.

He dropped the brush, and his head quickly turned from the canvas to Christine. "Huh," he stammered. "Are you alluding that you're pregnant."

"No. Oh, I'm sorry. I didn't mean it like that. It's my poor English."

"Nonsense, your English is coming along splendid," he said, picking up the brush and continuing to paint, "especially your contractions. It's my French that's horrible. I didn't inherit the genetic trait to be multi-linguistic. This language barrier is a constant struggle."

"Your French is fine. You can't expect to speak another language in such a short period of time. I've been studying English since grammar school. You've taught me so much."

"Now that I think about it, it wouldn't bother me if you were pregnant."

"It's conceivable. I don't use birth control. It's against my religious faith."

"What religion are you?"

"Catholic. But I'm not strict. I will if you want me to."

"It wouldn't bother me," he said. "I believe in God. That's for certain. But I disagree with the church on that issue. Children should be planned, not brought into this world by accident."

"I agree. I'll start taking them."

"Good. Because now is not the time for babies. But you, my lovely demoiselle, are far too young to think of having babies. Think of all the stretch marks. You'd look like a shriveled prune in the midst of your prime. You have such a youthful figure."

"I don't intend to shrivel like a prune," she said in an irritated voice. "I would never allow that to happen."

Feeling regretful, he said, "I'm sorry. That was a stupid thing for me to say."

"You haven't answered my question about children."

"Oh, ah, I like girls," he said. "Boys are a pain in the rear. How about you?"

"It wouldn't matter," she said. "It feels strange to watch you paint me. In a way, you are giving me immortality a second time. I'm being reborn on canvas again. I'm dying to peek at it. Can I please see it?"

"That might jinx it. But I'm almost done. I just need to finish your eyebrows and eyelashes. And I want Jacques and Dominique to be here for the unveiling."

"When are they coming?

"In a little bit."

"I can hardly wait. I'm so anxious to see it."

Clint was covering the canvas with a blanket, and Christine was laying out platters of hors d'oeuvres on a table when Dominique and Jacques arrived with a magnum of champagne just before sunset. Jacques popped the cork and filled three glasses with pink bubbly as they stood at the table, snacking on truffles and other delectable delights.

"The suspense is killing me," said Dominique, holding a saucer and demitasse of herbal tea.

"Me, too," said Christine. "I'm on the verge of having an anxiety attack. Please, Clint, take the blanket off."

"Unwrap the damn thing, Clint," Jacques quipped. "Why allow the ladies to suffer in agony. Now unveil it."

Clint laughed. "Well, in light of all this bellowing, I certainly don't wish to bring harm to the lady I love and her charming friends."

"Damn you," Jacques yelled. "If you don't yank that blanket off, I'm going to."

"Take it easy, Jacques, I will." Clint walked to the easel. "But bear in mind that I hate rejection and negative critique. So lie and pacify me. But please, no ridicule." Clint flung the blanket from off the canvas and stepped away. "Voila, 'Lounging Ballerina.'"

Quiet fell over the terrace as Dominique, Jacques, and Christine gazed awestruck at the painting. Their mouths opened wide, the three stepped closer and craned their necks. With the tension so great, Clint felt on the verge of bursting. Her eyes wide, her face trembling as she stared at the canvas, Christine turned and looked at Clint just before her legs wobbled and she appeared on the verge of collapsing to the ground.

In a state of confused commotion, mumbling, and shrieking in French and English, Jacques and Clint quickly grabbed Christine and carried her to the hammock. They laid her down, and Dominique charged into the apartment. A few minutes later, she came back out and rushed over with a bucket of ice and a wet towel.

“Is she okay?” Dominique said, packing the towel with ice cubes.

“She’ll be fine,” said Jacques, placing the icepack on Christine’s forehead. “She’s merely swooning.”

“Her pulse is okay,” said Clint, kneeling beside Christine, holding her wrist and gently patting her cheeks.

Several minutes passed when Christine twitched and jerked upright. “What happened?” she said with a bewildered expression.

“You fainted,” said Clint.

“I’ve never fainted in my life.”

“There’s always a first time,” said Jacques. “Dominique lost consciousness the day I asked her to marry me.”

“Jacques told me I was out for almost ten minutes,” said Dominique.

Jacques and Clint helped raise Christine to her feet. Following a few minutes of fussing and consoling Christine, they were back staring at “Lounging Ballerina” in silence.

“Hey, come on,” said Clint, “this mum stuff is getting on my nerves. It’s okay to talk. Say something, anything, there’s no need to rant or rave.”

Jacques, Dominique, and Christine took their eyes away from the canvas and stared at Clint with dumbfounded expressions.

“Hey. Give me a break. It’s my first attempt with oil painting. I’m a beginner for heaven’s sake, a novice.”

“You’re a prodigy, Clint,” said Jacques. “This is a masterpiece.”

“Jacques isn’t exaggerating,” said Dominique. “You are most definitely a master artist. Art is innate in your blood. You have captured Christine's playful innocence as well as her epicurean and concupiscent sides."

"You guys are saying all that to swell my ego because I sure as hell am not a prodigy."

Appearing mesmerized, Christine took Clint's arm and squeezed it. "We wouldn't do that to you," she said. "You're a wonder. It's as if I'm looking into a mirror."

"She isn't fibbing, Clint," said Jacques. "It's worthy of hanging in the Louvre."

Clint laughed. "Yeah, sure, hanging alongside the 'Mona Lisa.' Give me a break."

"You're blessed with a rare gift, Clint," said Dominique. "Christine is breathing life in your painting. You've captured the essence of her seraphic dalliance and her enchanting smile. She is ethereal and erotic."

With a look of admiration, Jacques patted Clint on the shoulder. "It's quintessential genius. I especially love the backdrop, the plethora of scintillating stars and the bulbous moon."

"And I love the genuflecting angels and nightingales," said Dominique.

Clint grinned. "I stole the idea from your husband."

"Your work is completely different," said Christine. "You have created a chef-d'oeuvre. I believe destiny brought you to Paris."

"My being here is beyond fate. I'll tell you one day why I came here, but now is not the time. You'd all think I'm crazy. I will tell you that you three have instilled me with inspiration and enlightenment. And thank you for all your tutelage, Jacques. This would not have come to be if I hadn't studied your work."

The four exchanged embraces and Clint looked at Christine and said, "Now what?" He placed his arm around her. "Geez, you're a pluvial rain forest. Why are you crying?"

"Because I am happy, because I love you."

"This is a time for revelry and rejoicing," said Jacques, "not crying."

"I can't help it. I'm sorry," said Christine as Dominique wrapped her arm around her, consolingly.

"Before you're catapulted into fame," said Jacques, "would you allow me the honor of displaying your painting in my gallery?"

"With pleasure, but it's not for sale. It's Christine's Christmas present."

"For me," Christine beamed. "Oh la la, I don't know what to say."

"There's no need to say anything except 'Merry Christmas.' Now bring on the resurgence." Clint thrust a clenched fist over his head. "I'm ready."

"Big rigs will start hauling materials in a few months, and the resurgence will commence at Miracle Meadow," said Jacques.

"In the meantime," said Clint, "may I paint your wife together with Christine at Fontainebleau?"

"Of course," said Jacques, "but nothing lewd."

"I was thinking of having them wear chemises and dancing in a forested garden. I'll name it 'Aphrodite and Venus Dancing at Fontainebleau.'"

Christine flustered.

"How flattering," said Dominique. "I would be honored."

Jacques scratched his nose. "Intriguing, a uniting of Roman and Greek myth."

Chapter 23

Seated underneath a large makeshift tent near the entrance to Miracle Meadow, Clint and Jacques were playing a game of chess, while formulating a strategy to launch the renaissance resurgence. Carpenters, plumbers and electricians across the grassy meadow were busy completing the barracks to house the throng of artists that were arriving daily from around the globe. Below a grove of maple trees, a forklift driver was unloading pallets of five-liter paint buckets, and stockpiling them on wooden platforms next to boxes of plaster. Spools of canvases dangled from a chain on the boom of a cherry-picker that was taking them to where workers were building, staging, and scaffolding in the center of the meadow.

"Your painting of Christine and Dominique has been stirring up considerable commotion at my gallery," said Jacques, attacking Clint's queen with his rook. "A former colleague of mine made a substantial offer yesterday."

"It's not for sale," said Clint.

"Don't you want to know how much he's willing to pay?"

"Not really."

"He's a quasi-famous philanthropist and a highly respected connoisseur of fine art with strong connections."

"I don't give a damn, Jacques. It's not for sale." Clint moved his pawn and checked Jacques' knight.

"Are you wealthy?"

Clint laughed. "No. Look Jacques, I just got untangled from a web of gluttony over money. I don't care about it anymore. I just want to paint. And this project is overwhelming. It's monumental, Jacques. This resurgence will knock this planet's gravitational pull out of whack. I can't wait till this resurgence kicks off."

"I'm glad you're so optimistic."

Clint pointed. "Look at the troop of artists marching in here right now. It's been like this all week. The energy of this force is ceaseless."

"I agree," said Jacques. "And the tenacious expressions on everybody's face, boggles my mind."

"You noticed that too."

Jacques brought out his queen and said, "Check. And the colony will continue to grow everyday. Belief coupled with determination and persistence is a powerful force."

"I can't concentrate on this game," said Clint, blocking Jacques' attack with his bishop, "I'm too excited. I had another dream last night."

Jacques grinned. "It seems you've been having a lot of dreams lately."

"Yeah, this one was a scene of 'Viking Warriors,' only it's even gorier than the one I showed you. I called my two Scandinavian college buddies. They'll make perfect blood-thirsty barbarians in the foreground. They've agreed to fly out when we need them."

"This is proving to be of omnipotent magnitude. I'm proud you're a part of this Renaissance re-creation," said Jacques, capturing Clint's bishop. "Check," he said. "Stay focused on "Viking Warriors. " How do you feel about Max and Hiroshi being in charge of "Hells Battlefield. "

"Those two are on fire with rage," said Clint. "They're perfect. I like that Antonio Giannini fellow."

"So do I. I've him teamed with Eduardo Sanchez to head up 'Heaven's Eternal Sanctuary' so I can concentrate on 'Magnum Opus.'"

"Those two collages will be epics," said Clint. "That's why you're the chief commander of this evolution. And we won't need models to pose. The disciples are here. Even Judas is here."

"I think I know who you mean," said Jacques. "That fellow Kozlovski, who looks like a cross between Hitler and Nixon with a smidgen of Stalin."

"Good eye, that's him."

"He'll make the perfect Judas.'"

"God, we're on the same wavelength," said Clint. "I'm so glad we connected."

"Hey, I've an idea," said Jacques. "A couple of old Brit colleagues of mine are coming. The blokes are brimming with enthusiasm and talent. What do you think about putting them in charge of your 'Swashbuckling Buccaneers'?"

"I trust your judgment. How about 'God's Kingdom'?"

"I'm giving that one to the Russian couple Ivan and Olga," said Jacques.

Clint covered his head with his hands. "Wow. Our minds are in sync, I've seen their work. Those two are masters. We're going to make history, Jacques."

"Time's dwindling," said Jacques. "Following the Ides of March next week, we stretch the canvases taunt in this Miracle Meadow and start sketching the layouts. Checkmate."

"This isn't fair, Jacques. I can't concentrate. My mind's in a spin-cycle overflowing with anxiety to get this project rolling."

"Another lame excuse," said Jacques. "By the way, do you have representation?"

"What do you mean?"

"An agent, a manager," said Jacques. "This resurgence will be generously rewarded."

"I don't give a damn about money."

"It's time you did. Dominique's father represents me. Claude has a great deal of influence in high-places. This project will fetch a tidy fortune for all."

"Kinda like the pot of gold at the end of a rainbow, huh," said Clint.

"You might say that," said Jacques. "Claude loves your painting of Dominique and Christine. He asked me to bring you by his office."

"Truth is, Jacques, I don't give a rat's ass about money," Clint said. "But I'd like to build a castle for Christine. I'm gonna ask that enchantress to marry me."

"She's waiting for you to ask her."

Clint looked surprised. "Really?"

"Yes, but ask her in French. She'll like that."

"Good idea," said Clint. "How do you say will you marry me in French?"

"Vous fera m'epouse."

Clint repeated the phrase several times.

"Not bad," said Jacques, "keep practicing. By the way, your French is coming along quite well."

"Bull, my French sucks big time," said Clint. "Everybody wants to speak English. When's the gala opening day ceremony of this resurgence going to kick-off?"

"Dominique and Christine are working out the details with Claude as we speak."

* * *

Amidst the roar of international banter on the first day of spring, trumpets blared as thunderous footsteps from the frantic herd of artists' rushed up the scaffolding in a frenzy of exhilaration. With zealous faces, artists, carrying brushes and buckets, began to slap goopy plaster onto the canvases, and the resurgence commenced. Dominique was glowing with motherhood when Jacques began to paint her on the canvas of "Magnum Opus."

* * *

Under an azure sky two months later, Clint drove to Orly Airport to pick up his pals Roy and his brother, Carl. Following some festive backslapping and hugs, the three piled into Clint's Citroen and headed to Miracle Meadow.

"Developing Sunshine City proved a mighty lucrative venture," said Carl, sitting in the passenger seat. "Every building and parcel is sold."

"We made a killing on the industrial park," said Roy from the back seat. "And people snatched up every house before we could stake a 'for sale' sign on the lawns. Sunshine City has become the technology capital of the world."

"So I've been reading," said Clint. "Glad it worked out so well for you guys."

"We're raking in sacks of dough," said Carl.

"Hell, there are so many greenbacks rolling in," said Roy. "We've had to stash 'em in numbered Swiss bank accounts."

"Even opened one for you," said Carl. "Hell, man, it was your concept."

"And your land," said Clint. "But thanks, I could use a little dough."

"Not a word from you in over a year," said Roy. "What's the deal on that?"

"Had to clear my head," said Clint. "I was messed up big time."

"I remember," said Carl. "Most everyone thought you did the hari-kari, a dead-goner. You could've at least called collect."

"Yeah, Clint," said Roy. "We were hanging on thin thread worrying about you till you called. You need to hone your communication skills."

"Can't blame it on procrastination," said Clint. "My mind was screwed up, way out of balance and distorted. It took me a while before I was able to regain my equilibrium. Glad you guys could make it."

"I can see by the paint splattered all over you that you're serious about this art stuff," said Carl.

"Yeah," said Roy. "The suspense has been eating away at us. What gives?"

"You'll see soon enough," said Clint. "All I can say is big. This project is so vast, it will skyrocket the planet. Anyway, how's family life, Carl?"

Carl's face turned sullen, and he wagged his head in disgust, ranting off a string of words that included constant whining, nagging, and being on the rag in reference to Bridget. Then he started spewing words like evil, fat bitch, and sneaky witch. He concluded with a tirade about private detectives, property settlements, attorney fees, and cross-country hide-and-seek chases.

"Do you want to hear more?" Carl asked.

Clint nodded his head and said, "No thanks, Carl. Sorry to hear that. How are things going on your home front, Roy?"

Roy rattled off a slew of words in the likes of goo-goo, gaa-gaa, stinky pooh-pooh diapers, burping, baby bottles, formulas, pacifiers, lullabies, terrible twos, stretch marks, and said, "Shall I go on?"

"Ah, no thanks," said Clint, "I think I'll pass, Roy."

"Oh, I almost forgot," said Carl. "I bumped into Dusty while spring skiing at Squaw last week. She was flying down the slopes like a damn tornado and crashed head-on into me. She told me to tell you that she always felt you should have been an artist."

"No kidding!"

"She also told me she regrets what happened and that she never had intercourse with that guy," said Carl.

"That's a crock of bull," said Clint.

"She told me she smoked too much knockout weed that night and was only seeking comfort and support," said Carl.

Clint laughed. "In bed in her underwear with some bozo hippie freak, give me a break."

"Anyway," said Carl, "she told me she'd like to see you again. She got your letter and asked me to tell you that she really appreciated it. She said she also wants to make amends."

"Is that so?"

"She looked like she damn well meant it."

Pulling up in front of a chain-link fence that encircled Miracle Meadow and parking, Clint laughed. "Not in this lifetime." "Well, here we are."

Carl gripped the dashboard and raised up from his seat and shouted, "Holy shit, you weren't jiving. This place is humongous."

"This sure as hell ain't no hoax," said Roy as they got out of the car. "There must be over a mile of canvas stretched out in that field. Carl and I thought this was another one of your college pranks."

"I have to admit that I was skeptical when you told me what you were up to," said Carl. "You weren't joshing, this project is titanic. And those paintings are massive."

"It's like an ant farm out there," said Roy as he and Carl stared out at the meadow. Where'd you dig up all the artists?"

"They're like bees swarming around hives," said Carl.

"The guy who conceived this resurgence placed ads in school newspapers and had ads posted on bulletin boards at every major art school around the planet," said Clint as they passed through the gate and headed to a large covered eating area. "The artists here are from every walk of life. The only requirement to be a part of this force is raw talent, along with an abundance of energy and acute vision."

"You're in charge of all this?" Roy asked as they sat at a large table.

"No one's in charge," said Clint. "We're a troop of the most gifted artists in the world, assembled here, painting in harmonious unity."

"Don't listen to him," said Jacques, walking over to the table, splotched with colored plaster from head to toe. Dominique and Christine were at Jacques' side. "Your friend is much too humble. He's our leader. Without Clint we'd be buzzing around aimlessly."

"He's putting you on," said Clint, standing up and embracing Christine. "This is the master. It's Jacques who ignites this force with inspiration and gets our imaginations soaring."

"You must be Carl," said Christine, taking his hand. "It's a pleasure to meet you."

"Same here," said Carl, as he and Roy stood up and exchanged hugs and kisses on the cheeks.

Jacques looked Carl and Roy up and down and smiled at Clint, "Excellent choices," he said. "Your friends will make consummate Vikings."

Following a lighthearted conversation while eating lunch, Jacques was back inside a bucket at the end of a boom crane painting Dominique on the canvas of "Magnum Opus. "

"Is that what I think it is?" Carl asked as he and his brother stood gaping at the canvas of "Magnum Opus."

"Maybe," replied Clint. "What do you think it is?"

"Looks like 'The Last Supper,'" said Carl, "except for Dominique and the two little children."

"Very good," said Clint. "This is Jacques' rendition of 'The Last Supper. He's named it "Magnum Opus"

"Who's the weird diabolical looking creep?" Roy asked.

"That's Judas," said Clint.

Christine smiled.

"That dude is freaky," said Carl. "His face is ghostly white, and all the other disciples have color and are smiling."

"It's a joyous day," said Christine. "Jesus is going home."

Clint smiled.

"Is Dominique pregnant?" Roy asked.

"She's almost five months along," said Christine.

"She's portraying Mary Magdalene," said Clint. "Jesus is married to her."

Roy and Carl looked stunned and said in unison, "Married!"

"Why are there children in the painting?" Carl asked.

"They're Jesus and Mary's children," said Clint.

Roy and Carl broke out in a fit of laughter.

"The Catholic church will condemn this," said Carl, shaking his grinning face. "The Vatican will accuse this assembly of blasphemy and call you all heathens, pagans, and atheists. The church will claim this is heresy."

"Gotta agree, Clint," said Roy. "The church will crucify everyone here. The Vatican will excommunicate the lot of you and sentence you all to hell."

Clint laughed. "Let 'em. I could care less. Everyone here knows what we're doing. This ain't a secret. Besides, I'm not worrying. I'm doing this for another reason. Come on, I want to show you 'Viking Warriors.' You two will be smack in the center foreground in three-dimension."

Standing in front of "Hell's Battlefield," Roy and Carl's eyes were transfixed on the canvas."

"Man, that evil monster looks just like Nixon," said Roy.

"More like Hitler," said Carl.

Clint laughed.

Roy and Carl looked to be cast under a spell as they crossed miracle meadow 200 yards past the fluttering canvases of "The Fall of Babylon," "Swashbuckling Buccaneers," "Jousting for the Holy Grail," "The Transfiguration," and "The Resurrection."

"You've captured my attention," said Carl. "This is beyond incredible. You've created a damn fantasy world. I'm impressed. Where's the media, the paparazzi. This should be on the cover of every magazine in the world."

"Yeah, Clint," said Roy. "This needs worldwide exposure. It's the scoop of the century. This is front-page headlines."

"In due time," said Christine. "But they will come. You can be sure of that. This colony is blessed with magic hands and wondrous vision."

"Those artists are something," said Carl. "It's like being at the circus watching a flying trapeze act."

"With all those cherry pickers and boom trucks this must be costing a fortune," said Roy.

"It is," said Clint.

"The scope of this project is beyond my comprehension," said Carl. "This is far bigger than Sunshine City."

A short distance later, they came upon "Viking Warriors" and stopped. Carl and Roy grimaced and wiped their rusty, wavy locks.

"Good grief, that's morbid," said Carl. "What's with all the mutilated bodies?"

"It's a battlefield," replied Clint. "What did you expect? The Vikings were ruthless barbarians, savages."

"That's way too grizzly for my innards," said Roy.

"Yeah, Clint," said Carl, "looks like a giant outdoor slaughterhouse. There's way too much violence. My stomach's churning just looking at all that gory bloodshed."

"That's the way it was back then," said Clint. "The Norseman war creed was kill, pillage, plunder, destroy, conquer, and rape. My ancestors were peace loving."

"Hah," Roy bellowed, "give me a damn break. The Irish, those thieving bastards were vultures, cannibals. They'd gauge out your guts, hearts, and eyeballs, and eat 'em raw."

Clint snickered. "There's some truth to that. A dark umbra fell over that monstrous period."

"Look, Clint," said Carl, "Roy and I didn't travel 7000 miles to pose as murdering butchers, chopping bodies with hatchets and axes in a damn bloodbath."

"That's the way it was, Carl," said Clint. "We're depicting legendary fact. This resurgence is about showing the children the atrocity and grotesque brutality of war. Maybe it will help save the planet. Even right now, it's one war after the next. Hundreds or even thousands of innocent bystanders are being mercilessly killed everyday. We must educate the children of the future that peace and loving thy neighbor are better than war."

"You and your brother will be immortalized for all eternity in a palace or a museum," said Christine.

"She's right," said Clint. "You two will be proud victors basking in the foreground of glory, the focal point, the center of attraction. Your mugs will be famous."

"And wait till you see your costumes," said Christine. Dominique and I scoured the northern continent to find the horned helmets, swords, and shields. It's all authentic. We even found real puttees and whips for the flogging."

"And you have the faces of real Nordics," said Clint. "Your humped noses are perfect. Drench you two in oil and blood until you're both glistening and you guys will look exactly like bloodthirsty killers. All you need to do is give me a gloating, murderous glint. What say?"

Roy and Carl looked at each other and then looked at the painting. Staring at each other, they wagged their heads and Carl said, "We're here. Let's do it. Curdle my blood."

"Why not," said Roy. "Now that I've got a ton of money, I may as well taste a little fame. Okay, have us dripping in blood."

"You'll be celebrities," said Christine.

"Hey," said Carl. "With so many diverse ethnicities gathered here, what's the common language, Esperanto?"

Clint laughed. "That mumbo jumbo never caught on. Most everyone here is almost fluent or speaks fair to middling English."

"What about security?" Roy asked. "You know, protection against vandalism and theft."

Clint swiped his forehead. "That's one of the reasons why this resurgence is strictly hush-hush."

"What about rain?" Carl said. "Hell, all this could be destroyed in a single storm."

"Or fire," said Roy.

"Hey, I appreciate your concern," said Clint, "but lighten up. Everything's under control. The owner of the property is about to start building some metal warehouses."

"They'd better be big," said Roy.

"They will be."

"When do we roll?" Carl asked.

"At the crack of dawn tomorrow."

"Will you join us for dinner tonight?" Christine asked. "I've a special treat."

"It would be a pleasure, mademoiselle," said Roy.

"Mademoiselle is an old woman," corrected Clint. "This charming, beautiful young lady is referred to as a demoiselle."

"Whatever," said Carl. "You got our blind dates lined up?"

"That's the special treat," said Christine with a bright smile.

"Yeah," said Clint, "and they're hot to trot. They love to shake their booties at the disco. You guys will cherish this night."

Chapter 24

Clint had finished painting his blood drenched pals Roy and Carl and was sitting on a grassy knoll with them as they looked down at the artists painting the background of "Swashbuckling Buccaneers."

"You're right, Clint," said Roy. "This is a mighty feat. I've a strong hunch you and Jacques are going to be catapulted into fame."

"No doubt," said Carl. "Look, I'd buy anyone of these paintings. But not one of them would fit in the mansion I'm having built. And it's capacious, over twenty thousand square feet. None of these paintings would even fit in the grand ballroom."

Clint chuckled. "I've gotta admit they're big. The proportions of this whole thing staggered my mind at first. It still has me blown away, especially how fast everything has come together. It seems we're moving at the speed of light."

"It's our faces," said Roy. "You've captured the very essence of rage in our faces. They're incredible."

"My brother looks like a snarling marauder with his cutlass crossed," said Carl. "And me with that ax, so much rage."

Roy shook his head in agreement. "You've done a damn good job of making my brother and I look like real murdering scoundrels."

Clint laughed. "Jacques' British friends Colin and Troy with their mimicking parrots, earrings, and eye patches crack me up. Those two blokes are incredible artists. The faces of those cut-throat pirates on that canvas are the epitome of viciousness and hatred."

"Yeah," said Roy. "I get a kick out of listening to Troy and Colin's tales of derring-do. Those two are a couple of raconteurs."

"Some of their stories are pretty far-fetched if you ask me," said Carl, looking up at the sky and pointing. "What the hell. Two choppers at ten o'clock."

"Two more whirly birds coming from the north," said Roy.

The three stood up and began scanning the horizon and spotted two more helicopters coming out of the clouds in the southern horizon.

"They're heading right for us," said Carl. "Guess word's leaked out."

"Hell, the sky's full of 'em," said Roy. "They're coming from every direction. Looks like you've got company Clint."

Within minutes a swarm of helicopters were buzzing overhead.

"It's the press," said Carl as the helicopters swooped down and hovered over Miracle Meadow. "Those choppers are loaded with reporters and cameras."

"Better than soldiers with flamethrowers," said Clint, scratching his head. "Well, I'd better get you two to the airport. This place is about to go into an uproar. Too bad you two are going to miss the hullabaloo."

The ecstatic throng of artists stood with their heads raised and screaming in excitement as Clint and his two pals crossed the meadow.

"Something big's brewing," said Clint when they reached the chain-link fence. "Check out the mob of paparazzi with their noses crammed between the wire links."

"The whole place is surrounded," said Roy. "A big ado is about to bust loose."

Clint shook his head when they reached the guard stationed at the gate, and Clint told him, "Except for the artists associated with this project, absolutely no one is to be admitted. If you don't recognize them, they don't get in."

"It's not going to be easy," said the guard. "There are a lot of people out there."

"Get on the bullhorn and put a crew together. Have 'em grab the 'no trespassing' signs in the shed and start hanging 'em on the fence."

The guard nodded.

"Might behoove you to string some barbed wire on top of the fence," said Roy. "These folks look mighty serious about getting inside for the big scoop."

"Electrify it," said Carl. "Tie it into two-twenty volts. Give 'em a jolt. Fry 'em. Better yet, zap 'em with four-forty."

"Maybe add some gun towers with machine guns," said Roy.

"Hey, Roy," said Carl. "Let's rebook our flights and stick around. Clint's right. This is colossal."

"I wouldn't miss this for world," said Roy.

A couple of hours later, sitting under a large tent, the three sat at a long table shooting the bull, ignoring the chaos.

"By the way, Clint," said Carl. "Have you told Christine you're married?"

"I'm divorced."

"It hasn't been finalized," said Carl.

"That's a legal technicality." Clint jerked when a shock wave ran up his spine as he recalled Christine seeing a picture of Dusty in his wallet. "Damn. That means I lied to her. I told her I wasn't married when I met her. And I was. She saw Dusty's picture. And I told her it was my sister. This is going to be a tough dilemma to overcome."

"You'd better tell her," said Roy, "if you want to keep her for a playmate. That babe's a fox and classy too. She kind of reminds me of Dusty."

Clint sighed. "I saw that the day I met her. She's got the same verve and dalliance and reeks of wholesomeness. But she's got another side to her verdant freshness. She really gets off on getting carnal."

"It's in her eyes," Roy said.

Clint shook his head and took a sip of apple juice. "It's like she has two pairs. Now what the hell can I do?"

"It's simple," said Carl, "Tell her the truth."

"She's been hurt before by assholes who've lied to her. Marriage scares the hell out of me and now I have to deal with this mess. I don't think I can handle another trauma."

"You'd best tell the lovely creature," said Roy.

"I'm scared she'll freak out because I lied to her," said Clint.

"That was a mere slip of the tongue," said Roy. "Tell her that you thought you were divorced."

"She's European," said Clint. "Divorce is far less prevalent here."

"Tell her divorce is rampant in California," said Carl. "Hell, everyone I know is either divorced or in the process of getting divorced. It sure ain't like it used to be back in the old days. Divorce has become the American way. Some asshole had the gall to introduce his wife to me as his domestic partner. Can you believe that. The only person I know who's not divorced, besides my brother, is your pal Matt."

"That's because Matt robbed the cradle," said Clint. "Bonny's also a Marilyn Monroe look-alike."

"You'll figure out something with your line of BS," said Roy.

"Those days are in the past," said Clint.

"Things could be a whole lot worse," said Roy. "Ya heard what happened to Dan?"

"No."

"It's ugly," said Carl.

"You gonna leave me hanging."

"He O-D'd on some hallucinogenic while sitting in a hot tub," said Roy, shaking his head.

Clint's face twisted. "You mean he's dead?"

"As a doornail," said Carl.

"Damn. You're kidding me?"

Roy shook his head. "Who would joke about something like that."

Clint grimaced and slammed his fist on the table. "Ah, hell. I loved Dan. He was so talented. Damn. That's a rotten shame. I saw it coming back in sixty-four. What the hell's happening to this world. I don't get it. To hell with bad news crap. I've decided to ask that enchantress to marry me right now. I cherish that lady. That is, if she accepts after I've told her the truth."

Carl laughed. "Best skip the part about sending the house crashing down the hillside in a cloud of smoke. The lady might think you have a severe case of distemper."

Clint wagged his head. "Good point. That's a tough one. But I have to tell her. She'd find out one day. Can't hide that crazy stunt forever."

"When ya comin' home?" Carl asked.

"Not for a long time. At least not until this project is finished. Besides, I like Europe."

"From what's happening up in the sky and outside those gates," said Roy, "I've a hunch this Renaissance project is going to be splattered on the front page of every newspaper on the planet tomorrow morning."

"Yeah, Clint," said Carl. "This thing's gonna make headlines. No doubt about it."

"We'll see," said Clint. "Hey, if she accepts, you guys coming to the wedding. I'm going to need a best man and some ushers."

"Wouldn't miss it for the world," said Carl, pulling out his wallet and handing Clint a folded piece of paper. "I was going it to give you at the airport, but now that we're staying, thought I'd give it to you now."

Clint opened it. "What is it?"

"It's the number of your Swiss account."

Clint's eyes perked. "Wow, a numbered account. Out of curiosity, how much is in it?"

"A hair shy of seven figures is all we're telling ya," said Roy.

"Wow!"

"You earned it, good buddy," said Carl.

"Think I'll spend the rest of the day looking at rings."

"By the way," said Carl, "Clay Thompson told me to thank you for all your hard work and that he wishes you the best. He chipped in most of the money."

"How's Matt?"

"Diligently working his ass off," said Carl. "He's going to be pissed off when I'm not in the office on Monday. The poor guy is running the whole show."

"I'll call him tonight," said Clint. "Right now I'm going shopping for a ring. You guys have fun enjoying the show."

Following an exchange of robust hugs, Clint headed into Paris.

* * *

Miracle Meadow was swarming with paparazzi when Clint arrived early the next morning, having to inch his way through the maddening crowd to the gate. Honking and mumbling, he finally parked and yanked the emergency break. He got out and pushed his way through the boisterous rabble of camera-packing press. He could hear the shutters clicking after he passed through the gate. Every artist he walked past was singing, whistling, or humming, with gloating expressions.

"It's like a zoo out there," Clint shouted up at Jacques and Dominique, who were inside a bucket 20 feet above him, putting the final brush strokes on the face of Jesus on the canvas of "Magnum Opus."

"We can see," hollered Jacques. "We're not wearing blindfolds."

Clint sat beside Christine, kissed her on the lips and said, “Bon jour mi amore.”

“Have you seen this morning’s paper?” Dominique’s father, Claude De Monet, said with an ecstatic expression. He was seated across from Christine, puffing on a cigar. His paisley silk shirt was half unbuttoned and his frizzy black hair fell to his shoulders.

“Not yet,” said Clint. “Why?”

“These paintings are on front page of *Le Monde*,” he said. “Take a look.”

Clint grabbed the paper. “Wow.”

Claude blew out a smoke ring and flicked an ash. “It seems your paintings have captivated global attention. My secretary says the telephone at the gallery hasn’t stopped ringing.”

“It’s a good omen,” said Christine. “You and Jacques have worked so hard.”

“You mean the entire colony of artists assembled here has been working hard,” said Clint. “Look around. This troop has been busting their butts from dawn to dusk seven days a week. There are no quacks on this Miracle Meadow.” He turned his attention to Claude. “What about that angry mob of priests out there. What’s that all about?”

Scratching his portly middle-aged belly and playing with his neatly trimmed Van Dyke, Claude shook his head. “Shallow-minded poor souls. The church’s reaction to a pregnant Mary Magdalene and the two young children is as I expected. It has been the intention of the Catholic hierarchy to suppress women since its conception.”

Clint smiled. “We finally agree on something.”

“The photographs of “Magnum Opus” and “Heaven’s Eternal Sanctuary” on the front page have sparked a controversial uproar amongst the local clergy," said Claude.

"Polluted parody, one archdiocese called it," Jacques roared as he lowered the bucket.

"Perverted deviation, one cardinal referred to 'Magnum Opus,'" shouted Dominique.

Clint laughed. "The hell with all this heresy crap. We should have made all the disciples women. That definitely would have freaked out the Vatican commandos."

"Jacques and I were hashing over whether to allow the press in for an hour," said Claude. "It will give this project worldwide exposure. Call it an early sneak preview."

"Sure, why not," said Clint. "Bring on the cattle drive. Let the herd stampede."

Jacques carefully assisted Dominique out of the bucket and brushed off her clothes.

Clint stared up at the face of Jesus. "His expression is so intense and yet so at peace."

"Wait till you see the model we found for Aurora," said Dominique. "She arrived a few days ago from Sweden. Not only is she a gifted artist, she has the face and body of Aurora."

"I think I know who you mean," said Clint. "I saw her as I was leaving yesterday. I thought the same thing. Her face was glowing like a dawning sun. If she's who I think she is. She's perfect."

Christine clasped Clint's hand. "I want to help paint. I know I'm not very good. But I want to try. I want to be a part of this force."

"Don't say you're not very good," said Clint. "You're an exceptional artist. Your talent is equal to anyone here."

"Let her paint Pegasus," Jacques said.

"If you don't like it," said Christine, "you can paint over it. I love horses. I used to paint horses when I was a little girl."

"Quit belittling yourself," said Clint. "And you're still a little girl. Of course you may. You paint the winged horse and I'll paint Apollo, mounted atop Pegasus."

"The scene in the painting is so high up. I should tell you that I've a little acrophobia."

"I'll hold you tight," Clint whispered in her ear. "We can do it in the bucket."

She gave him a curious look. "Do what?"

Clint winked. "Youuu knowww."

Christine blushed. Her mouth rounded and she beamed. "Oh la la. Can we take a walk. I've something important to tell you."

Clint noticed Christine's face turn serious. "Sure. I've also something to ask you."

Clint grabbed a bottle of Perrier, two glasses, a wool blanket from off the table, and the two walked away hand in hand. The sun was rising overhead when Christine shook the blanket and laid it on the grass below a spruce tree. Curious what she wanted to tell him, Clint untwisted the cap and filled the glasses with sparkling mineral water. He wondered what she would say when he asked her to marry him and dreaded her reaction when he told her he had lied to her. Christine sat silent and looked nervous when Clint handed her the glass and sat cross-legged beside her.

"Look, Christine, I've something important I need to tell you."

"What."

"It's been torturing me all morning."

She looked at him inquisitively. "Tell me. There must be no secrets between us."

"You're right." His jowls tightened and he blurted, "I lied to you. I was married and the girl you saw in the picture at the train station the day I met you was my former wife, not my sister. My friends told me that it's now been finalized."

She looked at him oddly. "That is all you wanted to tell me."

Half expecting her to turn furious and fly into a rampage, he was surprised by her calmness, and his heart stopped pounding. "There's one other little thing," he said.

Appearing unruffled, she asked, "First, do you have children?"

"No."

"Go on."

"There's one more thing. I snapped and demolished our house."

"I don't understand snapped or demolished."

"I think the French translation is demolir. Snapped means I went crazy and destroyed our house."

She smiled and started to giggle. "Your wife must have done something very horrible for you to do that. May I ask what happened?"

He went on to explain, and was further surprised at how composed she remained as he told her.

"You're not angry that I lied to you?"

"I value honesty. And you have told me the truth. You are deserving of merit for telling me. I appreciate that quality in you."

Feeling relieved, he said, "Now that I've divulged my secret, what is it you wanted to tell me?"

Her eyelashes began to flutter rapidly and she said, “I’m pregnant. With all the excitement, I forgot to take my birth control pills. I hope you’re not angry.”

His lips went ringent and he blurted. “Heck no. You’re going to have a baby?”

“We’re going to have a baby.”

“Man, this is some kind of joyous day. We’re going to have a baby.” He wrapped his arms around her and they kissed passionately. He dug his hand in his pants pocket, pulled out a small fuzzy box, and handed it to her.

Her face flushed with astonishment, she asked, “What’s this?”

“Open it.”

“Oh la la. Is it what I think it is?”

“Why don’t you open it and find out.”

Staring at the box, tears began to ooze down her cheeks. She slowly opened the lid and shrieked, “Oh, Clint. It’s beautiful and so big.”

Beaming, he said, “Vous fera m’epouse?”

“Oui, yes, but ask me in English.”

“Wanna get hitched, tie the knot, get married. Will you marry me?”

She threw her arms around him. “Oui, oui, yes, yes. Je t’aime, mi amour. I love you. I want to be your wife. I have been waiting for you to ask since we first made love. I don’t care if you were married. I want you to be my husband.”

“I can’t believe this. It’s almost too much. Paparazzi, helicopters, headlines, rings, a baby, a bride, anything more and I’ll probably have a stroke. How many months along are you?”

“This is my second month without a menstrual cycle.”

"Can I put my hand on your belly?"

"Belly?"

"Stomach, abdomen, but I prefer belly or tummy."

"Oh. But you will not feel anything."

"I don't care. I just want to do it."

She raised her blouse and he placed his hands on her stomach, and kissed the diamond in her bellybutton.

He gripped her waist tightly, looked into her teary eyes, and said, "I was thinking we could get married at Notre Dame Cathedral?"

"The wedding will cost a fortune."

"Who cares. Besides, it has to be a big church. Look at how many artists are here. Miracle Meadow is going to explode. We have to get you to the altar A-S-A-P. I don't want your parents to know you're pregnant."

"I've already told them. We're too close to keep secrets."

"Where would you like to go on our honeymoon?"

"San Francisco," she said excitedly. "I want to ride with you on a cable car and meet your family. But anywhere is fine with me. I love you. You're my lover, my teacher. But what about your work here. There's so much to be done."

"It will all come together," he said. "I'll invite my parents, and you'll meet them at our wedding."

"That's wonderful!"

"As for this project getting completed, there's nothing that can stop this force. We're unstoppable, invincible."

"I agree."

Clint squeezed her hand. "The voracious expressions on that maddening throng of paparazzi tell me we're onto something beyond notable. This is a chapter in the history books."

"Oh, Clint, this is the happiest day of my life."

"After the gala banquet you and I are going to light up Paris with the biggest wedding this city has ever seen."

"When can I start painting Pegasus?"

"Tonight, after I drop off Roy and Carl at the airport. Then we're going to do it in the bucket."

"Oh la la."

Chapter 25

Dawn was beginning to rise when Clint, wearing paint-splotched coveralls, wagged his head as he snaked his way through the clamorous crowd of press and cameramen in front of Miracle Meadow. Passing through the gates, he looked up at the slew of helicopters whirling in the pale blue sky in a state of wonderment. Stepping onto a bench, he scanned the thick crowd of artists in search of Jacques. A resonating echo filled the air as fired-up artists bustled about eating breakfast and conversing in a wild uproar under a circus tent. He spotted Jacques sitting at their usual table, jumped from off the bench and hurried over to him. Jacques was tapping his fingers on a pile of magazines and flipping through a stack of newspapers scattered on the tablecloth when Clint walked over to him and patted him on the back.

"You look pretty stoic considering the chaos," said Clint as he sat across from Jacques. "It's like crazed soccer fans trying to crash the World Cup outside."

Jacques grinned. "Next thing you know the Goodyear blimp will be hovering overhead." He smirked and tipped his beret. "Think we'll need to upsize the banquet facility."

Clint laughed. "The Palace of Versailles might not be big enough."

"Nor would Windsor Palace," said Claude De Monet, walking up and slapping Clint and Jacques on their shoulders. He plopped several magazines on the table and sat down. "Seems the force you boys have generated here has created a tidal wave. Every TV channel I clicked on this joyous morning had newscasters and reporters running live coverage, and now this bedlam."

Clint grabbed three of the magazines. "Well, I'll be damned; word's leaked to the states. This troupe's made the front cover of *Time* and *Newsweek*, and *Look* Magazine. This is unbelievable. It's a revelation."

Claude puffed on his cigar and exhaled. "Phone's been ringing off the hook since news broke out. It's not only the media calling, but art collectors and curators. Luminaries, royalty, presidents, dignitaries and other such aristocracy from across the globe are even calling. My secretary told me last night that she got a call from one of Queen Elizabeth's aides. She said the queen is interested in coming to Miracle Meadow."

"Wow," Clint said, "the queen of England."

Several artists overheard Clint's loud voice, and a boisterous chain reaction began to flow from table to table. In minutes, the artists around them looked stunned and began shouting, "Her Majesty the queen is coming." Moments later, Claude loudly mentioned that Prince Rainier and Princess Grace might be attending, and the tent erupted in jubilated pandemonium.

"You boys and your force deserve to take a breather," said Claude. "The warehouses are nearly completed. I got big rigs and cranes coming first thing tomorrow morning. Best get these canvases rolled under the protection of shelter."

Jacques stuffed the *Look* magazine in his leather bib and stood up. "Then let's get to work."

* * *

Following a couple months of whirlwind excitement, on a hot muggy night, Clint rubbed Christine's tummy as she reached from out of the bucket to paint Pegasus' wings. When she dappled the finishing strokes, Clint drew her back, spun her around and kissed her.

"You have a magic touch, my lady," he said. "Pegasus is alive and breathing. Miracle Meadow is a fairytale come true."

"You're funny," she said over the sound of twittering blue jays.

"Cuckoo's a better word. Hey, bright eyes, I've an idea. Let's skip Notre Dame and get married here on the day of the gala banquet. What do you think?"

"What a wonderful thought."

"Remember the abbot I told you about, Father Bernardo?"

"Yes, you've spoken so highly of him."

"I'd like for him to marry us. What do you think?"

"It sounds marvelous."

"I've spoken to him and he's agreed to perform the wedding ceremony. He'll come whenever I call him. I'll have the carpenters build a chapel by the grandstands."

Her eyes stopped twinkling. "But what will he think when he sees 'Magnum Opus'?" And all the controversy these paintings have stirred within the Catholic Church. The Pope and the Vatican have condemned them."

He nibbled her earlobe. "They're just depictions, theories of how it might have been."

"They refute the Bible. And he's a priest, an abbot."

"He'll understand."

"And I'm pregnant."

"You don't look it. Look, I know him. The man saved my life. He'll be happy for us and our child."

She grimaced and placed her fingers on her cheeks. "My doctor told me I might have twins or even triplets. Twins would be okay, but triplets. I don't think I could bear the pain."

"Anesthesia. You'll be asleep. They come out one at a time."

"I want to be awake so I can see our baby or babies. What do you think of twins or triplets or even quadruplets?"

"I think it's glorious, as long as they're all girls."

She smiled. "Be honest. What do you really think of Pegasus?"

He playfully pinched her cheek. "You need to change your major from English to art."

"You've been a good teacher."

He winked at her. "Wanna do it in the bucket?"

Looking rhapsodic she said, "Oh la la, mon amore."

* * *

Jacques and Clint were seated around Claude's desk inside his penthouse office, overlooking the river

Seine on a scorching midsummer afternoon. Claude's attaché lay open on the desk as they spoke in French, planning the gala banquet. Feeling as if he were riding on a magic carpet, wedding bells tolled in Clint's head.

"I'm starting to feel woozy," said Clint. "My head's spinning, can we speak English. It is the international language."

"I beg your pardon," said Claude, loosening his ascot. "I believe French to be the international language."

Clint laughed. "You mean used to be the diplomatic language. Things changed after the Second World War."

Looking infuriated, Claude leaned forward, tipped his straw hat, and a heated exchange over the Vietnam War began.

When Clint and Claude's voices escalated into a shouting match, Jacques intervened. "Hey, you two, cut out the bickering. Let's not get into a row over political ideals. We Spartans have a Herculean task looming. Now is the time for brevity, enough of this foolish arguing. Let's focus on the future."

Clint swung his seat around and faced Jacques. "I'm sorry, Jacques. But Claude irks me." He turned his attention back to Claude. "It was your country that botched things up in the first place. France turned that poor country into a damn shambles. Then your country abandoned the peasants, leaving the United States to go in and clean up your country's friggin' disaster."

Claude's face contorted, looking on the verge of blowing a gasket. "You fool, you idiot, you buffoon. You jest of course."

"Gentlemen, please," Jacques interrupted.

"I'm sorry, Jacques. But I'm fed up with Claude lambasting our country for being in Vietnam as if our country was the perpetrator of that holocaust. Ever since we started this project, Claude's been ranting an outpouring of hatred toward the U.S. It fries my ass." Clint threw up his arms. "It's outrageous. French missionaries attempting to convert Buddhist and Hindus to Catholicism, building missions, what a preposterous joke!"

Claude shrugged, raised his brow, and composed himself. The tone of his voice became softer. "The revolution was imminent. Yet, it might have been prevented had Kennedy not been assassinated."

"Well," said Clint, "we agree on something. Hey, I'm sorry for blowing up, Claude. It's the stress from everything that's happening. I'm way too tense. And the heat is almost unbearable."

"Apology accepted," said Claude. "But Jacques is right. Let's put an end to this morbid topic. We have pressing issues to discuss. It is a shame what happened to Kennedy, a pitiful tragedy. The French people worshipped that man and Jackie."

Clint shook his head. "I idolized him too until I found out about his affair with that bimbo, Marilyn Monroe." Jacques and Claude wagged their heads. "Now America has a sadistic madman at the helm, that perverted maniac hasn't the slightest clue how to navigate. It burns me. I can't for the life of me fathom how that monster got elected."

"It's one of the reasons I left the states and came to France," said Jacques. "But keep in mind, America is forever indebted to the likes of the European immigrants who fled the tyranny of kings, czars, sheiks, sultans, emperors, pharaohs, and all the rest of those self-proclaimed blueblood aristocracy. Bless the likes of

Washington, Adams, Jefferson, Hancock, Franklin, and the rest of the souls who drafted the Constitution and created a free democracy."

"Here, here. Aptly spoken," said Clint. "Those were some mighty wise men."

Appearing calm, Claude said, "I've been to America many times. I'm always impressed with how well such diverse, ethnic cultures meld."

"Except for New York," said Clint. "That city's a melting pot for racial prejudice. It's nothing like San Francisco."

Filling their glasses with wine, Jacques said, "Let us commence this monumental feat with a toast and plot a course to receive these nobles."

After the three men clanked glasses and swallowed them empty, Claude took a deep breath and said, "Now to why I called this meeting. A courier dispatched from Buckingham Palace informed me that her Highness Queen Elizabeth will definitely attend the banquet, along with an entourage of royalty."

Clint jolted in his seat. "Wow. She's actually coming. This is gargantuan."

"More like an epic event," said Jacques.

Claude reclined in his chair. "Indeed. I also received a reply that Prince Rainer and Princess Grace have accepted our invitation. And Giscard d'Estaing and his wife, Anne Aymone, will be here."

Clint's eyes widened even more. "Whew."

"There's more," said Claude, furling his brow. "J. Paul Getty and Howard Hughes have expressed an interest in coming."

Clint snickered and said, "Most likely incognito."

Jacques rotated his head. "Of course, what do you expect? They're billionaire recluses. That Getty guy is something else. Heard he's so chintzy, he has a payphone in his mansion."

"No way that Nixon fiend is getting in here," said Clint.

They smiled and began planning the banquet.

Shortly after dusk, Claude leaned back in his chair, undid the top buttons of his shirt, scratched the curly fuzz on his chest, and said, "Seems everything is in order, but costly. I can handle most every expense to stage this supreme occasion. But the catering and music tabs are well over what I can afford. Which brings to mind another reason for calling this conference, to be frank, my funds are nearly depleted. You boys have any ideas?"

"I just sold two paintings," said Jacques, "but a mere pittance to feed this extravaganza. With Dominique's inheritance tapped out from the magnitude of this project.."

Clint grinned proudly and cut Jacques off. "Not to fret, fellows. It's covered. There'll be no skimping on this gala banquet. I recently came across some unexpected good fortune. We'll have the best gourmet chefs in the world, and Napa wines, and the best symphony orchestra on the planet. Maybe get the Beatles to drop in and play 'Magical Mystery Tour.'"

Claude and Jacques' eyes widened.

"This is no time to be joking," said Jacques.

"Who's joking?"

Appearing surprised, Claude scrunched his chin and said, "I estimate the catering and open bar to run as high as a hundred thousand dollars. You have this much money?"

"I told you, it's covered."

Jacques shook his head. "You never cease to amaze me, Clint. You're an intriguing man."

"As you continue to fascinate me with your inventiveness, my fellow compatriot," said Clint.

"That puzzles me," said Jacques. "Why are you always telling me that you don't give a rat's ass about money?"

"I don't," said Clint. "This was a gift from heaven. Think I'll hire a plane and take Christine on a trip to Switzerland. Have the pilot buzz over the Matterhorn before I press some buttons and presto, instant money. This gala shebang is gonna happen. Oh, let me put my John Hancock on that personal management contract. Without your clout, connections, diligent hard work, this monumental event may never have come to fruition. We're going to be the pinnacle of acclaim, mister manager."

Claude pulled out the contract from his attaché and handed Clint a pen.

"I propose a toast to the man who conceived this great vision, to Jacques the visionary," said Clint as he scribbled his signature.

The three men clinked glasses and stood up.

"To the force," hollered Jacques."

"To the force," they shouted in unison.

Guzzling their glasses empty, they tossed them across the room.

* * *

Banderoles fluttered in the mid-morning breeze on the day of the gala banquet as winter was fast approaching. Clint sat between Roy and Carl with his arms draped over their shoulders. They were on the top row in the shade of the covered grandstands, looking out at the stream of limousines slowly crossing Miracle Meadow.

"Thanks for flying back to be in my wedding," said Clint. "Your presence here means a lot to me."

"Thanks for the blind dates," said Carl. "Those babes showed us more than the sights."

"I'll say," said Roy. "The chick Jacquelyn took me on a tour of her private hot spot last night."

"You ain't been cheating on your wife, have ya, Roy?" Clint said.

"Banish the naughty thought," said Roy. "This grand affair looks to be bigger than opening day of the Olympics."

"Never seen so many stretch limos," said Carl.

"This is the ultimate red carpet treatment," said Roy. "And a helicopter pad and a landing strip. This is extravagant luxury, musta cost a fortune."

"It did," said Clint, "thanks to your generosity. In a couple of hours, this place will be packed with the beaux monde, aristocracy, bejeweled royalty, philanthropists, and avant-garde. Not to mention, Princess Grace. Man, did I have a crush on her when I was a kid. She's drop-dead beautiful."

"Now you're going to bow before her," Roy said with twinge of facetious humor.

"Guess I'll have to," said Clint. "It's protocol, or rather savoir faire. But I'm going flick her a wink before I bow and kiss her hand."

Carl wagged his head. "This is a thousand times bigger than your first wedding. You should get married every couple years."

Clint laughed. "This is the last time I'm saying 'I do.'"

"Any kings coming?" Carl asked.

Clint grinned and rubbed his chin. "Hah, thanks for reminding me, you guys aren't gonna believe this, but yesterday my manager, Claude, told me the King of Denmark will be here. And catch this. He said the king's interested in purchasing 'Viking Warriors.' "

"You're putting us on?" Roy said.

"No bull," said Clint. "Your bloodthirsty mugs will be hanging in a mammoth palace in your homeland."

"I ain't buying that," said Carl.

Clint smirked and said, "You'll see. Hey, the Beatles were coming, but something came up, and they had to cancel. But I got Seiji Ozawa and the San Francisco Symphony Orchestra. That dude is wild."

"I saw him earlier," said Roy. "He was talking to your dad."

"They're pretty tight friends," said Clint. "That's the reason Ozawa came. My dad met him in the late sixties or early seventies in San Francisco. Their personalities clicked because they both have the same satirical humor. My dad's gonna open with a horn solo."

"Honeymoon in San Francisco?" Carl said.

"Just a couple days," said Clint. "After the girls have their babies, we're going to Spain to restore a basilica with Jacques and Dominique. After that, we're going to the Himalayas to paint a mountain, Ama Dablam. It means *Mother of Pearl* in Nepalese. It's a sacred mountain shaped like the blessed virgin Mother Mary. Jacques tells me it's unreal. Said he thinks a band of Neanderthals carved it back in the Stone Age. He told me people come from around the world to worship it."

Roy pulled out an envelope and handed it to Clint. “Almost forgot, Dusty gave this to me to give to you. She called it an amend letter.”

Clint pulled out his Swiss Army knife and opened it. “This should be interesting,” he said, unfolding the three-page handwritten letter.

“Wow, heavy duty,” Clint said after he finished reading it and wiped the tears from his eyes. “I’m touched. Why’d you tell her I’m getting married?”

“You told me to,” said Roy. “Don’t you remember?”

“Oh, yeah, so much has been going on around here that I forgot. Tell Dusty I wish the best for her, and maybe I’ll see her in the afterlife, but not while I’m on this planet. He tore up the letter and tossed it into a trash barrel. “This place is turning into a madhouse. He looked at his watch. “I gotta go, I told Father Bernardo I’d meet him at the chapel. Glad you two are here. Catch you guys at the wedding. I’ve got a ton of things to do. I’m getting married to an archangel.”

Half an hour later, Clint found Father Bernardo wandering aimlessly in a daze near the chapel and hurried through the bustling crowd over to him. Hearing Clint’s voice, Father Bernardo turned and his eyelashes flickered several times when he saw Clint.

With elated expressions, they hugged, and Father Bernardo held Clint’s shoulders. “My, my, look at you. Tan and fit. You and your fellow constituents have created worldwide excitement.”

“It all started with the vision you and I had, Father. Those children were right. Everything began coming together the moment I arrived in Paris and met the woman who had been appearing in my dreams. And she introduced me to Jacques. He conceived this resurgence. It's all so incredible."

Father Bernardo smiled. "You and this Jacques have accomplished so much in such a short span of time. It seems you just left the abbey."

"Miracle Meadow is blessed by the good Lord, Father Bernardo."

"I could tell from the photographs you have been sending me. It is even more evident now that I am here. I must say, you and this force have stirred some rather intensive drama around the planet. I believe God is quite pleased with your work here. I so look forward to seeing the paintings and meeting your bride."

"She's joie de vivre," Father, "and so talented. This union's gonna be for all eternity. This whole thing staggers my mind. Just think a year and a half or so, I was on the verge of committing suicide, and now..."

"Life moves in a zigzag pattern until it straightens out, my son."

Clint looked at the sky and back at Father Bernardo. "You're a wise man, Father. Those chats in the cloister got me through a serious crisis. I'm so happy you came. I've never divulged the vision you and I saw at Massabielle to anyone."

"Not even your to your soon to be bride."

"No. She would think I was insane. Maybe one day I'll tell her when we're old and gray. But my instructions have come to life on the canvases. I came to discover that God is a powerful person when I saw the same two little children we had seen in that apparition on a sketch drawn by Jacques. I couldn't believe my eyes. I've a strong hunch that Jacques also received God's message to stop war for the sake of the children. But I've never mentioned a word to him about what we saw."

Father Bernardo looked around at the crowd and turned back to Clint. "From seeing the expressions on the faces of the people here, you have succeeded in your mission extremely well. I thought Angelwings fountain to be a mighty accomplishment. But this is an unparalleled achievement. I'm anxious to see the paintings."

"You're not offended by the controversy they've stirred up?"

Father Bernardo gave off another rare smile. "Scandalized."

"Come. I want to introduce you to my bride and my family, her family, and Jacques, the mastermind of this force."

Clint took Father Bernardo's hand and led him around, introducing him to Jacques and Christine's families and Claude. Christine clasped Clint's hand when she and Dominique appeared with Clint's parents'.

"My goodness, my dear son," said Clint's mother, Sarah, as she heaved toward him and threw her arms around his neck. "Your lovely bride-to-be and her charming friend took us on an early tour. The frescos are marvelous. But some are gruesome and bloody. It made me queasy to look at them. I don't understand the need for so much violence?"

"There's a reason, Mom," said Clint. "I'll explain later."

"This is all incomprehensible," said Sarah. "It's inconceivable. This is an incredible feat you and all these artists have accomplished." She stepped backwards and stared at Clint with her big brown eyes. "I especially love

'Magnum Opus' 'The Transfiguration' and 'Heaven's Eternal Sanctuary.' Oh. I'm so proud of you."

"So am I, son," said Clint's father, Ian, stepping forward to embrace him. He was wearing the same tattered tam-o'-shanter Clint had seen him wear since he was a small child. "Your mother nearly fainted when she saw 'Hell's Battlefield.' I almost did too, for that matter. This is a phenomenal milestone. Even with all the gore, those paintings are masterpieces."

Clint wiped the tears from his eyes and scratched his scalp. "I'm so glad you and mom are here. This is all too much."

Her beauty radiating, Christine took Clint's hand and said, "Oh la la, you cry." She dabbed Clint's eyes with her handkerchief. "It makes me happy."

Smiling at Christine, Ian said, "Clint's a lucky lad that he met you, my dear lady. It seems he has inherited his mother's artistic traits. The paintings we have seen will be everlasting."

"Clint has your genes too," said Sarah.

"It's not just me, Mom. It's the whole colony of master artists here." Clint pointed. "Mostly, it's that man over there, Jacques. He deserves all the credit. My good friend is responsible for this incredible creation. Jacques conceived this international resurgence. Artists from almost every country in the world are here and everyone is getting along, and working in a harmonious atmosphere. The man's a genius. I mean it."

"Don't sell yourself short, Clint," said Jacques. "You're an integral part of this force."

"You must both come to my abbey," said Father Bernardo, "and see the fountain your gifted son built before you return home."

"We'd be delighted," said Sarah. "I have a feeling that I'll be in dire need of a retreat after all this excitement."

* * *

The sun was directly overhead when the royal procession was about to start, and Her Majesty's horse-drawn carriage trotted across Miracle Meadow. Surrounded by royal guards with shiny swords and beehive shaped black, furry hats, Queen Elizabeth and her entourage exited the carriages. A short while later, two white stallions, with Prince Rainer and Princess Grace seated in the back of an open buggy, pranced across the meadow.

Amidst the fanfare, with exalted eyes, the troupe of artists lined up to be greeted. Holding his trumpet, Ian took center stage and began to play one of his own jazz compositions. He was later accompanied by the members of his quartet, a bass player, a pianist, and a drummer. After the roaring applause had died, the maestro, Seiji Ozawa, wearing a turtleneck and looking wild-eyed, snapped a baton over his head and kicked off the San Francisco Symphony.

Jacques, Dominique, Clint, and Christine led the greeting procession of more than two hundred mesmerized artists. Ozawa was in a frantic frenzy, whipping his baton when Clint licked his upper lip, winked, and bowed before Princess Grace. Her face was flushed as she extended her hand for Clint to kiss. He was surprised when Princess Grace returned his wink just as Christine curtsied before her. He was completely blown away when Princess Grace graciously invited them to join her and Prince Rainer at the royal table. Clint and Christine eagerly smiled and accepted.

Christine looked to be feeling woozy when Queen Elizabeth, wearing a stomacher, invited them to come to Buckingham Palace for dinner.

A few minutes later, Giscard d' Estaing squinted, and in refined French accented English, he invited Christine and Clint to come to the Elysee Palace. Christine wobbled and Clint gripped her tightly around her waist to prevent her from falling over.

Trumpets blared and Ozawa and the San Francisco Symphony Orchestra revved into high gear while the guests were being seated. A throng of caterers began serving crab, shrimp, lobster and other gourmet delicacies, and filling fluted gold chalices with Napa chardonnays. The festive royal banquet launched into orbit.

"Are you okay?" Clint asked Christine when they were seated at the royal table opposite Princess Grace and Prince Rainer, munching on tender filets and succulent treats.

Looking annoyed and patting her lips with a starched white napkin, Christine leaned toward Clint and whispered in his ear, "I'm fine. But why is Princess Grace looking at you that way?"

"Huh, what do you mean?" Clint said in a soft voice.

"She's been giving you coquettish eyes since we sat down at the table."

"I haven't noticed?"

"She's flirting with you, and so have you. I've been watching you two."

Clint laughed and took a piece of fruit from the cornucopia.

"That's ridiculous. Your imagination is playing tricks on you."

"It is not. I saw you wink at her."

"I did not. Hey, sweetheart, let's not squabble on our wedding day."

"I don't understand squabble."

"Argue, quarrel, bicker," he said. "Hey, you're jealous."

"How would you feel if I was flirting with her husband?"

"I haven't been flirting with her. It's you I love. No one else matters."

"Oh, I'm sorry. I'm just nervous and tense from all this excitement."

"So am I," said Clint. "It's not everyday I'm dining with bluebloods."

"Please forgive me? Oh, I think the baby just kicked me."

"Really! Clint said excitedly and gently placed his hand on her stomach and kissed her. "Wow, you're right."

When the lavish banquet began to wind down, the large gathering of luminaries walked anxiously toward the warehouses and Clint's heart pulsed faster. To the sound of Clint's father's trumpet blaring, the wheels of the large doors rolled open, and the boisterous guests entered into the first exhibit.

Claude took his place behind the podium, adjusted the microphone and welcomed the audience in English. Standing proudly beside Christine, Clint's hands started to sweat as he watched two artists pull down on the ropes, and the large curtain slowly raised up. An eerie silence swept across the warehouse as the artists raised the curtain higher, and television cameras began to roll. Flickers of bright light from flashbulbs filled the warehouse until the canvas of "Magnum Opus" was fully exposed, and the gaping crowd erupted in thunderous applause and cheering.

The deafening volume continued when the next curtain was raised to reveal "Heaven's Eternal Sanctuary." Clint smiled each time he looked over at his parents chatting excitedly with Father Bernardo, Roy, Carl, Dominique, and Jacques. The sight of seeing Queen Elizabeth and Princess Grace clapping with their arms raised high was so enrapturing, Clint began feeling dizzy. Preceding each unveiling, except for Claude's amplified voice, the dazzled crowd stood silent. Upon each canvas being in full view, the warehouse erupted in thunderous applause and shouting.

Clint was on the verge of going daffy after the charged up crowd had gathered in another warehouse. As Claude began his commentary about the second exhibit, Christine and Clint stood embraced as the curtain in front of "Viking Warriors" slowly moved upward. The crowd fell mute when they saw the disfigured and mutilated dead bodies lying on the battlefield. Ear-splitting shrieks of horrid, ghastly, ghoulish, gory, beastly, and other such words echoed throughout the warehouse when the diabolical faces of Clint's friends, Roy and Carl, in the act of decapitating heads with axes, and cutlasses were fully revealed.

Spurred by shouts from all the artists, the crowd went ballistic and joined in the roaring clapper. Christine tightened her grip on Clint's waist and kissed his cheek.

Clint tensed when the crowd fell silent preceding the unveiling of "Hell's Battlefield" until it was fully revealed, and the ear-splitting shrieks returned. In the midst of the pandemonium and screaming, a sonic boom erupted and the building shook and swayed. The microphone dropped from Claude's hands and the crowd turned horrified. Panic broke out.

Christine quivered and gripped Clint's arms tightly. "I'm scared, what's happening?"

His mind in a chaotic delirium, Clint looked at Christine's terrified face and said, "I don't know." He turned and saw Father Bernardo with his arms stretched skyward.

Following a blackout, the hysterical screaming stopped when a bright golden aureole flashed overhead. The rumble and shaking of the building abruptly ceased and a child's voice warbled throughout the high ceiling, "Stop warring and killing. Educate your children to love and respect thy neighbor."

Christine's fingernails were gouged deep into Clint's ribcage when another child's voice sang out in a melodious loud echo, "Innocent children are precious. Show them the wondrous joy of living in harmony. Stop loathing your neighbors and teach the children to cherish peace."

The stunned crowd stood silent, gaping in awe up at the winged and haloed angels, singing and playing small harps.

In a magical puff, the bright light faded and the angels vanished.

Trembling spastically and clutching Clint tightly, Christine said, "Oh my God, that was an epiphany."

"You better believe it, sweetheart," said Clint. "It sure wasn't a mirage."

"I thought I would miscarry. Please Clint, can we go some place where it's tranquil. My stomach is cramping. I need serenity. I'm exhausted. I have to lie down. It's crazy in here. I have to relax and take a nap."

"There's no time for naps," said Jacques, appearing desperate. "Dominique's water bag broke. She's about to pop. We need to find a doctor or a nurse. Quick. Oh, Christine, your mother fainted, yours too Clint."

"Oh, no," said Christine.

"Good grief," said Clint, "we need doctors and nurses. I'll announce it over the loudspeakers." Clint released Christine's hand and charged through the stunned crowd up to the podium and cried out for doctors and nurses or anyone with medical experience. By the time Clint got back his mother and Christine's mother had been revived.

Amid the pandemonium, artists were scampering around, carrying the victims of shock into the barracks where people with experience in treating trauma waited. As most everyone in attendance, Clint was also in a state of shock, seated between Father Bernardo and his father inside a corridor, while a doctor and nurse were inside a small room delivering Jacques and Dominique's baby.

Christine opened the door and burst into the hallway. "It's a girl," she shrieked.

Clint smiled at Claude and shook his hand. "Well, grampa," said Clint, "you'd best get in and kiss your granddaughter."

"You too, Clint," said Christine. "And you too, Father Bernardo, Dominique and Jacques would like you to christen their baby if you have some holy water."

"I do," said Father Bernardo. "I always keep some handy for occasions like this."

"How's my mom and your mother?" Clint asked Christine.

"They're both fine and resting."

Looking madder than hell, Carl and Roy stormed down the hallway, and Carl shouted, "I need to talk to you, Clint."

"Hey, not so loud," said Clint. "Calm down." Clint turned to Christine. "I'll be back in a few minutes to kiss the baby," he said, turning to walk outside with Roy and Carl. "What's on your mind, Carl?"

Scrunching his chin with his fingers, Carl said in a gruff voice, "Did you stage that ridiculous farce with special effects?"

"Hell no," said Clint. "That was real. I had nothing to do with what happened."

"Are you sure?" Roy said.

"I might be a little on the wild side, but I ain't into pulling off a travesty."

"You were always pulling some hair-brained scheme," said Roy.

"That was back in my college days," said Clint. "Look, I've already told you guys that I had nothing to do with what you and practically the entire world saw. I ain't no fanatic. That was a genuine miracle."

Roy and Carl stood scratching their hair and looking at all the euphoric faces of the guests, wandering aimlessly around, staring at the sky as if expecting another phenomenon.

"You still getting married?" Carl asked.

Staring out at the artists singing and dancing on the grass, Clint said, "Sure am. Look, I gotta get in and see the baby. Then I need to gather a team together to keep everybody from leaving. I want everyone to stay for the wedding. You two mind helping me out. This place has turned into a madhouse."

Shortly before the twilight wedding, Clint sat with his parents and Father Bernardo, watching the mesmerized guests fill the grandstands around the chapel.

Holding her rosary beads in her shaky hands and gazing rhapsodically up at the sky, Sarah said over the sound of twittering jay birds, “Well, Father, this supreme message from heaven will certainly change the way people live.”

Father Bernardo’s eyes rolled and he humbly said, “Let us hope this timely, visual epistle puts an end to all the warring on this planet.”

Shaking his head, Ian said, “One would think that after what the world has seen today, there will be a ceasefire and an immediate withdrawal of troops in all the wars being waged this very moment.”

“Keep in mind,” said the abbot, “there will be those who will call this a great spoof. In the face of reality, perhaps this will help reduce the wars.”

“The commandment ‘thou shall not kill,’” said Clint, “kept me from going to Vietnam.” He gazed at his parents and said, “Wow, what a day this has been, and the Queen of England and Princess Grace are attending my wedding. This is some momentous day.”

“Momentous doesn’t sound a suitable word,” said Sarah. “I think epochal is more apropos. What do you think, Father?”

Father Bernardo scratched his chin and stared at the sky. “Quite befitting, but I like divine spiritual awakening.”

Clint’s parents’ beamed brightly.

“We’re so proud that you are a part of this, son,” said Ian. “I couldn’t believe my eyes. It’s all too much.”

"There is so much more to this than what you saw today," said Clint. "I will tell you later. Right now, I'm getting ready to marry a goddess."

"What will you do now, son?" Sarah asked.

"We're going to honeymoon in San Francisco and take a cable car ride. Then we gotta get back here and wrap up this resurgence. We've got a couple more paintings to complete. Claude told me a little while ago that every painting is sold or has an offer on it. Even the ones we haven't finished."

"What about 'The Transfiguration'?" Father Bernardo asked.

"Oh, I told Claude to hold off on selling that one until the pope has seen it."

"I am sure he will love it," said Father Bernardo. "Are you ready to say your vows and kiss the bride?"

Clint stood up. "I just need to change into my tuxedo."

Sarah looked at Father Bernardo with a concerned expression. "Is this allowable, Father?"

"You mean about your son being previously married?"

Sarah nodded.

"Some of the church's rules have long been in need of change. I know of your son's integrity and will use the privilege of my discretion to perform this holy matrimony."

At twilight, Clint joined Jacques, Roy, and Carl on the altar as Ian filled his jowls and began to blow into his trumpet when the wedding ceremony commenced.

"Have you heard about the world's reaction?" Jacques whispered.

"No," said Clint. "What's it like?"

"We rocked the planet."

Jacques' words were followed by the crying coming from his newborn daughter, Simone, whom Dominique carried in her arms as she slowly marched down the aisle in front of Juliet and Andre. Clutching her father's arm, and wearing a white Chantilly lace dress, adorned with pearls, and jeweled high heels, Christine glowed like morning sunshine. Seiji Ozawa raised his baton and the San Francisco Symphony Orchestra opened the ceremony with "Here Comes the Bride."

The End